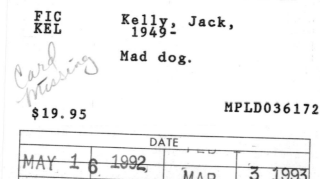

MAD DOG

ALSO BY JACK KELLY

Apalachin
Protection

MAD DOG

JACK KELLY

ATHENEUM

New York • 1992

MAXWELL MACMILLAN CANADA
Toronto

MAXWELL MACMILLAN INTERNATIONAL
New York Oxford Singapore Sydney

Atheneum
Macmillan Publishing Company
866 Third Avenue
New York, NY 10022

Maxwell Macmillan Canada, Inc.
1200 Eglinton Avenue East
Suite 200
Don Mills, Ontario M3C 3N1

Macmillan Publishing Company is part of the Maxwell
Communication Group of Companies.

Library of Congress Cataloging-in-Publication Data

Kelly, Jack, 1949–
    Mad dog / Jack Kelly.
        p.   cm.
    ISBN 0-689-12145-8
    I. Title.
PS3561.E394M34   1992   91-30275   CIP
813'.54—dc20

        10 9 8 7 6 5 4 3 2 1

PRINTED IN THE UNITED STATES OF AMERICA

FOR JOY

PART

I

1

FIVE MEN, CLEAN-SHAVEN, armed. The tires of the stolen Buick droned along the concrete. In the backseat Homer lit a cigarette. The sweet Virginia mixed with the essence of bay rum and toilet water.

John drove. The car's eight purred like a swarm of honeybees. John was humming to the tune of "Smoke Gets in Your Eyes."

The five men were bound the way that children are, bound by blood oaths, pirate loyalty.

Autumn rains had forced the streams. They snaked swollen toward Lake Michigan, brown and dangerous.

"My friends," Homer said. He angled his cigarette toward the ceiling and mimicked Roosevelt's round eastern voice. "I truly believe that we are going to have a grand time today."

John snorted.

"A grand time," Homer repeated. Homer was the scarecrow of the group. His clothes never fit him. Dressed in his business suit, he looked like a hick on his way to a shotgun wedding. His hands were large and thick like a farmer's. He bit his nails, bit tiny slivers off them that he would play with between his teeth. That morning a dab of pink alum marked a spot on his neck where he'd nicked himself shaving.

"She says to me," he continued, " 'I seen this morphodite at the fair.'

"I say, 'What in hell's that?'

"She says it's—half of it's a man, beard and all, half of it's a woman. What a leg, she says. And one bubbie. They made the women sit in one part of the tent, men in the other, and a curtain between. This morphodite goes back and forth.

" 'So it's a man one side, woman the other,' I says to her. 'What about in the middle?'

"She tells me, 'Oh, they don't show the ladies that. Anyway, there's some things a person just don't want to be curious about.'

"I told her, 'You missed the whole point of that one.' "

Homer laughed, a sound like an automobile starter way back in his throat.

"I've seen them sideshows," Red said. He sat in back beside Homer, watching out the window. The land drifted past his eyes, the hills, a bare tree posing. Now and then, when they climbed a rise, he could see the blue steel of the lake. His eyes, still clean from prison, drank in the sight.

Red had boxed. He remembered now the sensation he used to feel in the dressing room before a fight—anxious to climb into the ring, yet the awful work he had to do dripping panic into his gut.

John kept the Buick cruising at an even forty-five. The sun, low in the sky, cast the shadow of the car obliquely across the roadway in front of them. Scudding heaps of gray and white clouds laid a mottled pattern of sun and shade out over the autumn landscape.

John looked at his watch. Pete, who was sitting beside him in front, told him they were four minutes ahead of schedule at the last main crossroad.

"How do you think Henry Ford made himself rich?" Pete asked the others. The tension just before a job would make them say things out of the blue.

2

"How?" Makley asked him.

"Order," Pete told them. "Ford created a new order in the factory. Order is the key to everything. Science."

"Fear," Makley replied, long experienced as Pete's verbal sparring partner.

"No," Pete said. "Man is a herd animal. Everybody knows that. The government knows it. A dictator knows it. Order is power."

"Fear is behind it, I'm saying."

"Man is a herd animal. He has to be led. He's happy when he's led, when there's order. Take that away, he turns into a lone wolf. He turns dangerous. The uptake of the whole thing is what we call society. Get it?"

Pete had the vague, sensuous mouth and strong jaw you find in a lot of midwestern college boys. His people had wanted him to become an engineer. He'd constructed elaborate bridges and towers out of matchsticks. When he grew up, he acquired the bluff presence and large good looks that usually accompany success in life. His mind was clever, but not swift. A ponderous introspection weighed on his thinking.

At nineteen he shot a man whose car he was stealing. A year later he robbed his first bank.

They glided in and out of a cloud's shadow. They passed a filling station, the gasoline yellow-pink in the clear reservoir of the pump.

"I see the thing going wrong in two places," Pete said. "Coming in, those signs have to go up bam bam bam. You have the signs, Red?"

Red turned from looking out, nodded.

"The signs go up, the place is ours. Ninety seconds to get the officer back to the vault. That's the crucial one. After, it's clockwork."

"You jumping today, Johnnie?" Homer asked.

3

John turned and wrinkled his face. "Pete didn't schedule me any time to jump."

Makley laughed.

"Chaos is a woman," Pete said. "People fall for hysteria. Guys go bust because guys can't control themselves when the wild stuff starts. They lose track of time. People just don't know what time it is. What I'm saying, you hold onto the plan, the timing, no matter what. That's the beauty of the thing."

"I'll tell you the beauty of the thing," Makley said. He looked and talked like an uncle, like a banker.

"The timing," Pete said.

"Money, that's the beauty of the thing," Makley said. "You know that smell new money has? Know how they say somebody's stinking rich? That's the smell they mean. Like ripe quiff. How much is this baby worth, Homer?"

"Order. Order is organized terror," Pete said. "We don't just blow things. Because we don't want a war. There's no time for a war. We substitute our order for their order, the order of the gun for the order of—what? The paycheck."

"Thirty-five or forty thousand," Homer said. "With luck."

"Money is tomorrow. Planning is what it's about," Pete insisted. "You agree, John?"

"Of course. Planning."

"Nobody starts thinking they're bigger than the plan," Pete said to no one in particular. "Got that?"

"Sure, baby," John said. "Take it easy."

They crossed the state line. Pete checked the schedule. On time.

A poster for a circus three months gone was clinging to the side of a lame abandoned barn. A mass of starlings careened across the west. The flock changed its color in unison as it wheeled.

4

There was a subtle shift in mood inside the car as they encountered some houses, a store. More houses. A woman in a thin coat watched them from a bus stop, arms wrapped around herself, scarf over her head. A coal truck was unloading into the basement of a dilapidated two-family.

They quieted. Their words became clipped.

"On time," Pete said.

John stopped the car a half block from the bank. A fresh breeze brought the fishy lake smell from around the corner.

Passers-by saw five prosperous men climb from the black Buick. Camel hair, tailored fall-weight worsteds, gabardines in pearl gray and cocoa, tan felt snap-brims. Their polished shoes creaked. Their cuff links flashed the reassuring glint of gold. Pete slipped off his calfskin gloves, folded them, slipped them into his pocket.

Homer slid behind the wheel while the other four approached in pairs the green glass doors.

John made an effort to keep his feet on the pavement. Light as hydrogen, his body struggled to ascend, to sail above the brick and glass, above the slate roofs, to where he could gaze over the wide blue dappled lake, could look back the way they'd come all the way to Chicago.

For half a second he did see them from above, saw himself: One hat turned in at a doorway. Three more hats hesitated outside, followed.

He'd never tried to pretend that he was Douglas Fairbanks. That was never the reason he'd leapt over the tellers' cages that summer. It was just the lightness that came over him. He could not keep himself from leaping.

Banks, like post offices, all smell the same. It's a kind of official mustiness, a stale dusty smell. It's the smell you associate with paper shades in sunlight, with women's handbags and empty cigar cases.

Red is pasting up the posters to obscure the front windows. GIVE. RED CROSS.

Makley, affable, approaches the first teller.

"All right, stick 'em up."

"Go to the next window, please." Not even looking up.

"No joke, pal. This is it."

The man's eyes come above his half-glasses.

"Down flat! Everybody on your stomach!" Pete has a Thompson gun out.

The hum of adding machines and typewriters and conversations ceases. The vaulted room becomes suddenly quiet, holds its breath.

John's blood is crackling. He is marching the president back toward the vault. The man's colorless hair bristles on his neck. His collar is white as starch.

Red is behind the cages lifting the cash from the drawers.

"Ten seconds, move it!" Pete barks at John.

John jabs the officer in the ribs. The guy isn't used to taking orders.

Springs coil in John's legs. He fights an urge to leap to the ceiling.

The heavy man stands aside while John scoops the bills into a canvas bag. John sees the sack sag under its load, but cannot feel the weight. He prods the banker back to the lobby.

A uniform. Pete is tugging the cop's gun from its polished leather holster. The sight makes a laugh strike John's palate. The gun wedged, Pete jerking on it, the cop bouncing as if he were being goosed.

Another cop strolling through the front door. Machine gun. Somebody must have hit the silent alarm.

Pete shouts. Makley turns, holds out his pistol as if offering it, fires.

The sound flies to the ceiling, crashes around the lobby, returns as an applause of echoes.

The cop falls hard, cheek against the floor. Makley picks up the cop's machine gun. A woman screams.

John's nerves become music. The beauty is the planning. The timing. Time itself. The beauty is the money. The dancing marble that smacks your feet. The beauty is the massive steel door of the vault, the stacks of silent bank notes. Your face freezes in exhilaration, because suddenly the beauty is everything. Everything sighs, everything gasps.

Someone upsets a vase of yellow flowers. It shatters.

"Let's move!" Pete is saying.

Makley, "Quite a crowd out front."

"The back's no good," John says. Words hang in the air like objects. They have to be grabbed, squeezed for meaning. "We're going to have to shoot our way out the front."

A woman is hovering against the wall. Her black dress is printed with salmon-colored flowers. She looks down at herself. The flowers come to life. Spin. Pulse and spin. Sounds move away, leave her in a vacuum. She doesn't feel herself leave herself behind. She drops.

The air turns to a haze of smoke and dust. They gather the hostages. Three pretty girls.

To one John says, "You, lambie pie."

The bank president. Move! Pete swats him. The president's glasses skitter across the floor.

Time is piling up on them now.

"And the cop. Take him too!"

They move out. Hostages around them. John holds one girl by the elbow. Delicately, with two fingers. He can smell her perfume.

Two hundred and fifty people outside. They watch the group of prosperous men emerge. They don't know what to make of it.

They're filming a movie, somebody says. Two days before Homer stopped at half a dozen stores near the bank and mentioned the rumor a movie was to be filmed soon.

The invisible web of authority has dissolved. The bystanders don't know what to do.

Pete marches the president, a gun to his head. Makley has a grip on the cop's belt. John tries to herd the girls. One of them simply steps away, joins some people in an alley. Red carries the two bags.

As they reach the corner two uniformed cops approach, running from the station. One carries a shotgun.

"Mac," Pete says. He points.

Makley brushes the trigger of the police machine gun. First comes the clang and shatter of plate glass. Then the sound of the shots, at first a blur, seems to divide, each crack echoing its tattoo down the block. Then the white silence of the brooding lake rings in resonance, a giant bell. The sidewalk becomes wide and empty.

One of the girls breaks a heel descending to the parking lot behind the bank. She limps, struggling to keep up, obedient.

Homer opens the doors of the car. They make the bank president and one of the girls climb onto the running board on the driver's side. The cop stands on the other, Pete still holding his belt.

John guns the engine. They bounce over the rail tracks, turn south along the lake. At the end of every block they see the water, now snow-gray and tusked.

They round a corner.

The woman, her magenta dress rippling in the breeze, clutched the door with icy knuckles. She watched the deft hands of the man skim the steering wheel, watched his jaw work. Once he reached out and gently wrapped his hand around her waist. As if they were dancing, she thought.

She was being driven through a city that she'd never seen before, even in her dreams. The houses yawned and grinned. Windows were mirrors reflecting the sky.

A man turned to watch the car pass, scratched his scalp like some wiener-headed character in a Betty Boop cartoon. As they turned wide around a corner the woman felt another car's fender lick against her hips.

The car slowed to a stop on a street that smelled of burning leaves. The woman's strength drained away. She would melt onto the pavement. They would kill her now, but she lacked the will to resist the bullets.

They didn't shoot. They made her get inside the car. Mister Weyland sat between the two of them. One of them sat on the jump seat, two sacks between his legs. And she had to perch on the bony knees of the one with yellow teeth. Out the small oval window in back she saw the cop standing, his openmouthed image shrinking as they left him behind.

"Two point six. Right. Crossroad, crossroad. Church? Yep. Three point one, next left." The one in front, the one who looked like a movie star, was reading from a notebook. He would watch and read. "Elmwood, Kenosha, Prairie. Four point two. Right. By the gray house. Good. Easy does it."

Somebody lit a cigarette. The smell of smoke made the woman want to be sick. But it made her feel safe, too. As if she were coming back into herself. Could breathe. Could smell. She felt for the first time her fingers cramped from gripping the door. She felt the man's knees shift under her.

A forgotten jack-o'-lantern on somebody's porch watched them pass, its rotting face downcast.

They reached the highway, followed it for half a mile, then

9

turned onto a gravel road that led into the country. The sky was now overcast, the smell of winter tinted the air.

A hundred yards down the road, John stopped. Opening the car's small trunk he retrieved another set of license tags, which he quickly attached. From a small wooden box he scattered roofing nails, a man feeding chickens.

"This Arab's pretending like time grows on trees," Makley told Homer. "So our boy says, 'We don't think too much of bank presidents. We might just kill you for the hell of it.' For the hell of it." He laughed, jabbing John's shoulder. "That's funny, isn't it, Mister? What's your name?"

His name was Weyland.

"I don't think any of it's funny," Weyland said. He was a silver, lipless man with a barbed chin and flaring nostrils. "You shot an innocent man back there. You're causing Mrs. Patzke immense distress. Barbarians, that's what you are."

"She's shivering," Homer said.

"What we shot was not a man, Mr. Weyland," Pete said, turning in the front seat. "He was a policeman. What is a policeman? What is a prison guard? What is a banker? Scum trying to lord it over human beings. It's perfectly logical. Would you like my coat, Miss—?"

"Mrs. Patzke. I—I just—"

He removed his camel hair overcoat. Homer draped it around the woman's shoulders. She had brown curls and wide, pleasant eyes. She was stretching her mouth back at the corner to keep her teeth from clicking. She closed her eyes.

"The steno girl is saying, Can I help you with those signs?"

"Didn't I tell you timing?"

"See the look on the face of that copper?"

"House with a windmill, next right."

"Cops are so goddamn dumb, they must give them a dumb test before they can get on the force."

10

"Next window, he tells me."

"See the one in the yellow dress? The redhead?"

"What's one bank president more or less?"

"*Somebody* hit that alarm."

"No matter how bad it gets, you stick to the plan, it sees you through."

Weyland now was feeling the cold. He asked if he could drape a handkerchief over his bald head. Snickering, Pete tossed him his own fedora.

"So it's, your money or your life," Homer was telling Mrs. Patzke. "And the guy says, Take my life, I'm saving my money for my old age."

He yukked. After a hesitation, Mrs. Patzke gave out a high titter. She was immediately embarrassed.

They cruised at a leisurely pace along the undulant dirt roads. Coming over a rise, John said, "Trouble, boys."

Coats rustled. Metal clicked against metal. Pete put down his notebook and retrieved the machine gun from between his feet.

Ahead perhaps a dozen cars were lining the road. John tossed his cigarette out the window, gripped the wheel with two hands, kept going.

No one stood in the roadway to flag them down. As they mounted the knoll they saw people grouped in a field, figures silhouetted against the gray clouds.

All the eyes inside the car slowly swiveled as they passed.

"It's a goddamn funeral," Makley said. "That's what it is. A goddamn funeral."

Outside, the heads of several of the black-suited men turned to watch them go by. A crow leapt from a bare tree that had stood beside the church that was now in ruins.

"Mrs. Patzke," Homer asked, "why is life the riddle of all riddles?"

11

"What? I don't know. I'm sure I don't." She squirmed on his bony knees.

"Because we must all give it up, sooner or later." A laugh rose halfway in his throat, then blossomed as a smile.

2

THAT'S HIS STORY. John Dillinger. A boy in the Middle West, he became a man in prison. His life as an adult lasted only fourteen months. During fourteen months of freedom in the pit of the depression he blazed. He made himself the patron saint of bank robbers. A martyr, a lover, a man who dared.

That's his story. I'm going to tell you some of my own story, too. And if sometimes I get the two stories tangled—well, dreams have a way of turning into memories.

I'm an old man now. What I'm talking about happened more than half a century ago. It was the autumn of '33 that John and Pete and the others drove north to knock off the First National Bank in Racine. By the next spring a lot more had happened. Everybody in the country was talking about Dillinger. The town fathers of some little burg in Ohio put up a pillbox in the square to ward off their Dillinger fears. Women dreamed about him.

That June of '34 I was working small towns in western Michigan, down Benton Harbor, Kalamazoo way. I mean small towns. Leave the main street, walk two blocks, and the corn silk was tickling your ear. And when the honey wagons would turn out the winter manure onto the loam it would raise a smell up Main Street you could chew on.

Saturday afternoon. I had the back of my little blue Chevrolet opened up, my wares on display, and a decent tip of maybe twenty frozen-faced farmers listening to me pitch.

"Men, you are born to die. Every one of you is on that slippery slope. You are condemned to extinction and the calendar is your executioner. No man will continue to act on the stage of life after the final curtain descends. Whatever the quality of your performance, you will be asked for no encores. The man who thinks he will continue to strut and fret is born a fool and will die a fool."

I was a traveling man in those days. And I had found out that there is no difference between people so great as the difference between the rooted and the transient. The farmer and the city slicker, the villager and the suburbanite, they're all joined by roots. Permanence separates them from the vagabond, the wanderer, the vagrant and the drifter.

Those who sit still are a majority, and they have always eyed with the keenest suspicion that other class, the stranger, the gypsy, just passing through.

During those days nomads were everywhere. Bonus marchers had carried their righteousness to Washington. Families would engineer midnight moves to duck overdue rent bills. Oakies lit out for the promised land in the West. Young people with nothing to lose hit the roads and the rails. They all joined the mountebanks and carnies, the salesmen and musicians and cowboys for whom home was a memory.

"Ponder well that stark reality as you ask yourselves the questions that every man—every man—asks himself: Has Death, who so jealously guards his own frontiers, has he not invaded my territory? Has his bony hand not touched certain of my most precious faculties? Is he not already upstaging the few short scenes that it is my destiny to play out on life's great stage? Has he not sapped my most prized, my most God-given possession, my manly vigor?"

Two years earlier Hoover had offered Rudy Vallee a medal
if he could sing a song that would make people forget what
was happening. But that time was long past. One in three
people was out of work in the country that winter. The rich
were keeping machine guns in their country homes. Ordinary
folks hated to see Christmas coming, the kids talking Santa
Claus.

"And isn't there some way I can win back my full powers?
Can't someone show me how to banish death's meddling
hand? Is there no source of the innate vitality that was mine
a few short years ago? Remember? Remember, men?"

I slept in my car plenty of nights. I bought cans of beans
and ate them cold while the rain pecked my roof and I figured
ways to get enough gasoline to carry me to the next town
where maybe I could sell a few Kaiser Belts, enough to keep
on going.

And if sometimes I stopped my car on the top of a hill on
a cloudy day and sat on the running board looking at some
mundane scene—a bramble-clogged gully or the crooked sur-
viving trees of an abandoned orchard—and wept, it was not
from any remorse at being cast in my life as an itinerant. It
was only because of the times, because the things I saw on
my travels primed my eyes to overflow. And because it was
such a goddamn lonely life.

"Remember the energy that drove you forward? Remember
the hot, urgent energy that tingled through your every muscle?
Is there hope that you can recapture that vital essence? Is there
hope that you can regain that virile desire? Is there hope that
you can once again be the man you were in your glory? Men,
if there wasn't, I wouldn't be here."

They were all listening, wondering how I'd found out their
secret. I had them.

My mother wanted me to be a priest. For the Irish a vocation in the family was a blessing indeed. She pinned her hopes on me. She told me to pray, that God would show me a sign if I was meant for holy orders. I wondered what this sign could possibly be. Given my practical bent, I guess I figured it would be fire dancing over Lake Erie or a voice hailing me when I went fishing down in the creek. I always felt bad about not taking the collar.

"Science is the answer. What separates modern man from the Neanderthal? Science. What separates our fragile civilization from that of the wild men of Borneo? Science. What has lifted us from the ignorant hovel of pagan barbarism into the mighty cathedral of Christian wisdom? Why nothing less than science."

But my mother knew me. I'd been a grown man ten years then and I was still looking for the spiritual sleight of hand by which I could pierce the stubborn skin of the world. I always wanted to be an insider. An actor, an impresario, a priest, they're in the know. They have the goods; the ordinary Joe doesn't. They see behind the scenes. Sitting in the audience never satisfied me. I had to know what it looked like backstage, work the rope that raised the curtain, watch the dancing girls lace their silken costumes.

"And by science, I mean true science. I mean double-A grade finest copper annealed wire. I mean solid soldered connections. I mean triple-celled, silver-plated, eighty-gauge, long-lasting batteries. Batteries that supply your precious organs with a constant flow of vital, soothing, health-giving electrical energy. Electricity, my friends, that most versatile and magical servant of modern man."

In a lot of those hick towns the electric was brand new. It was heap big magic. Lit your lights and made your radio sing. Why couldn't it cure what ailed you into the bargain?

"I know you've had doctors take advantage of you. I know

you've put your faith in quacks, in institutes, in so-called specialists, and have been sorely disappointed. And maybe you've given up hope. Maybe you've said to yourself the only thing you can do is to suffer in silence. Well, men, I'm not offering you promises. I'm not offering you empty words or useless medicinals. I'm offering you the Kaiser Belt, the only proven, totally effective, guaranteed electric belt in the world today and I'm offering it to you below the wholesale cost and I'm telling you that if you don't get real genuine relief in five days, five short days—and I'll take your wife's word for it—that I will give you double your money back, no questions asked. And listen to this, listen carefully. The first man to walk up here and buy a Kaiser Belt—don't rush now—that first man gets his not for the regular store-bought price of twenty-seven-fifty, not for the less-than-wholesale price of twelve dollars that the rest of you will pay, but for a mere nine dollars and forty-nine cents."

I sold seven belts that day. Five of them went right after the spiel. Then I loitered around the car awhile. A couple more guys would always come up, say they wanted to pick up one "for a friend."

My usual practice was to clear out, move on after a Saturday pitch. I didn't want to be available to argue with some hick about his second thoughts, have to sell him all over again.

But that town had a decent hotel where I'd taken a cold-water room for fifty cents and I had a long drive to the next burg. Anyway, it was one of those late spring evenings that are as delicate as an eyelid and perfumed with willow blossoms. It was the kind of night that you're only blessed with half a dozen times in your poor life. I wanted to get drunk and enjoy it.

After supper I wandered down to the town tavern, or cafe they called it. Six months after repeal and it was harder to get

17

a drink of good whiskey than it had ever been during the dry years. A reputable bootlegger would have hung his head to have sold some of the rotgut that was passing over the counter those days.

I was in a gin mood. They served me a kind of pink oily fluid that gave me a burn in the throat and a kick in the head every time I swallowed. It made my skin prickle.

I was watching the yokels dance to a broadcast of the Whiteman band from some ballroom in Chicago. Farm couples were shuffling their feet as if trying to wipe their shoes clean. I had my eye on two girls dancing together.

One was a brunette, sharp-faced, a line of concentration between her brows. She was leading. The other was a slim redhead with Little Orphan Annie curls.

They were flowers blossoming in a drought and you could already see the wilt beginning. There was nothing for them in this town but to scrub floor or sling hash or pick rotten cherries off a conveyor in a packing house.

Whiteman took an intermission and I moved over to their table. I suggested I join them and did. I ordered rickies all around.

A fire was burning in my gut. The booze set it off, but the fuel was loneliness and the warm young flesh of these two girls. I had just turned thirty and was thinking I'd never get any younger. They were closer to twenty.

"When Whiteman plays 'Rhapsody in Blue,' look out," the redhead, Brenda, explained. She had a whole arsenal of dimples and smiled like she'd just learned how. " 'Cause that's his theme and it means the end."

"And Cab Calloway's is 'Minnie the Moocher,' " the brunette informed me. She was Aline. Her narrow eyes looked almost Chinese.

"Yeah, and Gus Arnheim has 'Say It with Music.' And I

wish they'd play Frank Crumit on the Melody Hour singing 'Abdulla Bulbul Amir' the way he used to."

"Don't she look like Myrna Loy, though?" Aline asked me. They were a team, see.

"I thought she was her for a minute," I said. "That nose."

Aline was hot on flying. "I want to try it. Just to see what it's *like*. Just once, just to try it, just to get *up* there, just to get off the ground, just to see what things look like, to fly. I want to fly."

She looked at the pressed-tin ceiling as if she might ascend right through it. I examined the line her throat made.

"I've flown," I said.

Brenda pursed her lips and brought out dimples in the backs of her cheeks that made me swallow fast. Aline's worry line disappeared for a second, then came back, deeper.

"You have?" Brenda said.

"You have not."

"Is it true," Brenda asked, "men look like ants from up there?"

"You never went up in no aeroplane."

"Sure did," I said. "You get up there, you can see the world is round. You *see* it. Men are ants and the sky's so big it takes your breath away."

"How's it work?" Brenda said. "You look *down* at the sky?"

"Sure. You're God up there. You're God Almighty looking down on his creation and seeing the vanity of vanity, because a man ain't nothing but an ant."

"You scared?"

"Nope. You're riding the wind and you just figure, well, if I crash, okay, at least I've seen this."

"At least you've flown," Aline said, her eyes now shining at me.

19

You meet two girls in a hick dance hall, chances are one of them will be pretty, one friendly, you know what I mean. I was beginning to believe that I'd beaten the odds two ways from Sunday.

We had more drinks.

I danced with Aline. Our thighs touched. She whispered something in my ear. Her hot palm came into mine as we strolled back to the table.

Brenda licked her pink tongue over her bee-stung lips. Aline's cheeks were flushed rose. The lights over the bar glowed a soft pink. I swallowed some more of the pink gin. It didn't burn, it cooled. It didn't kick, it billowed and pillowed. I stared at the light red stain on Brenda's cigarette.

I knew there would be a moon out that night. A tea-rose moon. I knew my number had come up. I knew the sweet songs were prayers, that prayers are answered—

"That's all, John!"

I turned my head just far enough to catch a glimpse of the black revolver he was holding against my neck. I could see the snouts of the bullets packed inside the chambers. The gin all of a sudden turned to kerosene in my belly.

Imagine yourself marched naked in heat before all your female relatives. That's not exposed compared to the kind of exposed you feel when you have a gun barrel resting against the back of your neck. It's a cold, cold feeling.

A commotion had already started in the room. People came to life as if they'd been waiting all evening for nothing but this.

Another man stood on my right. I could sense him. He leaned over and started to go through my clothes. He patted me. He ran a hand up between my legs hard enough to hammer an ache into my groin.

Brenda was smiling and frowning, smiling and frowning, as

if she couldn't decide whether this was a joke. Aline said, "Hey!" but, looking at the man with the gun, fell silent.

"He's clean, Buck."

"You try something, John, your brains are going to be against the wall."

"Mister, you are under arrest."

"What the hell—"

"Shut up!"

I'd had trouble with the law before, you bet. Times, the local pharmacist or sawbones would get the constable to escort me to the town line. I'd been inside for vag, for the odd Saturday night drunk, once on a morals thing—or did that come later? Anyway, all misdemeanor stuff. This was different.

I could think of nothing except what it would feel like if he pulled the trigger. A blinding pink light? Or just the click of a switch? Or not even that?

The man on my right put his face close to my ear and breathed onions on me. He wrenched my hands, snapped on cuffs. The metal pinched.

Brenda's lower lip rippled. She pulled together the top of her blouse—earlier she'd let me eye her shadowy mounds.

The bar was buzzing now. Every face was turned toward me.

"We got 'im!" Onion-breath shouted. The crowd quieted. "We got John Dillinger! This is the famous bank robber, John Dillinger. We got 'im!"

In the stunned silence, I turned my helpless gaze to Aline. A smile crept across her mouth. A fevered, glittering look took over her eyes. I knew that if I hadn't been manacled and under arrest I could have had my way with her then, no questions asked.

And what I wouldn't have given for the chance. My Christ, I'd never seen such an inflamed expression on a woman's face.

But my mind was quickly gripped by other concerns. Twenty-eight people had been lynched for various crimes, real or imagined, the year before. I'd read in the papers about a case out in California. A young man was kidnapped, killed, his body thrown in the river. A mob took the two guys who did it out of jail and strung them up. The governor called it a patriotic act. So many people stripped pieces of bark from the hanging tree they killed it.

A group from the cafe had already joined their voices to create that persistent incoherent murmur that is the sound of a mob. They all trooped along as my two captors led me out into the night.

3

NOTHING, Billie Frechette would tell me later, had ever happened to her before that night in the cabaret in Chicago.

As a girl, she used to make the world spin doing cartwheels in the village. If she could make it spin, she owned the world. She kept her eyes open to see the trees tumble. She lived among the pines and paper birches of upper Minnesota. On the reservation. Where winters were death. Where the ice-clear water sang in spring.

Naked beneath her little smock, she would wheel and wheel. The women of the village would click their tongues at her boldness.

In church Billie loved the Virgin, the plaster pallor of her skin, the tiny rosebud of her enigmatic smile, her mild hands—one glued at the wrist—opening her veil. What fascinated Billie was the Blessed Mother's holy calm as she crushed with her foot the head of a serpent. Always afterward, Billie knew the highest beauty was the beauty of serenity. Blue would be her favorite color all her life.

Billie walked a long way into the somber woods. She was at home there. She invented her own names for ferns and mosses and salamanders.

Once she caught an especially big milk snake. She wrapped him in her mother's indigo shawl and carried him to a secret place. There she crushed his head with a rock. She broke into an icy sweat. She draped the shawl like a veil. She rested her bare toes on the snake, whose back twitched and whose mouth still gaped open and closed.

Her father was a small French Canadian who taught her to say "Bonjour" through her nose. He tickled her with his fuzzy chin. When he drank his rye he would talk too loud. Sometimes she would hear him wander into the woods shouting, or upstairs shouting at her mother. She imagined that his thin body was packed full of sound that the rye let loose. The sound must have hurt him because sometimes she found him crying.

Then he coughed forever and died.

They dressed him in his Sunday clothes. Grown-ups came to look at him. Billie wondered where the reservoir of fierce sound inside him had gone to.

They sent her to a government school for Indians in South Dakota. It was the first time she'd left the forest. The wind out there was not a lilt in the treetops but an angry animal that dragged itself across the plains and roared. It would blow for two weeks, never once inhaling. The anxiety of Billie's adolescence expanded to exactly fill the open void of plains and dry hills.

One summer she snuck down to the creek with two other girls to watch the boys swim naked. The girls crept dangerously close, lay under the drone of cicadas. Billie watched the sunlight flash on the boys' arms, turn to fire their wet torsos. She stared, fascinated, at the jewels of light in their fragile pubic hair. The girls giggled. But the light made Billie's eyes ache. It seemed to shine inside her own body, too, and make her tremble.

At eighteen she came to live with her sister in Chicago.

Chicago was a city on a spree. Rumors of fortunes filled the streets. Intoxication was a universal light switch. Billie saw it from behind the scenes. She scrubbed the floors of the stockmarket millionaires on the North Side. She handled their soiled laundry. She served them their meals in restaurants. She learned to curtsy. She wore a uniform. The men would pinch her. She brought a soup ladle down hard on an employer's hand when he tried to touch her between her legs. His nostrils stretched as he laughed, encouraged.

Once she was walking along Armitage among stately residences on her way home from her job as a waitress. The sky was gray, flecked with snow. She found herself tangled in a crowd lining up to enter a brick building. She joined them, hoping to see something memorable.

She waited in the cold, shuffled slowly forward. The steps were flanked by Corinthian columns. Yellow light silhouetted the patterns on the leaded glass. In the center of each window a cluster of fruit glowed in liquid color, grapes and cherries and saffron lemons.

Inside the sanctuary the first hint of incense made her light in the head. The hot air prickled her skin. They moved haltingly along a velvet rope. The scrutiny of mahogany gargoyles quieted conversations.

At first she could only see the flowers. Great banks of pale roses. August lilies. Violets and camellias. Flowers she knew as shooting stars. Pale jonquils and brilliant nodding anemones. Thousands and thousands of flowers. Cascades of dahlias and carnations. Blossoms of such glory that they couldn't be real— yet they must be real for the air was rank with their perfume.

Among all these brilliant curls and colors, reposing on a mattress of flowers, lay the corpse. She understood now why so many strangers waited to see him. He had died young. Impossibly young. His translucent wax face was youth itself. It glowed as if lit from within. The lips were set with a hint of a curve, as if he were tasting a butterscotch lozenge. His hands, folded on his chest, were tipped with immaculate fingernails. His lustrous hair still bore the marks of the comb.

This, Billie decided, must be the son of some affluent family broken by the Crash. Brought up as a prince, he could not bear to face the harshness that had descended on his world. He had slit his mild wrists while lying in a tub of warm water and had let pink death seep into his brain.

Billie felt her own brain begin to tumble. She could not draw a breath into her chest. She fought an urge to kiss those tender lips. She felt her own hands shaking with the sheer beauty of this death.

She hesitated until the large woman behind pushed against her, leaned myopically over the coffin, and said, "He don't look so tough."

Later Billie found out that the young man had been a pontiff of the underworld. He dealt in bathtub gin and needle beer. His life had not bled away into tepid water. Instead he had had his gut ripped open by bullets from a passing car. She began to marvel then about this magical place known as the underworld.

At night she would go out with girlfriends from work. They became devotees of movie palaces where they watched bejeweled ladies in breathless silk mouthing love.

Billie wore raspberry lip rouge and told lies. Her father had been a fur trader, she said. He'd gone down with the Titanic when she was still a baby. An unscrupulous partner, an Italian, had embezzled her birthright.

In November—this would have been in '33—Billie went with Marjory, a fellow waitress, to a cabaret on the North Side called Swans. It was a foggy, dank night. During the coming on of winter Billie often had flashes, stark reminders of the huge winters she'd endured as a girl. She would think she didn't belong in this dirty growling city. Didn't belong anywhere.

Under the low ceiling they joined another girl and a couple of fellows at a table near the dance floor. The place was crowded and loud. Billie looked around eagerly.

She had become an inveterate trier of cocktails. Sensitive to alcohol, she made keen distinctions among the feelings different drinks generated in her. A Stinger would cast a minty orange light over her thoughts. She would imagine she had turned into perfume, her nails and teeth the only solid parts left. She would hear clarinets on Stingers. A Tom Collins, on the other hand, made her feel jumpy as a hare.

Tonight she ordered her favorite, a Champagne Dove. That was gin, crème de menthe and lemon juice topped off with cold champagne. That was the one that dissolved the top of her head and let the stars in. It made her wise and made the high notes of the trumpet stab right through her. It turned her eyes liquid and made her aware of her naked body under her dress. It was what she always ordered when she needed a lift.

She danced with one of the fellows. He stooped a little because Billie was short. He talked at her, his breath stale. He talked about the president, pronouncing it "Jewsevelt." He bounced his large Adam's apple.

Back at the table she sipped another drink. She watched the singer, a long-legged woman with skin blacker than any Billie had seen. She sang "My Old Flame," waving her long yellow gloves in the air. Her sequins flashed. When the band swelled her voice seemed to ride up, buoyed by the music, until it went right over the top, beyond the range of voice. That gave Billie a physical thrill. The Champagne Doves were taking effect.

Blue votives burned on the tables. Three yellow spots converged on the band. When people passed in front of them their bodies cast shadows along the smoky air.

27

Marjory was talking to a man who'd just come to their table. Billie was tracing the coronet solo with her finger against the tablecloth.

". . . my friends Tess and Billie. You know Tess, don't you? Tess? Jack Harris? Where have you been, Jack? Isn't this band the most? I want them to do 'By a Waterfall' again. Oo, new tie?"

Billie was looking across at the band, imagining the whole room, the dancers, the singer, the cigarette girls, the lights and candles, all reflected in golden miniature in each of the brass horns.

". . . care to dance with me?"

No one said anything. Billie realized the man was speaking to her. She looked at him. He was in shadow. Then someone moved and the light caught the side of his face. His mouth was tucked into a hint of a smile. His eyes were looking. The drinks made a shower of static electricity wash her skin. She nodded.

He danced awkwardly, stiffly. But Billie was taken by his crooked smile. His suit had a crisply expensive fit. She could feel his eyes on her.

When he made a mistake, missed a beat, she murmured, "Oops."

The music stopped. They separated. Suddenly she felt all wrong. She could not return to her friends, could not break the connection with him. She looked into his face and saw that he felt it, knew the feeling, understood it, accepted it. How could he, so fast? She licked her lips and started a sentence three times without a clue as to what she wanted to say. He touched her elbow as if to lead her somewhere, but they remained standing in the mist of smoky yellow light.

The band started up again. "Stardust." He held her closer. She could feel him breathing as if the air belonged to him. And when he became very still she knew that he was holding his breath to feel her breathe against him. Nightingale, fairy tale.

The trumpeter stood and blew out the first four notes of the melody. Love's refrain. Billie felt the man's arm on her back.

"That was long ago," the singer toned. Everything, Billie thought, was suddenly long ago. Her life was long ago, before this night.

"Lookit Johnnie," Red said. He spoke with the accent of an emigré remembering his native tongue. "Dance number three with that package."

"He needs a regular," Elaine said. They were sitting in a booth by the wall.

Red said, "I can see his heart going pitter-patter."

"She's dangerous. I can tell the dangerous ones. I can always tell."

"Dangerous?"

"I can tell," she said. She took a drag from her cigarette and puffed the smoke out without inhaling, jutting her lower lip beyond the upper. "She's cute, but she's dangerous. She thinks of herself some, I'll wager. I believe she likes him too."

"It's so easy," Red commented.

"What?"

"When you've got the swag they fall so easy."

"Oh? Who do you think you're talking to?"

Red laughed his innocent laugh.

Red and Elaine both watched the dancing couple. John's eyes looked sleepy. Billie's emerald dress was cut low in back. She had sleek hips and a sheen in her black hair that caught the lights. They stepped, stepped, stepped. The reed section made a dozen loops. The drummer ran off six quick rim shots and dove back into the beat with a splash of cymbals.

Elaine hummed, "Though I dream in vain." She was a pretty

29

redhead with a long upper lip. Life had dealt her some bad hands in husbands—a hard-faced drunk and a hotel clerk full of five-and-dime dreams. Her strategy was to throw in her cards and go with the luck of the draw. Twice divorced, she had a daughter she boarded in the country.

"Johnnie had a coy broad before," Red observed. "He paid for her divorce and she fluffed him. She thought coy was peachy."

Elaine didn't know exactly what game Red and Johnnie were playing. She knew it was a serious game. She didn't like to think about it.

She preferred to dwell on the story they kept up among themselves, to have it fresh for outsiders. In the story, Red was a businessman, the son of a wealthy family from Des Moines, the Lewis family. He was Orval Lewis. Johnnie'd come up with that name, Orval. Red laughed when he said it. And Elaine herself had decided on the Lewis's business: soap. He would be a soap heir.

Red became a soap heir. She taught him the habits of the rich, as she understood them from magazines. He bathed two or three times a day. Sometimes she would help him wash. He liked that, liked being a big baby. She had him drink tea, listen to phonograph records of Caruso.

Eventually, Elaine came almost to believe the story.

She snapped her cigarette, missed the blue glass ashtray, spilled ashes onto the linen.

"There's the one," she told Red, pointing to a woman across the room. "My friend went to her party. They had a pig."

"Who?"

"With the polka dots."

"Oh. A pig?"

"At this party. A pig, a hog. A little piggie. Made him drink martinis."

"How?"

30

"How do I know? The pig got tight and didn't they think
that was a laugh. That's her."

"Gee."

"Isn't that something?"

John and Billie joined them in their booth. She carried a little
bead bag and Elaine thought that bead bag was the cutest.
Billie smiled a shy smile.

They ordered drinks. The perfumed tang of the Champagne
Dove tickled Billie's nose. She looked more carefully now at
the face of this man, this Jack Harris. His eyes, the spin of
the cocktail made her feel like a dirigible coming loose from
its mooring.

Elaine said again about the woman who'd brought the pig
to the party and they all laughed. Billie laughed too long,
could hardly catch her breath.

"Seen you doing the cakewalk out there," said the big-faced
man, Orval. "Swell."

"Ever seen such beautiful hair?" Jack said. Flattered, Billie
reached to stroke her cascade of black silk.

They danced again. The lights, as they turned, would shine
in her eyes and make them water. A man blew a birdcall from
a sax, a long golden evening note. Jack Harris whispered in
her ear. When she looked his eyes were beaming at her. She
nodded. Oh, yes.

They left soon after. He drove her to Lincoln Park. They
walked along the autumn-scented paths. Down to Lake Michigan.
She'd never seen the lake at night. Near shore the water played
with the reflection of lights, sparkling. Farther out, a cold and
final darkness took over. The water lapped and lapped against
the beach. The cold wet air got up her dress and chilled her,
thrilled her.

The Champagne Doves were cooing to her. A girl has to let

a little madness come over her, she imagined. A girl has to take a chance in life.

She watched his shoes, brown and white bucks, odd, elegant shoes for the time of year.

He held her around the waist and told her how he liked to come down here where everything ended. The dark water did not depress him, it made him feel clean, whole.

He took her to his apartment. It was so natural, she felt she'd done this all before. Had waited for him to open the car door for her before, like a lady. Had felt him lift her coat from her shoulders. Had seen this red and blue carpet before, this fringed lamp, this maroon plush davenport, the picture on the wall of the Pyramids of Egypt. Had stood at the window while he tuned in these very words on the radio, ". . . it's a honky-tonk parade . . . a melody played in a penny arcade."

She felt a heartbeat in her belly as his hand gripped her shoulders from behind. She knew he was going to say those words, what were they? Yes, "I had a dream about you." In his soft twangy voice.

He ran his hand up her neck, smoothed his fingers over the small hairs that patterned her nape. She turned to him, her legs pivoting deliberately. She saw his scarred lip smile, as she knew it would. She pressed her mouth to his.

She said something to him as they stepped to the bedroom, spoke as if she were recalling lines or prayers learned by heart long ago.

The steam heat was gurgling in the pipes, but the window was open in there. The breeze off the lake billowed the white curtains, curled around her pretty legs.

4

"HE'S A MAD DOG!" Buck insisted. His voice bent. It sounded like a nail being yanked from hardwood. "He's killed twenty people. This is him. This is John Dillinger."

Buck was some kind of a lawman, probably a dry goods clerk they deputized for the Fourth of July parade. His two front teeth overlapped like crossed fingers. He'd taken me into an office that served as the local police station and jail. Twenty other men crowded into the little room. More pressed against the windows.

The constable had just arrived. He was a heavy man who looked perpetually as if he were about to belch. I could imagine him in overalls slopping hogs, but I later learned that he doubled as the town barber. He must have been at dinner: just as he settled behind his desk his tongue found a dollop of gravy at the corner of his mouth.

"I'm not Dillinger," I said. I added, "I can prove it," though I had no idea how.

"Shut up!" Buck roared. "You shut your lying mouth! I've seen your picture. You filthy liar."

"I'm not him."

Buck nodded wildly in contradiction. His original accomplice, of whom I'd seen nothing more than an bristly Cro-Magnon chin, yanked my collar from behind until it sliced into my windpipe.

"It's him, Hollis," Buck told the constable, who was in the

33

process of stuffing a bulldog briar full of Duke's Mixture. "I've studied them pictures. This is John Dillinger. Spotted him down to Mason's Cafe vamping a couple of girls. A ladies' man—everybody says Dillinger's a ladies' man."

The constable's eyes narrowed at me as he sucked wetly on the stem, sending blue-gray puffs out the side of his mouth.

"They got a reward out for him, Hollis," Buck continued hoarsely. "Fifteen thousand, I heard. The federals are looking for him. Everybody is."

The word "reward" echoed through the crowd. I heard somebody quite close to me murmur, "Fifty thousand" to his neighbor.

A reporter had pushed his way inside. They cleared a space for him. He held up his camera, squatted a little, aimed, and blasted us with titanium light. The air took on the smell of mica. I still have a copy of that photo somewhere: a dozen men craning to get into the picture, myself impossibly young, on my face the sick expression of a man who's just had a gin high kicked out from under him.

But the reward talk had given me an idea.

"Got to hand it to you boys," I said. That brought a few chuckles. "Yes sir."

"This ain't Chicago, John," somebody said.

"Sure ain't."

"You looking to take the Fidelity National, John?"

"Your gang around here? We'll grab 'em if they are."

"That's not Dillinger," the constable said. This quieted them.

Then a wave of protest broke out. Somebody produced the WANTED poster. Buck looked, pointed his finger at it, pointed at me, pointed at the poster, back at me, grinned.

"That's him, Hollis. I'll swear on my private parts that's him. Look."

Hollis took the poster from him but didn't look at it.

"Reward, Hollis," somebody said.

"Call them, Hollis. Put us on the map."

"Sitting in Mason's as bold as a blue jay."

"He's a killer."

"Turned white when Buck grabbed him."

"They're all cowards, comes to it."

The constable spoke with his teeth clamped onto the stem of the pipe: "This fella ain't killed nobody. Look at him. Look at his eyes."

A low grumble answered this assertion.

"Check that picture, Hollis," Buck demanded.

"Sure, he looks like him. And that Congregational minister down there, you put spectacles on him, he's the spitting image of FDR. But that don't make him president."

Buck shook his head vigorously.

"What's your name," the constable asked me. I told him. He read from the flier: "Half-inch scar back of left hand. Scar middle of upper lip. Brown mole between eyebrows."

I was quickly examined.

I watched a yellow cast come over Buck's face. Somebody laughed.

"Why you dirty skeesicks!" the deputy said. He slammed a fist into my gut that emptied the whole world of air. My hands, remember, were still cuffed behind me.

I don't know as I could blame him. Poor Buck was from that moment destined to go through his life as the man who'd grabbed "Dillinger." An act that he was convinced would effect his redemption now promised instead to turn him into the perpetual butt of every wag in the county.

He stormed out of the office, the rest of them close behind. Some were already guffawing over the incident. Others cursed me for a no-good polecat.

The constable unlocked the handcuffs. My fingers tingled as the blood came back.

"You do look like him," he said.

"Is that a crime?"

"No, ain't no crime. Just, fellas get restless. Half those boys in here tonight been busted off their farms. They're used to doing things. Somebody took that away from them. So they all got the jimmies."

"I was a little worried there."

"Good reason. You take my advice, you'll shave off that mustache, part your hair different."

"Why should I? It's my face."

"Not any more it ain't. You mark my words. That Dillinger's fooled around too much with the law. They ain't going to give him a chance. Certain lines a man crosses, there just ain't no way back. It's true with women and it's true with the law. You'll see." Like every barber he had a little philosopher in him.

I said, "Hollis, you been feeling like you lack a little vim lately?"

How come I'd never noticed before that June this resemblance I bore to a man whose picture had been staring at me from the papers for months? For one thing, I never had occasion to see a photo of myself. You always look different to yourself in a photo than you do in the mirror. That intimate companion whose cheeks you shave, whose teeth you brush, is constantly beguiling you with winks and smiles and grimaces. But the frozen cross section that turns up on emulsion is a total stranger. They say Eleanor Roosevelt, in person, was an attractive woman—she just wasn't photogenic.

Studying the photos of Dillinger, the likeness grew on me. I had the small cleft chin, the high forehead, the hair receding along the part line, the flat eyebrows and jug ears.

I didn't have the smirk behind the lips that I saw in every one of the Dillinger portraits. The tilted smile. But, you know, yes I did too.

My face began to change. Every time I'd look in a mirror— I'd be sitting in a bar and I would glance up to see myself behind the bottles staring back with cold gray Dillinger eyes, my mouth casually twisted upward on one side.

And not just my face. When it comes to resembling some-one, posture is as important as the nose or the cheekbones. Dillinger had a powerful build and a fluid way of moving. I'd seen Movietones of him when they caught the gang in Tucson and brought Dillinger back to Indiana on a plane. He walked with a confident swagger, light on his feet. Short, like I was, almost bandy-legged, but with a presence that came over even in the jerky newsreel.

I acquired that strut. When I stood I held my hands at my sides loosely, the way a man with a gun in his pocket might stand.

Walking out of that hick jail, I began to see with new eyes. Banks didn't look the same. Or cars. Or women. The steak I treated myself to later that night, the glass of amber beer I drank with it, the way I held my cigarette in my mouth, it all meant something now. I had been touched by the light of notoriety.

My entire outlook on life changed. Now—that was the ticket. Not tomorrow. Not yesterday. Time became precious. To be satisfied with getting by, the way I'd been until then, was sacrilege. Loneliness? I would never ache with loneliness again. I was connected to the world at last. Millions had seen my face. I was tied into something serious.

What I couldn't fathom, what I've spent a long time trying to fathom since then, is how Dillinger himself must have felt. The luster that I experienced must have been a mere gleam compared to the sun that illuminated his life.

37

* * *

"John Dillinger, alive," I was saying a week later. "Alive is what people want these days. Yes sir, watch him walk right onto our stage and act out his robberies, his escapes, before your very eyes. Ask him questions. Gentlemen—and ladies, too—all the family—you may never have another chance to see with your own eyes John Dillinger, the most daring criminal of our day, Public Enemy Number One."

Sparky Masterson sent furrows shooting up from the bridge of his nose and said, "Nah, you're glorifying."

"Crime does not pay!" I countered. "This man is a hunted animal. If they don't shoot him down he'll go to the chair. He's already spent nine years behind the walls at Michigan City. His loot can't do him any good. His life is a warning. He knows it now, and he wants every girl and boy to know it—Crime does not pay!"

Sparky uncrossed his arms and scratched his head, scattering cigar ashes onto his gray cowlick. He was touring the Middle West at the time with a one-ring circus. I'd worked for him briefly the year before, talking folks into a tent to see a collection of human embryos in formaldehyde. That was a popular show back then. It was supposed to say something about evolution.

"How do I know if this Dillinger thing is going to last?" Sparky was one of these ageless guys, weathered like old tent canvas.

"Look at the James Gang. Who doesn't know Jesse James to this day? Dillinger's bigger. They've seen his picture, the newsreels, they want to see him in person. I'll bet as many people know Dillinger as do Lindbergh. Next big job he pulls, people will be stampeding to get in and see this act."

"What's so hot about him? He's a punk like a lot of other punks."

38

"You've been reading those Hearst papers, Sparky. I say the Dillinger story is a human story. Story of a poor boy gone bad. Story of a youthful mistake, bad companions. It's a familiar story. Could have happened to any of us."

"Hold up a bunch of banks, where's the mistake?"

"I'm talking about ten years ago. He tried to rob a grocer. Just a boy, he's egged on by a grown man. Looking for thrills. Demon alcohol. Threw himself on the mercy and there was no mercy. No mercy, Sparky. The hard heart of blind justice."

"He went to prison?"

"Nine years. Imagine that. The nine most precious years of a man's life. Imagine it. His balls are churning juice and he's got nowhere to dump it, nowhere natural. Imagine nine years without seeing sunlight in a woman's hair. Without tasting a glass of beer. Nine years in a sweating cell.

"So he comes out, he's changed. He's bitter and the world's collapsing. It really is, this depression. He's paid his debt, he's paid ten times over. Society owes him and he's bound to collect."

"Owes everybody."

"Okay, but some dare to collect. He never hangs his head. He walks in and takes. He puts style into bank robbery. He's the Douglas Fairbanks of the heist. This is a stickup, sweetheart. Put up those pretty hands, sugar. He puts science into it. Timing. Outruns the law in fast cars."

"You want to show this on stage?"

"With real money, Sparky. Big bundles of bills to wave under the hicks' noses. Real guns firing blanks. Let them know what it's like inside a bank robbery. They see him captured—not once, but twice. No jail can hold him."

"I don't know," Sparky said. "I don't know about gangster shows."

"Not gangster. Capone's a gangster. There's a difference between a gangster and an outlaw. A gangster is a politician's friend. He's tough, but he's an egg-sucker, too. An outlaw may be mean, but he's out there, he's willing to pay the full price. The gangster wants it for nothing. A gangster's a pimp."

"What do you think we can charge to see this?"

"This is something special. This is an opportunity, Sparky. How many men out there are certified Dillinger look-alikes? Huh? Thrown behind bars as dead ringers?"

Sparky bit off a tatter of his cigar and chewed on it, his forehead furrowing into a dollar sign. The idea was sinking in.

"I'll take a chance," he said. "You can draw the people you need right from the crew. We won't have to hire anybody."

"On display, the very car he drove. The doubting Thomases will be lining up to put their fingers in the holes the bullets left."

"Where do you get that item?"

"He's driven a lot of cars. You buy a Terraplane and shoot it up. Listen, he's big. He's bigger, right now, than Jesse James. He's the greatest of the great outlaws. Greatest because he's the latest. Not just the latest, the last. You'll never see his like in this country again. I'm telling you, six months from now, he'll be bigger than Lindy. They'll be dancing the Dillinger Two-step and drinking Dillinger Slings. They'll be naming children John Dillinger McGillicuddy."

"It's—basically you see it as a clean show?"

"Sure, clean. The Methodists will walk out smiling. Not only that, but something for the ladies. See, Dillinger has this love, Billie Frechette. She's an Indian squaw, but he loves her. And she's quite a package. Let the men imagine how he makes up for lost time with her. Let them think how it took a wild Indian, a lovely savage, to satisfy his lust. And let the women join her tears, because Billie knows her man is doomed."

"Is there anything we could sell along with it?" Sparky said. "Souvenir-type items?"

*   *   *

They'd talk about that summer of '34 until Pearl Harbor, how damn hot it was. End-of-the-line heat that's like a claw.

The heat was just getting going on that Wednesday morning, second day of summer, when I met with Sparky's crew to choose my players. They had the sides of the big top rolled, but the sun was beating on the saffron canvas without mercy. The air was a cooked vapor of sawdust and elephant shit. I was afraid I'd sweat right through my pearl-gray Dillinger worsteds.

The circus workers were lounging in the bleachers, sucking on tin cups of burnt coffee, smoking, knuckling particles of sleep from their eyes. It was quite a group. Some were the men who drove the moving stock, who handled the rigging, cleaned the animal cages. Some were wives of clowns. There was a fat lady, a tattooed man, a geek who swallowed small frogs whole and bit the heads off milk snakes.

"I'm Dillinger," I started. Somebody coughed. "I don't care what you think of me. I'm no bellyacher. I take. I take, I run, I kill if I have to. I love women in a way the poets only talk about. I'm alive, and I need live people."

They weren't looking at me.

I glanced quickly over my shoulder. On one of the middle rows of bleachers behind me a midget—he went by the name Count Baroni—was mimicking me. He had his hands clasped behind his back, as I had. Apparently he'd been imitating my movements.

I reached into my pocket for the .38 pistol I'd picked up in a pawnshop. I fired a shot close enough to his head so that he'd feel the zing. The bullet splintered a bench behind him. His face ashed over. He tiptoed down the bleachers and headed toward the exit.

I held up the gun. "Alive! Live ammo. Live people. Dillinger alive. Pierpont alive. G-men alive. Billie Frechette alive. That's what will draw the tip, not wax dummies, not cardboard cut-outs. The Dillinger of our dreams alive. And we have to have him alive, onstage, to feed those dreams. I am John Dillinger. The people I choose here today will *be* these other characters. If you don't think you can become a criminal, don't hang around. If you're not willing to enter into the soul of a desperate man, I don't want to talk to you."

Five or six of them left. From the rest, I selected four bohunks who looked like they got their hair cut once in a while to play the G-men. I told them they'd each get a navy-blue suit to wear during performances. I had them stand with their arms crossed to see if they had the right bureaucratic effect. They'd do.

Red Hamilton was no problem. Half the roustabouts were shanty Irish with big blank faces who could have passed for the Canadian any day. Unfortunately, none of them were missing fingers. I chose the one who had the wickedest glint in his eye. His name was Eddie Moran.

I'd picked out one of the clowns to play Homer, but he turned it down. He was such a hit with the kids Sparky wouldn't make him double up. I settled for a bean pole named Silas Wellington, a distant cousin of the Duke of Wellington, according to him.

The one I chose for Pete Pierpont, every so often he'd pretend to spit between his teeth, emitting nothing but a little sound, "tit." But his right-angle jaw was the closest thing there to the handsomeness that Pierpont was noted for. I never did like him in real life but he would prove to be a reliable performer in the show.

I walked over to a kid who was sitting in the front row cleaning his fingernails. He was the Elephant Skin Boy in the Ten-in-One. Wearing a loincloth he would lie on a bed of nails. He also helped cook meals for the crew.

"Baby Face," I said.

"What?" he said.

"How's the weather down there, shorty?"

"Why you—" He jumped to his feet. I'm not tall, but the top of his head came only to the level of my nose. He clenched his fists.

"You've got spunk, I like that," I told him. "I want you for Baby Face."

"Yeah? Well, lay off the cracks."

His name was Marty Burke. He had just the kind of round features, assertive chin, and small eyes that I wanted.

Unlike the men, whose natural shyness made them drag their feet, the women were eager to get involved in the drama. They wanted to show off. I selected a skinny blonde with big eyes and a plump Polish girl to act as all-purpose molls, ready to flash a little leg to spice up the show when we weren't too deep in the Bible Belt.

For Billie, I needed somebody special. To begin with, her picture had been in the papers a lot. There had to be some likeness. I wanted her to be a dish, somebody I wouldn't mind making mock love to for the next how many months.

I had my eye on a dark-haired Italian woman sitting up in back. She sold cotton candy and told fortunes on the side. She had a wide eager mouth. Her peasant blouse draped a lot of shape. But when I asked her to come down and try out I was sorry to find that she was two inches taller than me. She expressed her own disappointment with some succulent dago curses.

I considered another one, but she was just too bony. I thought I'd scored with my third pick, but she opened her mouth and let out a fat Natchez "y'all."

I settled for a small woman who'd been watching me intently, dropping cigarette ashes down the front of her dress without noticing. Her hair was copper-blond, but a wig would fix that. I could tell she bleached it, she had the umber eyes that never go with fair hair. She looked about as much like an Indian as Greta Garbo did, but she had a small enough build and a blank face that you might have called cute.

In fact, up close there was something a little depraved about her that I liked. You got the impression she was dreaming about some other life that she'd had, or that she planned to have. It was as if the present was a minor inconvenience that she was being forced to endure.

She said she was Ivy Holcomb. Her husband was Harry Holcomb, the high wire man.

I asked if she was enthused about becoming Dillinger's lady. She said yeah she could use the extra money.

"One question," she said. "Who is this Dillinger character anyways?"

5

ONE DAY during the summer before the market crashed, John trotted out onto the ball field to play second base against a team of Legion boys, Indiana state champs who'd been brought in to challenge the inmates. He was five years into his sentence. Prisoners, guards, politicians and invited guests waited on the bleachers. Seated among them was a scout for the Cubs.

A scout. To boys growing up in the country those days, the big leagues were Valhalla. You would never see a game, only read the names in the papers or hear them through the static of the radio: Kiki Cuyler, Hack Wilson, Gabby Hartnett. And Gehrig and Ruth and Lefty Gomez, those giants from the East. Big league ball was played entirely in our imaginations.

And in our dreams a scout would one day appear, sent down from the bigs with a single goal: to stretch forth a hand and beckon the one whose agility and reflexes destined him for glory.

John played ball. Played games at dusk back in '22 when folks were breathing hope. He had it, people told him. He had the eyes, the fever in the nerves you need to jump on the slashing ground ball. Chance he could play pro ball. Good chance.

A voice that day said, "Johnnie."

They were warming up in the outfield. John effortlessly scooped a rolling ball into his pudgy, frayed-leather mitt. He fired it to another player. He stepped to the foul line to shake hands with Pete.

"What are you doing?" Pete asked.

"Ah, you know."

"You're a clown, Johnnie. I don't know about you. Didn't we talk?" With his chin, Pete indicated the subject of their conversation, the field, its patches of grass and dirt.

"We're going to knock the socks off these yokels today," John said. "I'm ready, I can feel it. I can see the ball. Understand? See it."

"They dress you in pajamas and send you out here to perform. You're a little boy."

"Lundy's throwing steam. These greenhorns won't be able to touch him. We're going to show them something."

"You've got time to do, fella." Pete wasn't going to let him off easy.

"They see you've got talent—genuine talent—and—"

"Stop it."

"I'm serious. It happens. They give you a shot at pro ball. If you've really got it. And today—"

"You're dreaming. You let them parade you like a monkey. You're not ready. Know what I've been telling you? You have to be ready every second. Every chance you get you spit in the man's eye. He slaps you down, but you're alive. If you want to eat his fairy tales, play his games, you might as well sit in the hot seat and let him turn on the juice."

"It's a game, Pete. It's all a game."

Their eyes locked for a second. John flashed his crooked smile. Pete moved up to sit in the stands.

Pete had tried to escape three times. He'd received sixty days in the hole, ninety days, finally six months. Six solid months stripped in a stone cell, without light. When he came out, they marched him around the prison naked, a skeleton from a diet of bread and gruel. Marched him, blinded by the light, as a warning.

Two days after that, when Pete managed to open his eyes a slit, he swung on a guard and drew another month in solitary, his two broken fingers left to heal on their own.

Backpedaling for a high fly, John noticed a spiral of gulls. From the guard towers of the prison, it was rumored, you could just glimpse the azure of Lake Michigan. But the prisoners never caught sight of the water. Their only clues that they were on the shore of this enormous inland body were the watery, fishy smells that came over the walls with a north wind and the gulls that streaked their sky. Today the birds were soaring in white circles on the updrafts, a sure sign of rain.

Lundy took the mound for the Michigan City team. His motion was a pastiche of all the photographs and movies of pitchers he'd ever seen. He would reach up as if retrieving the ball from the back of his neck, lift a leg, cock an elbow, wag a knee, peek out from behind his glove, pivot, jerk his head, then undo these movements as he came around to fling the ball.

When he received the ball back from the catcher he would glare at the batter and give a little involuntary jerk of his head, his bottom teeth jutting. His fastball came in like a ripe apple, but dropped through a trap door just before it reached the plate.

Doc Lundy himself was a quiet young man of twenty-five. He had no medical background to explain his nickname. Nor had he ever let anyone in on why he'd strangled his mother and thrown her out of the second-floor window of the family home in Terre Haute. He would complain that such-and-such a guard "gets on my nerves." Or it would be the summer heat. Or a politician he read about in the paper. Or the smell of cabbage soup. "It gets on my nerves." His mother, they assumed, had gotten on his nerves.

He struck out the side in the first inning.

John led off for the prison team. He hammered at the first pitch and struck air. The pitcher, Adam's apple bobbing, had fooled him with a screwball. John choked up and watched two balls and a called strike sail by. He smiled at the blue-eyed hurler and cracked the next one down the base line. John beat the third baseman's throw by half a step, but the umpire, one of the guards, called him out. The convict spectators jeered.

Years before, John had known another umpire. Ed Singleton, a man with his ring finger and pinkie webbed together. The guys would make fun of Ed off the field, but the man had a papal authority calling balls and strikes. The bat frozen on your shoulder, you would watch a curve ball veer from way outside to nick the corner of the plate. You'd know that you had been fooled. But Ed hadn't. He would scream, "Steee-ha!" and point both hands toward the gasworks beyond right field.

Singleton was a thirty-one-year-old who had never grown up. A lonely man who looked up at the world as from the bottom of a lake. A no-account, semipro, boozing umpire.

He had told John they could make some money together.

Ed Singleton was a drunkard. John, who'd never had a taste for liquor, got into the habit of going with the older man to small-town speakeasies. The scalding bootleg rye would soon set John to dreaming. He would become fascinated by a piece of dirty yellow silk that trimmed a woman's dress. Fascinated by the way her mouth moved when she talked. Fascinated by the idea of easy money.

"Easy money, John," Singleton said. "And lots of it."

Never afterward could he imagine why Singleton's scheme had made sense. But it wasn't the plan, it was the gun—the gun, the booze, the thrill, the daring. All it took, Singleton assured him, was to dare. You could have anything, be anybody, if only you could master your fear. John knew that was true. Maybe he knew in his heart, too, that Singleton was a coward.

A young man has wires in his blood. A pistol in his pocket and easy money within his grasp set those wires singing. John had spent the early evening drinking with Singleton. Dutch courage, the umpire said. You'll need it.

Each sip of whiskey ratcheted the tension in John's belly, made the light crackle in his eyes. When they walked out of the speakeasy the pavement felt hard as ice under his feet. The November night swarmed with the smell of leaves and coal smoke.

Simple. The grocer would be walking along with his cash.

"You take a sock loaded with a bolt," Singleton instructed. "Whack him on the head with it. Grab the loot. I'll be waiting at the end of the block with the car."

Simple. In an alcohol-tinted dream John was already crowing at the take. So simple.

But in life a man does not go unconscious because you hit him with a bolt. He turns. Screams. He screams the Chihuahua yelp that is the Masons' distress call. The night goes loud all over.

You pull the gun. He won't stop screaming. He lashes. The gun drops. Fires. Shades are going up. Porch lights come on. Doors open. You run.

It's a dream you can't wake up from. The car is gone. Singleton is gone. Steee-ha! The night is threatening. You're sweating. You're burning. You try to walk but your blood says run.

John endured the dark menace of his sorry act for two days before they came for him. He told. His repentance was sincere.

"Tell them the truth, Johnnie," his father advised. "Say you're sorry. It was evil companions. They'll understand. You're not a bad boy. Just say you're sorry. Very very sorry."

Guilty, he told them. Sorry. His father didn't show up in court. The judge, maybe he'd eaten spicy stewed tomatoes for lunch. Maybe he looked at John and saw a smirk lurking in the lips. Wheels turn. A man can be picked up and lifted to the sky. Or crushed. The judge said, twenty years.

Singleton hired a lawyer and drew a different judge. He got off with eighteen months.

That prison day in '29 was warm, pregnant. The sun still shone, but clouds were moving in, clouds so bright you couldn't look at them. The grass was scruffy. John trotted out to his position. Behind him, past right field, was the looming brick wall.

For the Legion boys the game with the inmates was a lark. When they first took the field, they laughed with the heady superiority that touches any visitor to a penitentiary, the knowledge that you can walk out of this cage, that others can't.

Their first baseman led off the inning. A pink-cheeked Norwegian youth, he turned to his bench and made a remark after the first pitch. Without hesitation Doc Lundy reached back and slammed a hard one that backed up on the hitter and walloped him in the kidney.

As the next player approached the plate, Doc hefted the ball as if it were a hand grenade. He heaved a looping curve that started for the kid's head, then dove across the plate. The batter dropped to the dirt. The inmates laughed. The Legion bench quieted.

Doc threw hard for four innings. John pivoted a slick double play in the third, but had few chances to show his range and style in the field. He hit a double in the fourth, but two innings later the Legion pitcher made him look bad, made him go after an outside sinker.

The game went to the bottom of the seventh scoreless. Then the prison right fielder, a button man for Capone, walked and stole second. He went to third on a fly ball. A Pollack, in for check kiting, came up and walloped a fastball into center. They proceeded to the eighth inning with the prison team a run ahead.

The heat had grown tropical. Clouds now formed enormous hot-white columns above them. The sky swirled, carrying aloft dust and scraps of paper.

The first Legion boy up hit a squibber back to the mound. Doc, who had to take some time to untangle himself after every pitch, bobbled the ball. The runner reached safely.

The next batter smacked a huge fly into right. The horsehide sphere drifted one way, then the other. The Capone man ran in, faded to his left, scrambled back to his right. He dove. He caught the ball.

The high brick walls made a funnel for the wind. Dust men rose up and scurried across the outfield. The rumble of thunder burst from underground and crashed off the walls.

Doc straightened his cap, pushed up his sleeve, scratched behind his knee. The Legion batter came up, swinging three bats. His enormous hay baler's arms swiveled about his head. He flung two bats away. He knocked the remaining one against his cleats. He pounded the plate. He turned the lumber

51

around and tapped the handle on the ground. Finally satisfied, he stepped in and glared out at all the captive men.

Doc aimed a fastball down the center of the plate, defying the lummox to hit it. The batter swung, throwing a foot out to keep from falling as his bat sailed through nothing.

The infielders barked their encouragement to Doc. A drop of rain as big as a fist hammered the dust between first and second base.

The batter puffed his cheeks. Doc wound up and threw with the identical motion. Only this time he pulled the string. The ball floated in. The big hitter groped with the bat. He managed a rolling foul ball.

A guard adjusted a casement window in the gun tower, reflecting for a moment the sky.

Some of the prisoners in the stands were holding newspapers over their heads. The warden, most of the visitors were already leaving. The batter called time to adjust his socks.

The rain was pocking rhythmically now. The air reeked of dust.

Doc tried a lazy curve. The batter watched it. Ball. Doc paced behind the mound in what was quickly becoming a downpour. He marched to the rubber, wound up, and threw the ball. It was a steaming fastball straight down Broadway.

The sky cracked. The clouds tumbled, leaving a brilliant, eye-aching white from which a torrent of rain poured.

The ball skidded off the bat and tore up the center of the infield. John saw it with stunning clarity. He broke toward second. The ball's english caught and flung it upward. John leapt, speared it. He twisted in the air so that he landed on his back. He let his legs continue over his head. He sprung back onto his feet. Took one step to touch the base. Leapt to avoid the spikes of the sliding runner. Reached back against his direction of motion. Put his whole arm into a desperate throw to first. The ball just beat the lunging batter, ending the inning.

The ground was now alive with the pelting drops. The sound was a white rush.

The scout, if there'd been one, had already departed. The game was called.

As the others ran for cover, John walked slowly across the field. Wheels turn. He would never again have as keen an edge for baseball as he'd had today. He was twenty-seven years old and he still had at least five more years to serve for a single boyish mistake if he couldn't get a parole.

He felt a slap on his back. Pete's wet face grinned at him. "Nice play, Johnnie."

6

JOHN NEVER DID make it to the big leagues. He gave up baseball, started to focus on doing his time. He sewed the yokes onto Big Yank shirts. He ran the machine up and down the stitches. Up and down, up and down. Each shirt perfect. He was proud of his work. Shirt after shirt after shirt.

In the summer, the odor of piss and disinfectant would mix with the caustic fumes from the soap factory. Men on the steaming upper tiers would awake under a bluebottle blanket, the flies too lazy to stir as their hosts jerked and swatted.

They would draw lines in the dirt of the yard. Here's the door. The cages. Here's where the guard stands. The light's coming in these windows. It's ten in the morning.

Red would step into the imaginary space. To a counter. Then John, Pete. Homer would stand with his back to them, his hands cradling the shape of a machine gun.

"Change, please," Red would say, stepping up to a teller's cage of air.

"Everybody down!" Pete would shout.

They would move to their positions.

"No," Pete would say. "You just walked through a wall." And they would start over, do it all again.

"Intelligence, logistics, lines of maneuver," Pete would explain. "It's all so simple if you break it down. So damn simple. We're fighting a battle, we must win it. We will win if we stick to the tactics planned in advance. It's science."

You had to case a bank for days, he said. Learn who worked there, how they might react. You had to check the location of the cages. Of the cages, the offices, the vault, the closets. Everything. Every window. You would watch the guards, their patterns. You would look at where the police station was. You would know that bank better than the people who worked there. That was science.

So they would do it again. Pretend, laugh, spend the imaginary money they stole from imaginary vaults. Only Pete never laughed.

"You have so much time inside the bank," he'd tell them. "When the time is up, you quit. You move. It doesn't matter if you're reaching for fifty thousand at that second. You leave it behind. You stick to the timetable. You're outside and you haven't fired a shot. You plan the escape route, rehearse it."

Pete saw patterns. Not just the layout of a bank. He had maps in his head that charted worlds. He saw through to the bones of life. That's why they had confidence in him.

This was how they spent their time, dreaming.

Dreaming to fight the daily, minute-by-minute boredom of prison. To forget the meals of watery beans and cornmeal mush. To forget the crackle that drifted from the guards' target range.

In the spring of '33, two months after Roosevelt took office, they released John on parole. What was it like to move, to be driven along the Indiana plains after nine years in one spot?

His second day home, a man came to the back door of his father's farmhouse. John opened it. The man stared down at his own dusty shoes, up at John. He screwed his mouth to one side, smacked his lips. His eyes came up again, down. Up again quickly. He cleared his throat.

"What do you want?"

"Ahem. You wouldn't have some work for me, wouldya? I ain't eaten today. Yesterday neither."

John brought him in, gave him cold chicken and bread and a slice of gooseberry pie. This was something new, strange. Hoboes would come around for handouts, sure. But this man was not a hobo. He was broken. He told John he'd worked eighteen years in the mills in Akron. He wiped tears away.

"Eighteen years. And now it's all shot. Know what that feels like, Mister? Things are bad up there. My neighbor, somebody stole his dog. Et it. And that was a year ago. Before this latest."

"Bad all right."

Imagine John's eyes those first days out. Nine years of gray, nine years of brick, nine years of steel. Then suddenly, color. Moss green and apple green and the lush yellow-green of still-sticky leaves. New cream roadsters and midnight-blue coupes, models he'd never seen, glittering with chrome. A roadside clogged with poppies. A wind rippling fields of young oats.

And women. Everywhere radiant women. Their molded calves and round arms and delicate hands. The way their eyes flashed and their crimson lips pulsed and their clothes fell in shifting shadows over their curves. What a feast for his eyes.

And what a disappointment. Because the world can never match the splendor of anticipation that has been hammered out during a hard prison sentence. Never.

John's disappointment went deeper even. He was out, but he couldn't feel freedom. He'd hungered for it until he'd imagined that the prison walls were the only obstacle.

They let him go, but they robbed him. They stole his youth. Now he realized the price he'd paid. Now he knew Pete was right. Everything that happens, happens forever. You don't leave prison to return to the life you left behind. You pass through to a different life. You can never go back.

Following Pete's instructions, he contacted people. He scouted Pete's list of banks. Half of them were closed, victims of the financial collapse. He robbed a bank. It was easy. Terribly easy.

He robbed other banks. He put the money into an escape plan. In October he helped Pete and the others break out. The real fun was about to begin.

Billie moved in with him that November.

There's something about a small woman that's very appealing. They're not much bigger than a child, so they inspire some of the affection, the protective feeling that a child does. Especially if they have some nice curves.

Billie had firm hips and high, round breasts and eyes full of outdoors. John could pick her up in his arms effortlessly.

She took him to the movies. They would enter the big picture palaces in the afternoon. Watch the shorts, the newsreels, the cartoons. They would thrill to the eye play between Dick Powell and Ruby Keeler. Then they would come out into a different world than the one they'd left, a strange, sparkling night.

John was fascinated by *The Three Little Pigs*. He heartily endorsed the wisdom of the pig who built his house of brick. It suggested something to him beyond the simple moral. They saw the cartoon four times.

"I'm going to huff and puff," John would say. Billie sang the Big Bad Wolf theme for him in her thin contralto, making up personal and erotic lyrics.

The underworld remained a fascinating enigma to Billie. She

knew now he was John Dillinger, not Jack Harris. Some people had heard of him. She knew he didn't earn his living honestly. Who did? He was assured about it, capable. He was sober—he drank beer but forbade boozing. She imagined his life as something solid and unassailable. What underworld? She was about to learn.

John had come down with a skin rash and wanted to see a doctor about it. He made an appointment with a specialist on Irving Park. They stopped in one afternoon, parking in an alleyway. Billie waited in the car.

She saw John come out a short while later. She was listening to Eddie Cantor on a radio John had had installed in the car. She watched him look up at the sky for a long time, as if judging whether the low evening clouds would deliver rain. He walked toward her, his gait wooden.

"Well," she asked, "did he give you something?"

He turned his face toward her but flicked his eyes to the front. He started the engine, threw the car into gear, and backed at full speed the length of the narrow alley. Billie had to brace herself against the dashboard.

The acceleration jerked her back against her seat as they spun onto the roadway. Behind the squeal of the car's tires she heard a different sound, a crackling as of pine logs on a hot fire. The back window shattered. She felt the bullets thud into the car.

She could not stand it. It was exactly what, in some hidden corner of her mind, she'd imagined and feared.

John was accelerating the car down the road, swerving in and out of traffic. His face alarmed her. He appeared totally unconcerned. Small crinkles by his eyes indicated his concentration, but otherwise his expression was blank.

She turned reluctantly, hoping that the danger had disappeared, that John was driving fast just to make sure. But the police car was gaining on them. It had a chrome siren mounted on the left fender. She could just barely hear the wail. A red light was flashing on top, a steady pulse.

"John, oh God!"

"How far?" he asked her.

"I don't know, I don't know. A hundred yards, maybe."

A man leaned out of the passenger side of the car and pointed a handgun at them. She saw the puff of smoke but the sound was lost in the wind.

"Okay," John said.

Billie was nearly thrown into the back seat as he punched the accelerator to the floor. She turned in time to see they were speeding toward a crossing. Two streetcars were about to converge. He couldn't possibly stop in time. He wasn't trying to stop.

Warning bells were clanging furiously as they skimmed through the closing arms of the scissors. They gained two hundred yards on the police.

But the prowl car rushed forward. John wrestled the wheel to turn the Terraplane down a side street. The police car banged their bumper.

"Hail Mary full of grace! Hail Mary full of grace!" Billie blurted.

Another shot sounded.

Billie scrunched on the seat. She could see only the blur of tree limbs and housetops and sky. John hit the brakes. She slid onto the floor. A squeal. The blur revolved. She was thrown back hard into the seat. She huddled, watching John's feet pump the pedals.

After a minute, she saw him reach into his pocket, shake a cigarette from a pack, pull it out with his lips. They slowed. John was weaving through the back streets.

Normally she didn't smoke. Tobacco was big medicine with

her people, not something for every day. But now she asked him for one. She sucked the rich fumes and let them seep up into her sinuses. She reached to brush the hem of her dress where it had been soiled. She looked at him from the corner of her eye.

He saw her looking. He smiled. She frowned. He chuckled. She wrinkled her nose and gritted her teeth. He laughed. She shivered and let out a long, high-pitched sound midway between a howl and a giggle.

"You're all right," he said.

It was the best compliment she had ever received in her life.

In the middle of December the first dirty flakes of snow were swirling. Pete watched them out the window of the apartment John had rented on the North Side. They seemed to have no intention of landing. They were scouts sent to reconnoiter and report back to legions in the sky.

"Down there you spend all your time outside," John was telling him. "The days are mild as hell year round. They have trees a hundred feet high. Flowers, the smell of them can knock you cold. Fruit growing in your bedroom window. You'll have servants. They worship the dollar. Worship it."

"I don't like Mexicans," Pete said.

"The ones down there are different. Those South American girls, Pete . . ."

"You're fooling yourself. I've told you. If you had ever talked that way inside, guys would have puked on your shoes. I'm telling you now, you can only go, really go, to the places that are inside you. Maybe south-of-the-border is in you. It's not in me."

"Where are you headed, Pete?"

"Nowhere, John. I'm here. I have arrived."

Pete moved away from the window. Now John glanced out.

"The other day I was having a cup of coffee in Berghoff's," he said. "I noticed a guy looking at me. Know what I did? Took my pinkie and shoved it right up my nose like this. That makes them turn away, it really does. But it got me to thinking, maybe I'll dye my hair, grow a mustache."

"Can't hurt. I can see you, platinum blond. John Harlow."

The doorbell rang. They both tensed until the code was played out.

John got up to let Red Hamilton in.

"I thought you were bringing Elaine over."

Red just looked at him, rubbing his jaw with the three fingers of his left hand as if somebody had just bounced a punch off it.

"The cops grabbed her," he said.

Both the other men stared him. For a minute Red didn't seem inclined to amplify.

"I went to pick up my car at the garage," he said finally.

They waited. Hamilton blinked more than usual, but his face was as blank as ever.

"They fix it?" Pete asked him.

"I think they did."

"Don't you know?" John said.

"There was some trouble up there."

"Bad?" Pete said.

"Yeah."

John and Pete looked at each other. Red crossed to the window and separated the drapes a crack. The sky was limpid, the streetlights already glowing a sick yellow. He turned back toward them.

"He says is this your car? I say no it belongs to the wife. Elaine shows him the receipt, she has it in her purse. He says to me keep your hands away from your pockets."

"Who?" John snapped.

"This, I think, cop."

"And he took Elaine in?"

"No." He started to turn back to the window again, stopped. "Keep your hands away from your pockets. I held them like this." He positioned his arms as if he were dripping water down his elbows.

"This guy is a cop?"

Red nodded. "He started to pat my pockets. I had the .38 under here, I just reached in and pulled it."

John crossed his arms. He tilted his head to one side.

"Red, what happened?"

Red half-formed his hand into a gun and twice mimicked removing it from under his coat. He shook his head.

"I caught him right here," he said, massaging his shoulder as if it ached. "And he's fumbling with his coat and I hit him again."

"Where?"

He pointed to the lower part of his breastbone.

"Fucking Christ!" John said. He took two steps and kicked a bentwood chair by the wall, fracturing its leg and sending it sprawling.

"Elaine was going nutso by then. I pulled her out of the garage. I could hear them running. I ran. I left her."

"Will she talk?" Pete said.

"You know what you've done, Red?" John shouted at him.

"She knows just what to say. We've gone over it."

"Answer me!" John screamed.

"She knows where you live," Pete said. "She's been up here, hasn't she?"

"You've shit in your bed, pal. A Chicago cop?"

Red said, "Yeah, she's been here. But she knows what to say."

"You've burned this goddamn town down! The great Chicago Fire? Forget it. From now on all they'll talk about is how Red Hamilton burned down Chicago."

"Things to talk about, John," Pete said.

"We should kill him," John said. "Throw his body out there and let them have him. That's what we should do. A Chicago cop!" He opened the drawer of a secretary and lifted out a big .45-caliber automatic. He hefted it in his hand as if he intended to throw it. Red watched him, shifting his feet uneasily on the carpet.

"Go easy," Pete said to John.

John ranted. Chicago was their base. You simply didn't do what Red had done. The police wouldn't just comb the city for them. They'd knock down every crap gang, every fence, every hook shop in the city. Suddenly a lot of characters would have a hundred good reasons to turn up the gang. It was impossible.

"I think there was an imbalance," Pete said. "I don't blame you, Red. You taught them a lesson. They needed to learn it or they wouldn't have come at you like that. This is what it's about, John. Not South America. We're all up for a one-way trip if they take us. More, a hot squat for that sheriff in Lima. If we can do the human race a favor, take care of some of these monkeys, I say hip, hip. Balance things out."

"I'm sorry, John," Red said.

"What was he supposed to do?" Pete said to John.

John lifted his hands to heaven. "Do? Give him some grease. This is Chicago."

"I really am sorry," Red repeated. "He came up on me so fast. One minute I was kind of dreaming. Next thing, he's standing there. I never saw him coming. I didn't think. I'm sorry." Red's eyes watered. His hand moved tentatively toward his face, as if he were afraid to acknowledge his tears.

63

"Kill them all," Pete said. "And all the legionnaires and the politicians and the drunken judges. That's the way to get some order. Kill them, clean up the world."

Red sat down on the davenport, his back straight, head hanging.

John had returned the gun to the drawer and was pacing the length of the room. Suddenly he said, "Hell," and came and sat beside Red, draping an arm around his shoulder.

"Listen, don't worry about it, honey," he said. "You did what you had to. I'm just getting soft living on the fat of the land. We all need a little change."

"I'm sorry, John," Red said once again. John could feel a movement in the man's body like the tremor from a distant earthquake.

"Don't think about it. It takes it out of you, a thing like that. You're worried about Elaine. That's okay, baby. You did good."

"John," Pete said, "we'd better get on it."

"I'll walk over ten cops to shake your hand, Red. You know that don't you?"

"He dropped down and he sort of lurched. I think—"

"When and where?" Pete said.

"I think he was dying."

"Florida!" John said. "Let's go to Florida. Billie! Pack the bags!"

7

AFTER RED KILLED the detective in the garage, the Chicago police assigned forty men to hunt the gang. Sergeant Reynolds was in charge of the night shift. He spent two hours on the practice range every other week, not shooting mechanically but pinning his mind through the sights to the target. By that December in '33 he had already killed twelve men while carrying out his official duty.

Snow was forming a white cap on each of the iron spikes in front of the apartment building. Snow was heaping on the ledges of the first-floor windows, from which seeped light the color of weak tea. Snow dusted the sidewalk to record the steps of passers-by, then slowly erase them.

Reynolds and five of his men moved quietly up the carpeted stairs of the building. They gathered in front of a door. Reynolds knocked.

A man opened it. Reynolds fired his revolver. His round face flaming red, he moved into the dark entryway. The man he'd shot dropped to his knees beside a settee. When the man turned he was holding a Luger. Reynolds flattened against a shadow. The man advanced on his knees. Reynolds placed a bullet low in the man's belly, another in his chest. The man tipped onto his face.

Another, the one who'd been reading the evening paper by

the light of a fringed lamp, watched his friend die. His brows peaked. A frozen grin flashed onto his features. His hand moved toward his pocket. Reynolds shot him in the shoulder, the spleen, the left lung.

Reynolds dropped his empty pistol. A gun behind fired a shot over Reynolds's shoulder to take down a short, chubby man who appeared from a dark room beyond.

The officers stepped carefully into the bitter, ringing room. The short man was grabbing at the oriental carpet. He wanted to pull himself along, but the carpet was bunching in his hands. Reynolds drew a second .380 revolver from under his coat. He shot the man in the head.

One of the officers went right to the phone. He called headquarters and told them to put out the word. They'd gotten the Dillinger gang. Reynolds pushed his hat back on his forehead. With his toe he rolled over the last man he'd shot.

"This guy's a Jew," he said.

"This is Dillinger," one of the officers said, pointing to another of the corpses.

"This one looks like Pierpont. I'd know him."

Reynolds was lighting a cigar. "It's not them."

"They found out their names were Ginsburg, Tattlebaum, and Katzewitz," John said, laughing. "First victims of the Dillinger Squad."

He carefully clipped the story from the Chicago paper that they paid a boy to bring out every day from town. He added it to the others, about the Racine robbery, the break from Lima. He added it to the editorials. Why haven't our officials brought this mad dog to justice?

A strange experience: John's every gesture multiplied and distorted, as if he stood among a hundred fun house mirrors.

He especially liked to read the accounts of robberies that

had been pulled around the Middle West since the gang had arrived in Florida. Four men took off a bank in Fort Wayne. Witnesses were positive it was the Dillinger mob. A ball bearing factory had been robbed of $8,000 in payroll by three masked men—one of them walked like Dillinger.

Dillinger had been seen everywhere. He'd bought a used Dodge off a lot in Joliet. He gave an unemployed man five dollars on Milwaukee Avenue. The very same day a waitress served him roast beef and peas in Muncie. John hated peas.

It was fame. It rained on him like a mystical shower. How can we imagine it? A young man, free only seven months, robs a dozen banks. Suddenly his name is shouted and whispered across the country.

Everyone knew who he was. Everyone read about him.

Dillinger, they were all saying. Dillinger. And you're him. Imagine it. Imagine that glow.

They had their pictures taken. John and Billie stood before an assemblage of sheet metal palm trees, and pelicans, with a boat in the foreground, a painted alligator. Real palms tossed their hair right behind the photographer, but he told them the ersatz ones showed up better on film. Pete and his girl Mary had theirs taken behind a board painted with the headless bodies of a man and woman. Both figures were mincingly holding red and yellow striped towels to cover their nakedness. Pete smoothed his hair before he positioned his head. Red had his taken in his bathing suit holding a deep-sea diver's helmet as if it were a trophy he'd just won.

They were living a dream. Daytona Beach. One of the girls, the first day, ran in reporting an impending flood. They laughed their heads off. The tide. She thought the tide was a flood.

Here was life. Flush with cash. Relaxing in a tropical scene.

The world was awaiting his next move while he basked in the sun, in the light of the world's eyes.

"Over there there's a whole 'nother world," John told Billie. They were standing on the hard sand. The waves were frolicking, grabbing bits of sunlight and eating them, swirling up the beach green and foamy.

"What world?"

"Europe. Africa. South America. You wouldn't believe it, would you? The world stretches out so. I never thought about it. Anywhere you want to go, you just have to keep going far enough."

"I like it here, but I miss Mother."

Makley had rented a big villa on an uncrowded stretch of beach for himself, John, Pete, Red and the girls. Billie still hadn't gotten past the artificial feel of the climate.

"Any time you want to blow—"

"I don't want to blow, John. Why do you always say things that way? I miss Mother, that's all. It doesn't seem like Christmas down here."

"Wait till you get your presents."

"Santy's going to be good to me?"

"You betcha."

She laughed. It was late afternoon. The rollers caressed the sand with mild fingers. One reached and touched Billie's toe. She squealed.

"Hey, where are you going?" she said. "We're getting too close."

"It's easier walking down here."

"Stop it, I don't want to."

"Come on. The water's warm as anything."

"John, look out! Let me— Oh!"

"Feel good?"

"What are you doing? You're crazy!"

"Oh oh, here comes a big one."

"You're crazy. Please. Oh, God, John. Ah!"

They fell into the foam. John stood, laughing. Billie sputtered, wiped the water from her face. Her black hair slicked, she looked like a young girl.

The wet plastered her new yellow-print summer dress to her thighs, her belly. Her dark nipples poked at the fabric. John stopped laughing.

"Let's go for a swim."

"What? John, there's people."

"So?" He already had his shirt off. "Come on. We can do anything."

She unfastened one button, hesitated.

"Do it," John said.

Her hands, beyond her control, mechanically moved down the opening. She tossed the dress up on the sand, peeled off the clammy slip. His eyes followed each movement. A wave inhaled, thudded. The brightness of the sun pressed against her skin. Grass nodded on the dunes. In a moment they both dove naked.

Billie had learned to swim in the icy lakes of Wisconsin. She dolphined through this bath water, stretched in the salty buoyancy and let her toes and breasts kiss the air. John swam an awkward trudgen.

"See?" he said. He meant it's no dream. He meant he was the king of all he looked at. He was known. He was free.

John splashed. Billie spit a fountain. They both stared at the bobbing blue sky. The current carried them as they swam. When they returned they had to run up the beach a little way for their clothes. She watched the sun on his white limbs, remembering the naked boys of her youth.

The prickle of the salt and the clinging of her cold sandy dress sparked an urgency in Billie. She sprinted for the house.

69

The softness under her bare feet slowed her. She fell. Her arms became sugarcoated. She tasted the glassy glint of sand between her teeth.

"Just before we left Chicago," John said on Christmas Eve, "I phoned Leach." Matt Leach was the head of the Indiana State Police. "He knew it was me right away, but he pretended he didn't. I made him guess. I said, You imbecile. You're never going to grab me. Why don't you stuff your head up your hole?"

"If you can find it," Makley snorted.

"He starts sputtering like he wanted to call me the worst name he could think of, but he couldn't think of it. I said, in a voice just like that high voice he has, I said, Hey Matt, how about a date? Yeah, I think I love you, you queer."

They had finished eating but the four men were still sitting around the table an hour later, smoking cigars. Billie and Mary were on the veranda.

The table was crammed with dishes. They'd eaten almost a bushel of raw oysters. The hacked remains of a standing rib lay on a platter. Dishes and bowls were still loaded with candied yams and pearl onions, pickled watermelon rind and glazed ham and fruitcake and bright coin-shaped slices of carrot.

They talked about prison, about guys they'd known, about a guy who'd built a false back for the truck that took the trash out. He'd gotten through two checkpoints and clean away. Half the prison knew and the warden was scratching his ass to this day over it.

They talked of prison the way old army buddies talk of combat. Prison was their nostalgic reality. Everything that had happened since seemed insubstantial, infused with the helium of fantasy.

Once they all pricked up their ears for a moment, but it was only people down the beach shooting off fireworks to celebrate the holiday.

"Look what I got for Mary," Pete said. He opened a plush box. A diamond watch glistened. He said he'd driven up to Jacksonville for it. They talked about the price.

"I went for pearls," John said. "I love pearls. Pearls and silk go together. I think Billie looks good in pearls."

Pete snapped the box shut as he saw the two girls coming inside.

"Gin go bells, gin go bells," Billie was chanting.

"What's with you?" John said.

"Billie, let's go upstairs, huh?" Mary suggested.

"I want to go home," Billie whined. "This is not Christmas. Palm trees is not Christmas."

John sucked in a breath and let it out slow. All the men straightened.

"What are you, a lush?" John spat at her. "I told you."

"I wanna go home, Johnnie," she said in a tiny voice.

"Who's stopping you?"

"Oh, big man. Big bad man."

"You do whatever the hell you want. Just don't do it around me. You got her started?" he pointed a finger at Mary.

"We had a couple to celebrate. You know how she gets."

"I know how she gets? You don't?"

"Take it easy, John," Pete said.

"Go upstairs," John told Billie.

"No."

John said, "The world stops because it's Christmas Eve? That what you think?"

"Just wannata have some fun."

"The world doesn't stop on Christmas Eve, baby. The world never stops. That's something I know. I may not know as much as a race car driver, but I know that."

71

Red fidgeted nervously. The race car driver was a wheelman who had run with the gang briefly in Chicago. He always used to invite Billie to come for a ride with him. He was a fancy dresser with a weakness for the bottle. They'd given him the bum's rush before the Racine robbery.

John continued, "How many people know the world never stops? It's one long go. They grab you on Christmas Eve— what? They let you out the next day? It's just one long go."

"I'm homesick, Johnnie. I want to see Mother."

"You want to go home to your mother, you want to go home to your race car driver."

"Don't start that one, Johnnie," Mary said.

"That slime son of a bitch. You want to go back to him so the two of you can get lickered up together, go running up Wacker in your bloomers out of your minds together? That what you want?"

"I don't want. I liked him all right, but I never—"

"You what?"

"He doesn't tell me to not to drink."

"You what?"

"Don't."

"You what?" He slapped her face. In the quiet that followed, Billie stared at him, her mouth twisted, inhaling audibly.

Suddenly she lashed back at him, making small fists. He held her arms. She kicked his shin. He threw her to the floor.

"I'll kill you," he said, pointing. "Think I won't?"

"Oh, big man. Lookit the big man. So big."

"You squaw."

Her mouth closed abruptly. John had once broken a man's nose for using the word in his presence. Billie's eyes became weapons.

She stood, her silence now potent.

"You want to go?" he said. "Go. Go on, get out. Go back to your reservation. Here's the keys to the car. Take it and get out."

Her lips were tight. She picked up the car keys and marched to the stairs.

"Big man!"

Billie left that night.

The next morning's sunshine and soft breeze made a mockery of Christmas. After breakfast they exchanged gifts. Pete sat nervously licking his lips, rocking in his chair, his hands clasped, waiting for Mary to open the beribboned velvet box. She screamed when she saw the jewels. She fastened the watch around her wrist just above the other one, the one he'd given her for her birthday in November. Bigger diamonds encrusted the new one. They sparkled brighter. He loved her more.

Red gave John a gold pen and pencil set. In prison John was always writing letters to his family. Red, who hadn't made it through grade school, marveled at the mysteries of the written word. John snapped the writing instruments into his shirt pocket and said, "How do I look?"

In the afternoon John walked a long way down the beach. Clouds lay spread over the sky. The choppy sea was a sick green. He watched the cold way that the water slicked the sand and withdrew.

As he walked he fingered the strand of pearls in his pocket. He stroked their smooth opalescence. He took them out and looked at them, his eyes burning. The pain a boy might feel filled his chest, choked him. He reached back and hurled the necklace. It dropped into the ocean and disappeared without a ripple.

No one mentioned Billie during the next week. Pete and

Mary took long rides in their car. Makley slept late, read magazines, and sunbathed. Red went out a couple of times with a woman who ran a photography studio in town.

Life is a river, John told himself. Everything, sooner or later, is carried away to the sea of memory and regret. There's no time to worry about one who becomes separated, who lingers in an eddy or is sucked down a whirlpool. At any minute, you have to be ready to shoot the rapids.

But he couldn't think of anything to do. At the movies he was not transported. He always remembered where he was. He looked around at the others in the theater, at the flickering light washing their faces. He felt like a foreigner. Twice he walked out in the middle of a picture.

One of the stories in the Chicago paper bore the headline DILLINGER REPORTED DEAD. It dealt with vague, groundless rumors, but it drove John into a rage. It terrified him. It was as if the reflections in the hundred mirrors had begun to move on their own, to dance and gesture without him. He wasn't Dillinger. They'd made Dillinger into something beyond him. They could make the image that he'd created into whatever they wanted.

He cursed them. But he cut out the story of his death as always and stacked it with the others.

The ocean boiled. Rain streaked the screens of the porch. John thought about Billie's lustrous hair when it whipped across her face. He didn't know what to do with his hands.

He drove into town New Year's Eve to buy two cases of champagne. It was the first New Year's since Repeal. On the way home, John saw a car wrecked against a pole, a woman on the running board laughing uncontrollably—or maybe crying. A man wearing a broken boater stood in front of the auto waving his arms as if he were conducting a brass band.

John slowed, asked if he could help.

74

"Sure!" the man shouted cheerily. He held out a pewter flask. "Help yourself."

Back at the house they all drank champagne from tumblers. John drank more than he usually allowed himself. The giggle juice unclenched him.

At midnight, Roman candles and firecrackers began to go off up and down the beach. Rockets sparked out over the water and exploded in red and chrome-yellow sprays. John unlocked the closet where they kept the guns and took a Thompson out onto the porch facing the ocean. A white wafer of moon was shining high over the horizon. He pointed the gun upward and fired off a couple of rounds. They all laughed. John swigged champagne from the bottle. He squeezed the trigger. The gun hammered out bullets until the canister was empty.

The next day everything had changed. It was 1934.

In Florida the sun shined. Bright thoughts suddenly flooded John's mind, bright possibilities.

He announced that he was going to drive north. He was going back to Chicago to unload those bonds they'd taken in Racine.

They should all get out, Pete said. Sitting still was wrong. Keep moving, they never pick up your trail. Always keep moving.

Makley had a friend in Tucson, a guy he'd run a black market sugar racket with during the war. They could spend the rest of the winter out in Arizona. It was all cactus and sand. It was the Wild West.

Suddenly everyone became enthusiastic about moving. Red decided to keep John company. Later they would all meet in Tucson.

And while he was up there, John announced, he thought he'd drive on up to Wisconsin. For Billie.

75

8

SPARKY MASTERSON, a second cousin to the lawman Bat Masterson, was born in a circus tent. At the time, his father, wearing an odd combination of both cowboy and Indian getup, was performing a knife-throwing act with the Pawling Brothers Show. His mother left Sparky in the care of a tattooed Eskimo an hour after she gave birth in order to take her usual place in front of the target.

A young man at the turn of the century, Sparky performed in Wild West shows. He rode horses for Wild Bill Cody, suspending himself in the chaos of hoofs under their bellies while firing blanks from a six-shooter.

He saved enough money to open his own three-ring show during the twenties. He toured Europe four times. In '28 his big top caught fire outside of Buffalo, New York. The flames leapt over and started the menagerie burning. He lost most of his animals, including five Siberian tigers. "My children," he would say.

So when I joined him he was traveling with a single ring, playing the kerosene circuit—small cities and county seats on a path from Pennsylvania to Arkansas. A small circus needs a strong side show to boost revenue and to send folks home with the idea that they've seen something. That's where I came in. Dillinger Alive.

Sparky ran an honest operation—honest within reason. "I'd rather talk a man into a tent to look at nothing than short change him," he often said. If one of the freaks or sensations he displayed was fake, well, the suckers were paying for the thrill of the anticipation. That was Sparky's view of show business, and of life, too.

He carried a "Circassian Snake Charmer," a breasty Polish girl with a tiny waist. In the towns Sparky knew to be loose she and two other girls would put on a hot cooch show in a tent on the back of the lot. If farm boys would lay out four bits for a close look at a woman's privates, Sparky wasn't about to deprive them.

Another act was the Weeping Wonder, a man by the name of Horace Naismith who could express any emotion at a moment's notice. He would sit on stage and cry, the tears pouring down his cheeks. Just when his sobs were getting some of the people in the audience going, he would burst into a maniac giggle. Then he would laugh his bubbling, infectious laugh until he had the house roaring. He could go on like that for hours. Folks left that tent like wet clothes out of a wringer.

Sparky had others, a roller skating parrot, a human pretzel. Of all his acts, Harry Holcomb was probably the best known. He'd signed with Ringling Brothers in '26 but had had a dispute with them when they brought in another wire act just before the market crash. Hard times had driven a lot of shows over the edge, so Harry was plying his trade with Masterson's Extravaganza.

I wanted to have the Dillinger show going by the Fourth of July. I worked out skits. I supervised the carpenters making sets for the East Chicago job, Crown Point, Little Bohemia. I did some running around trying to get hold of a couple Thompson guns. I wanted to get the thing up and running fast. To Sparky I'd pitched Dillinger as an immortal. But if

77

Mae West broke her leg or some idiot flew the Pacific, a week later people might be asking, John who?

None of the cast members were born thespians. That was okay, I would do most of the talking myself. "Red" and "Pete" managed to memorize "Stick 'em up," after a little practice. They came into our makeshift bank, took their places with guns drawn and looked tough.

We did a bank job that mixed details of all the bank jobs. We called it by what city we thought would be known best where we were putting it on—Racine or Montpelier, Mason City, Sioux Falls or Daleville. As Dillinger I was invariably courteous and good-humored during these robberies. Pete would raise his voice to a girl we had playing teller, and I would wave him off, reassure her that we meant no harm, we only wanted the money, the bank's money.

We leaned on that. In the East Chicago robbery Dillinger refused to take the cash deposit a farmer was getting ready to make. Keep your money, he told the man.

In real life, people told me, John was a little tight with his money—there was still something of the frugal hick in him. And the gang on one occasion stole the wedding bands off the fingers of bank customers. But the Robin Hood thing played well. That was what mattered.

And animosity toward banks was running high at the time. Imagine putting your life savings into a granite and marble institution, then finding out that the establishment had gone under and your dough was gone. And on top of it, the bank president is still driving a Packard and eating porterhouse. It made some people mad.

A Dillinger fan club started up that spring. They were urging him to run for governor—and they were only half joking.

Marty Burke, who played Baby Face Nelson, was the one member of the show who really displayed some theatrical talent. He filled the stage. He scared people.

"Baby Face *is* Dillinger," he explained to me. "They seem so different, but Dillinger has this crazy streak and Baby Face acts it out."

I got to know Marty well. He'd been an exercise rider, following the tracks from Hialeah to Saratoga. One spring at Pimlico a horse had kicked him in the left temple. He spent almost eight months unconscious in a hospital. He came around with a suddenness that surprised the doctors, but he suffered from complete amnesia. Not only did he not remember anything about his life, but everything associated with him up to that time, his name, the face of his pretty young wife, horses, all struck him as foreign and menacing. He never returned home. What he liked most about circus life was the traveling. Too long in any place and he began to acquire a kind of ominous déjà vu.

I asked him what it was like not to have a past. He didn't understand the question.

His personality offstage was the one I imagined that Baby Face himself had. When he laughed, he was a balloon released from a child's grip, absolutely free-floating. Despite his stature, a quick temper made him big. I saw him knock four teeth out of the mouth of a drunk townie, and, still rubbing his hand, whisper something in a pretty girl's ear that made her go upstairs with him. He could return any bird call note for note.

His voice was his main weapon on stage. To hear a loud gravelly baritone coming from this little man, you thought he was possessed. He would rant and stomp around the boards waving his machine gun. Spectators would cheer him on at first. They would laugh. Then they would gradually fall silent, thinking he was going out of control.

I worked up some love scenes between Dillinger and Billie to serve as breaks between the robberies, escapes, and shoot-outs. I fixed up Ivy, Harry Holcomb's wife, in a jet-black wig, headband and fringed buckskin dress. I knew Billie didn't go around that way, but the papers had made a lot about Dillinger's Indian girlfriend so that's what the people wanted to see.

We would act out a little vignette where Billie was scared for me when I was going off to do a bank job. We had one general-purpose love scene to show how devoted we were to each other. Then we would reenact the couple's shooting escape from the apartment in St. Paul. Finally she would kiss me good-bye, promising love eternal, and I would watch, horrified, while she was grabbed by the cops for the crime of loyalty.

"Harry says he don't know about this," Ivy told me before the dress rehearsal. I was working on her costume.

"About what?"

"He don't know if he likes having somebody pawing me."

"Who's pawing?"

"Smooching."

"This is going to be wholesome as hell," I assured her. "Family stuff. Try this."

She pulled the wig on, tucked loose strands of her own strawberry hair underneath. I started making up her face. I'd never done that to a woman before, but I had very exact ideas about the brows and lip rouge from studying Billie's picture.

She asked me about Billie.

"She's a girl who's willing to go all the way," I said. "She loves her man, and she never looks back. He loves her in a way we can't really imagine. She soaks up his love, lives on it. They have what every couple dreams of."

I was making a mess of the lips.

"Lemme," she said.

I told her how I wanted them, narrow. Her own lips had soft bulging curves.

"She knows that his love is pure love," I told her. "It isn't something that she brought to life in him. It was there. Like lightning is in the sky. She was just the rod."

I explained how I wanted her eyebrows. "What happened to her?"

"She's in jail right now. They sent her up for harboring."

"That's not fair. It was love." She added, "I wish Harry had some love in him."

She fixed up the powder. I stepped back to look.

"Stand up. Turn. Good. That's very good." I was surprised by the resemblance to pictures I'd seen of Billie.

I explained a little how she should walk, move. I had nothing to go by at the time, Billie hadn't been in any of the newsreels. But from photographs, from knowing who a person is, you get a sense of it.

Ivy had a careless, slightly superior attitude toward the show. She was the wife of a star. She often made me search the lot for her instead of showing up for rehearsals. All the same, I became rather fond of her. She had a shy little grin and subtle dimples. She was quick to laugh.

We planned to open in Findlay, Ohio. Dillinger was known around there. He'd robbed a bank in Bluffton, just down the pike. We expected a heavy holiday crowd.

As the day approached, I began to get cold feet. I kept looking in the mirror. Hell, I didn't look like John Dillinger. No, I did. I *was* him, that was the important thing. I had to perform, but I had to play it the way John would have. Cool. With the confidence, the authority that a loaded gun gives you.

But nights I'd wake up with sweaty thoughts. What if they laughed? I expected hecklers, but what if the illusion broke down? It wasn't just the embarrassment I was thinking of. I needed this job. We were passing through towns, I'd see guys younger than I was sitting on porches, town benches, holding their faces in their hands, their eyes focused about six feet below the ground. If Dillinger Alive took off, I'd have some breathing room. I'd be able to put together some cash, a cushion.

"I'm all excited," Ivy told me as we were getting ready to go on that first night. Her little white hands were shaking.

"You're going to do fine," I told her. "You're Billie."

"Yeah," she said.

I walked onto the stage, looked into the arc lights, drew a pistol from each pocket, and fired a dozen blanks right at the audience. People startle, they can't help it. They startle and it wakes them up a little. They think brave is easy. But nobody can control his nerves when the action starts. Think about that if you feel like laughing at a guy pretending to be John Dillinger.

You breathe a different air when you're onstage. Your awareness ratchets up. You feel a force at your back, pushing you. Because for those few minutes, you are creating the world. That's the pleasure of theater.

Cold lines of sweat traced down my back. My voice cracked a couple of times, but I loved it. All those faces packed onto the bleachers were rapt—at least I thought they were. And the show never lagged.

"Go to the next window." Bang.

"Stick 'em up!" Bang.

"Everybody down on the floor!" Bang bang.

"We don't much like bank presidents, Mister Bank President."

"They're waiting for us."

"We'll have to shoot our way out."

Bang. Bang. Bang.

"No jail can hold me."

"Sure I rob banks, but I don't go and get myself elected president of them first."

Bang.

"It's your girl, Johnnie. It's Billie Frechette."

We waited for Ivy to come out. "Red" repeated the cue. We waited some more.

Finally she appeared from the wings. Not hesitant. Too bold. I could tell from the look on her face that she'd drawn a blank. She was operating on pure adrenaline.

"Billie, my love," I said.

She stopped, turned to look at the audience, and became hypnotized by their eyes. Her knuckles were clenched white on the bead bag she carried. She tried a little smile. She lifted her chin.

"Billie!" I opened my arms to her. She was supposed to say a short speech at this point. How she was worried sick about my next job. She said nothing.

"Johnnie," I whispered.

"Johnnie!" she said, stepping forward. Her arms came up around my neck. I leaned to kiss her.

In rehearsal we'd filled in these parts by just saying, "Kiss, kiss." This was the first time our lips had met. Hers were soft, torrid. It wasn't the stage kiss I'd expected. Her mouth opened. Hot as I was, I felt my skin flash. I inhaled her talcum and the tar soap she used on her hair. I could feel her breathing.

It took several hoots from the audience to bring me around. I broke off and gazed at her face, pretending to be Dillinger the lover but in fact trying to lasso myself and sort out where I was. I heard applause and a good deal of cooing from the ladies in the crowd.

While I told her not to worry, I pulled out the long-barreled forty-four revolver that I'd be shooting off in the next scene. Some of the yokels must have seen an unintended symbolism in this, I heard them chortling. Maybe I blushed, I don't know.

83

Ivy tried to apologize backstage while our G-men plotted how to surround John at Little Bohemia.

"I goofed up."

"You did great. They loved you. Keep it up."

"I couldn't think of anything or anything."

"They didn't know what you were supposed to say. They like to look at you."

She put on her corner-of-the-eye look, wet her lips, and whispered, "Johnnie!"

"Perfect. You do the lovey-dovey stuff great."

She grinned.

We enacted a version of the escape John and Billie made from the law in St. Paul. She handled that okay, giving out with some real icicle screams. Toward the end we had another love scene. This time I stopped her just as we began to embrace. I held her face in both my hands and gazed at it. I kissed both her eyes before laying my mouth on hers. We held it. Whistles cut across the warm tent.

I was seeing stars when I came up for air. And far away I heard a voice saying, Look out, boy. I heard it, all right. It was my own voice. And I paid it no mind.

Then it was time for questions.

What's your favorite kind of pie?

Raspberry.

What's it feel like to kill a man?

You don't like to have to shoot a man. Something deep down tells you not to. But it's him or you. See? If you're willing to face death too, right along with that man, what more can be asked of you? And after, once you've seen how easy it is for somebody's luck to turn, why, you feel pretty good being alive.

84

Do you think this blue eagle business is going to pull the country out or not?

I generally leave politics to those that know something about it. I'm just trying to do my bit, spreading the wealth around.

Do you believe in the Almighty?

I was raised a Christian. I believe in God to this day. But only for His sake, you understand? Not for my own. If He needs me to believe in Him, all right. But I can't see He's done much of anything for me.

What happens to the money in these banks that close down? Where does it go?

It goes from the people whose rightfully it is into the pockets of other people who know more about shuffling papers and foreclosing farms.

Why don't you and your Indian girlfriend have a bunch of kids?

Kids wouldn't be a good idea for me just yet. I've got some running around to do before I can settle down.

They ever going to get you, John?

They may catch me, but they'll never hold me.

Why'd you do it, Johnnie?

We can't all be saints.

It was over and they gave us a good lot of applause. We took five curtain calls.

I sold pictures of myself and signed them "Love, Johnnie." Ladies would crowd around me, giggle and blush. Men shook my hand. Kids wanted to see my gun. I let them touch the barrel, still warm from shooting.

So we were rolling. After that night we did two shows a day every day the circus was up. Word of it got around. News-

paper reporters swore I was the perfect image of the desperado. I still have those clippings somewhere.

We were able to locate a year-old Terraplane that had
dropped a rod. I let Marty load a live clip into the machine
gun and practice shooting at the car. We kept that behind a
curtain next to the stage and charged an extra dime to see it.
We sprinkled some bull's blood on the front seat. I told everyone that that was where Red Hamilton lay after the East Chicago
job. For free we displayed one of Dillinger's actual suits, a
box of roofing nails found in his car, the wooden gun he'd
used to escape from Crown Point, and a container of dark
magneta lip rouge that had belonged to Billie Frechette. Not
all of these things were genuine, but they were genuine
enough.

I hired a first-rate talker to draw the tip. He knew how to
convince people that this was a once-in-a-lifetime opportunity.
They'll pay money for once-in-a-lifetime. Sometimes we were
able to bribe some of the circus bandsmen to play for us before
they set up in the big top. I asked them to swing some hot
jazz instead of the usual circus honk in order to give the hicks
a taste of Chicago.

Ivy's interest picked up after that first show. Before, I was
exasperated by her who-cares attitude. I would explain points
to her about the show, how she should act, the meaning of
what we were doing. "I know," she would say. "I know."

But after she'd gotten a taste of the spotlight, she became
avid. She began to think herself of things she could say. "Our
love is bigger than the world, Johnnie." Her gestures became
more theatrical. She learned how to weep real tears on
demand. The audiences loved that.

Ivy found adulation exhilarating. She became cocky. I was
tickled by her buoyancy. I was tickled by everything about her.

But more than that, I found that I looked forward with ever

more fevered anticipation to our onstage kisses. I knew she did, too. I would take her in my arms as if embracing a ghost. She would shoot me the little narrow puckered Billie smile I'd taught her. I would give her back my lopsided grin. She would grip me very tightly around the neck. Once during the first week I felt her dart her tongue across my lips. We built on that, turning it into a loving duel. The audience screamed for more.

But we never spoke about it. Does that sound strange? Offstage our relations were as casual as ever. In fact, I rarely even joked around with her the way I did with the other cast members.

One day she said Harry would like to meet me. I'd seen him around the lot plenty, of course. We had a nodding acquaintance, but we'd never spoken. The town we were playing didn't allow shows on Sunday, so the three of us planned to get together at a restaurant for Sunday dinner.

The meal started with the atmosphere of a papal audience. Harry was not a big man, but was very powerfully muscled. His face was frozen into a perpetual frown that suggested eternal skepticism or maybe long-suppressed mental anguish. His hand, when he shook, felt like it had been cast in bronze. He indicated where I should sit and suggested that either roast chicken or a ham steak was the best bet at eating places of this type. I ordered a beer with dinner. Harry was drinking milk.

Small talk was not Harry's specialty. He asked me half a dozen questions about the Dillinger show. He had somehow gathered from Ivy's descriptions that Dillinger was associated with Teddy Roosevelt's Rough Riders. He had no sympathy with lawbreakers. He had money in banks himself, he told me. Why would he cheer a robber?

Most show people take the attitude that any act was a success if the rubes ate it up and it made money. But Harry's view of the matter was evangelical.

"You can't just give people what they want," he said. "Otherwise it would be nothing but bare-naked women and gunfights."

I saw Ivy, who was unusually subdued in his presence, glance at him nervously at this point. She'd recently had her costume altered to show a slice of her shapely leg.

The waitress brought our meals. Chicken for Harry, ham for Ivy and me.

The conversation was as lumpy as the red-eye gravy that came with that ham.

I asked Harry about his act. I'd seen it and I knew he was good. I fully realized how good only years later, after I'd watched a lot of others walk the wire.

He launched into a well-practiced monologue about his art. You had to stretch your nerves as taut as the wire, he said. Wire walking was a feat of the nerves. He'd perfected the front flip on the wire—which was harder than the back because going forward you couldn't see the wire until after your feet met it. He'd practiced the move fourteen thousand times over three years before performing it in public. The wire was a perpetual challenge, he stated.

I asked him if he really took chances out there during the act. His frown deepened.

"You must take risks. If you don't, they won't watch you. Every show, I skirt the brink of eternity."

Ivy did not enter into the talk except to every now and then murmur her agreement with Harry. I noticed her warm brown eyes shifting throughout the meal. I was used to seeing her with the black wig; she looked strange to me now with her bleached curls.

We sipped coffee after the meal. Ivy stepped away from the table for a minute. As if waiting for this opportunity, Harry leaned to me and said, "Do you know how many times the movement of a watch beats every year?"

He gave me no time to make even a guess.

"One hundred fifty-seven million," he said. "Imagine it."

It was a subject on which Harry finally showed a full-blown enthusiasm, his hobby, watch repair. He was full of information about double-cut expansion balance wheels, polished patent regulators, and French enamel dials. Above all he was adamant about the regular cleaning and oiling of a fine timepiece.

This meeting confirmed my suspicion that Harry was not fulfilling Ivy's romantic needs. She rarely spoke of him; but she always hurried to change and remove her make-up so that she could watch Harry's act, which came near the end of the show in the main tent. She couldn't miss it, she told me, "In case he falls."

In spite of the fact that I was developing a complicated fascination with Ivy, we continued to keep an arm's length between us in real life. I would see her mornings sitting in the sun mending Harry's tights and I'd want to approach her, but I couldn't. For one thing, a circus crew during the season turns into something resembling a big raucous family. An act of adultery would have had a special stigma to it, sort of like a romp with your own sister.

Then too, I felt that Ivy was becoming the ideal person to play Billie. The romantic angle of the show accounted for a good part of its popularity, and I couldn't imagine anyone else in the role. I didn't want to jeopardize that. I had the idea that becoming too close to Ivy would keep me from believing in her as Billie when we put on the greasepaint.

But sometimes when she'd see me on the lot she'd flash a roguish, sidelong grin that made my heart swell. I'd think, What would the real Dillinger do in this situation?

The predicament intrigued me. There was a delicious conspiracy between us. We were engaging in a secret liaison right there on a public stage, yet in the most private of places— inside two other people.

Anyway, along toward the latter part of July we'd made our way across to downstate Illinois, a town called Mattoon. Through Indiana we'd drawn big crowds. Outside Indianapolis a woman fainted during the show. A rumor got out she was Dillinger's sister. We ballyhooed that one. Dillinger's own sister struck down by shock at the remarkable likeness!

To tell the truth it was the heat that laid that woman low. And it had gotten worse. People were dying in the cities. The fire escapes were packed with would-be sleepers at night. Out on the plains, the bluish-yellow heat was piled a mile high, crushing crops. People said more dust storms were certain.

That July we sweated through performance after performance. The smell of baked canvas inside that tent would get to where it would scald your throat. I began to work in my shirtsleeves.

One night during the worst part of the heat wave we finished our act and the perspiring crowd was wandering out and beginning to make their way toward the big top for the main show. We were outside the back of the tent waiting for a cool breeze. Pat Winston, one of the animal handlers, was hosing down the elephants. They didn't mind the heat, really. But if you cooled them off they would act a little livelier. Inside their dark cages, I could see the lions panting, stretched out as if they had melted.

Sparky came over to me wearing his ringmaster suit, top hat and all. His face was red and glistening but he was smiling.

"Well," he said, "get ready for bigger crowds than you've ever seen."

"Why's that?"

"Dillinger's dead."

I remember the time they told me my mother was dead. My mind went out of control, went into overdrive for about ninety seconds while it reevaluated ten thousand different things that I knew about the world. When I opened my eyes again, everything had shifted minutely.

The same happened that night. The word *dead* gripped me like a fist for a minute. Then I could breathe again, but a different air. Sweat dripped into my eyes and brought tears.

Sparky twisted his cheroot in his mouth and laughed. It was going to be big news, he said.

"The federals waited for him outside a movie theater. Shot him down like a mad dog. They say he was betrayed by a woman. It's going to make a perfect finale for you. Mark my words, we'll be turning people away every town we hit."

He hurried away to start the show in the big top. I sat on a bench for a long time, lost in thought. What was Dillinger to me? A guy I looked like? A meal ticket? Somebody destined from the word go to die in a pool of blood? A killer? A man who dared for all of us?

Whoever he was, the future without him loomed grim just then. And what kind of a clown was I, pretending?

The big cats let out that primitive growl that you feel in the bottom of your stomach. The handlers were moving them into position.

Emulating Dillinger, I'd been going easy on the booze lately. Now I felt a yen moving up my spine. I would go into town and tie one on and ask everybody if they knew John Dillinger.

Or, no, I would rob a bank myself. Nothing precipitous, nothing careless. I'd plan it just the way John would have. Down to the second. The getaway, every turn. I'd take Marty Burke with me. And a wheelman. And afterward they'd say, Dillinger's alive. That couldn't have been him they gunned in Chicago. He's alive.

"Johnnie."

I looked up into Billie's darling naked eyes. It was Ivy but she still wore Billie's wicked hair and smile. She rested her hand on my neck, slid her fingers along my jaw until they touched my lips.

"I had a dream about you," she said.

The night turned sweet for me. I reached my hand under her skirt and felt the damp silk of her stockings, her smooth bare skin. She wrapped her arms around my head. I laid it on her breast. She smelled of hot darkness, of sawdust.

Inside, the arcing spotlights were all aimed at Harry. Hundreds of eyes followed him across the wire. Hundreds of throats gasped as he teetered, skipped, spun. Beyond, in a marsh, frogs croaked frantically, as if they knew something the rest of us didn't.

It was the first time Ivy had ever missed Harry's act.

John Dillinger's body was lying on a porcelain slab at the Cook County morgue. The paths of the bullets had been traced. They were beginning to pack ice around his torso.

We sat there, clinging together in the heat. She never spoke my name. All I remember, like the whisper of a lost child, is her voice saying over and over, "Johnnie."

9

THE ROADS THOSE DAYS, the majority of them were gravel and not in any great shape. Even on the concrete highways you'd get a damn lot of vibration.

John loved to drive. He was always fascinated by machinery, by the feel of the gears when he shifted, the hum of a tuned engine.

That January he and Red drove nonstop coming back from Florida. John was halfway through his short career. The Biograph was still seven months, a lifetime away. The furnace that would ignite that summer was unimaginable in the January chill.

"You know how in the can everybody was always looking to get situated?" John said. "They wanted the right job, the right cell, the right angle on the screws."

"The right group of pals," Red said.

"Exactly. And you had to get your time positioned in your mind just right, too. Me and Pete used to talk about it. You didn't want to grab hold of too big a piece of it. You couldn't let it bury you. You had to keep on it. And the way you nailed that was the way you looked at things. The way you looked at the walls. The way you looked at the gun towers. The way, sometimes, you looked at the first speck of sun hitting the block windows. A sight like that could ice you. Anything could. And if you got it all right, got everything balanced just so, then you could live. Then—yeah it was bad you were locked up, but you could dodge the wrong feeling. Know the one I mean?"

"Closed-in feeling."

"Like something was eating your guts, something invisible."

"I had that."

"That kind of thinking gets to you. You can't avoid it. And you take it with you when you leave the can. That's what surprised me. It was like, getting out can't possibly be what you imagine it to be when you're inside. Because you take that thinking with you the rest of your life. Once you go in, you never do get out. Never, because the world you go back to is different. You don't fit."

"I never had it plush as this before I went in," Red said.

"Do you fit?"

"I don't know," Red said. "I guess. I'm wearing a diamond crucifix."

"What I found was, to fit, I had to work one of those jigsaw puzzles everybody's so wild about. You find the pieces to fit and you see a picture of a sunset over a river. This, driving back to Chicago, it's a piece. You're a piece. That sad sack farmer right there watching us go by, he's a piece. Billie is a piece. There's a million broads. Why her? Why an Indian with a booze yen?"

"I like Billie."

"She's part of the picture. Calling Leach, taunting him— why did I do it? Because it fills up this section here. Going to Florida, robbing the jug in Racine, it's all pieces. And when I get them all together, when I see a picture, then I feel at home. Then I feel lucky. But sometimes the pieces don't fit."

"That's one thing you've got, John. Luck. You're a lucky son of a gun, that's no lie."

"I'm lucky, huh? Seven weeks ago you were behind three

yards of concrete fingering your dick and wondering how many days makes a life sentence. Who's lucky?"

Red snorted lightly through his nose. He looked out at a movie poster on the side of a chicken house. The man in the picture was watching the road with defiant eyes. The woman he was about to kiss appeared horrified. Half her face was ripped off, gray boards showing behind.

John said, "I think there's something to that Lady Luck business, though. It's not just a saying. You really have to treat your luck like a woman. Keep her entertained. Talk to her, whisper in her ear. Give her gifts. Offerings, like."

"You mean like at church?"

"Remember telling me you climbed the chimney? Hundreds of feet high. You said you could see twenty miles from the top. That kind of thing. You flash signals to her up there in the sky. You court her."

"That was on a bet."

"How much?"

"Dime."

John slowed the car to a crawl as they limped over two sets of railroad tracks.

"I used to be a wisher," he said. "Even after I got out of lockup. My stepmother died the day of my release."

"You told me. I'm sorry."

"I mean, that, plus seeing Dad and my sister, seeing Audrey's kids, it made me wish. Jesus, if only I'd gone to Tech. Jesus, if I hadn't paid any attention to Singleton when he said let's rob this joker. Jesus, if I'd gotten a lawyer who could have beat my rap. If this and if that. Then I said, who are you? Answer: somebody who's along for the ride. Just like everybody. It's not a matter of wishing. It's not a matter of if. Some people are afraid to get into bed with their luck. That's the up and down of it."

"Take it as it comes down the pike."

"Pete's got it right. It isn't the money. People all over the country are talking about me. Who are they reading about in the papers? Me. Who are they going to remember? Me. Who are they going to tell their grandchildren about? Me. Why? I'm not the one with the money. Morgan's got that. The Astors. It isn't the money, it's what you do. It's luck."

As they plunged north the sky took on the sad familiar light of midwinter. The pavement grew harder. Tattered rags of snow appeared on the fields. For a long time their eyes watched out the windshield side by side in silence.

"You figure Billie's waiting up there for you?" Red asked him.

"I know she is. The reason I like Billie, she's got spirit. She needs to blow off every once in a while. That's her Indian blood. But she's okay. When she scrammed I never for a minute worried about her shooting her mouth. If they'd hooked her coming through Chicago, she'd never have said a word. That's her."

"She's a sweet kid."

"Yeah. But I don't care if she is or isn't. I'm gone on her. Totally gone. In the songs they call it love, but it's not love. Not like you love your mother. Not like you love to fuck either. A part of you goes haywire and this woman just gets like an itch on your insides."

"That old black magic, that's what they call it."

"It's a drive."

"That's it," Red said. "A drive. It's driving you right across the country."

"You know the way you used to think about broads in prison? The way they became more real than real? The way you could taste them and see them and feel them and fuck them clearer than you ever could in life? She's like that to me in the flesh. She's the end for me. I'm not ashamed to say that."

They skirted Indianapolis on the back roads. For all its

industry and activity, the city had never seemed to John more than an overgrown hick town, the illusion of a city. The endless farmland stretching out around it invaded downtown. People grew vegetables in their front yards and kept pigs in cramped sties out back. The wind blew harvest smells from ten miles away.

Chicago—that was the center of the universe. Long before the skyline came into view, John felt they were descending into a maelstrom, a bubbling sinkhole of corruption and danger and excitement. This was where life was happening, where burlesque girls were whipping their spangled hips, where the tom-tom scrimmage was running down the avenues at two in the morning, where fire blazoned the eyes of office girls, awakening dreams in sweating bellies. Where hogs and men and rails reached their terminals.

That was a city. Walking past the corner of Wells and Monroe, John went by a brothel where on the shade in every window they'd written in big letters: Why not?

And in Chicago, he was Dillinger again.

But they weren't able to unload the bonds. The certificates were too hot. All over town patrolmen were petting their side arms. The underworld had turned its back on him.

John sent word to Wisconsin. Billie would meet him in a few days.

He went to see a movie called *Lady Killer*. James Cagney played an usher who becomes a star.

John eyed the society women shopping in the Loop. He walked over to the lake near the Century of Progress. In the January wind the grounds of the closed world's fair looked hard and sad, a look that shot through him, like tinsel in the gutter.

He met Red in a German restaurant. Over a plate of bratwurst John said, "Say we could get a good wheelman?"

"Okay, say it."

"You and I, Red."

Red stopped with piece of sausage on his fork. "Are you serious?"

"Completely. We pick a place out in the sticks, somewhere with an easy in and out. We wear vests. We walk through it."

"Think we can?"

John's mustache slanted up on one side.

Two days later they drove out toward East Chicago, Indiana. Out across the flatlands south of Lake Michigan, out among the gasworks and scrap metal dealers, out where sulphur tinted the winter sky, where cold air gulped the flames that burned refinery gas. A big brick building dominated the crossroads of the hamlet. It was a temple to Money built during a time when Money was king. Corinthian columns were etched into the stone facade. Griffins and eagles and anonymous Roman patricians stared down on the cloth coats, the idle, worried faces of the townspeople.

Inside, a milky glow poured from the central skylight. Rose and cream marble, waxed to a luster, reflected panes of light. Inch-thick sea-green glass countertops offered chained pens and cups filled with damp sponges, like holy water fonts, for wetting your counting thumb. Art deco stainless steel vases emitted sprays of electric light.

John felt the world smiling at him as he unsnapped the clasps on the satchel. A hank of maroon velvet draped the tommy gun as if it were a jeweled bracelet or a musical instrument. The mild light reassured him, the sweetness of it. The way that the voices, the clanking noise of the office machinery ascended to the vaulted ceiling reassured him. He was inside a cathedral of dollars. The service was about to begin.

Red stood by the door. They exchanged a look. They saw through time, the two of them. They knew what was going to happen, no one else.

John's voice when he announced a job was an enigma. Witnesses failed when they tried to characterize it. He was not by nature a loud man. They reported that he hardly raised his voice at all. Yet they heard perfectly what he said even across a large space. He spoke with no scream in his tone, but his words reached every ear clearly. Some said it reminded them of a chant.

The announcement now leapt to the ceiling. Faces turned. Hands stopped moving, stopped counting. The click and whiz of adding machines, the jangle of coins and drawers, the forest-fire crackle of paper, the clatter and ding of typewriters—all ceased. With the delicacy of a single falling leaf, silence descended. The high room held its breath, listening.

Pale frescoes decorated the walls up where the marble left off. Armored knights were frozen in an eternal duel.

"Everybody back to the rear," John ordered calmly. "There might be shooting."

He stepped into the low corral where the officers' desks were. He ordered a vice president to come with him. The man stood. He was shaking.

Red rushed behind the cages. A stainless steel design on the front of each teller's window depicted a radiating sun.

"Take your time," John said. "Get it all."

John held the vice president in the middle of the room. John's eyes swept the eyes that were watching him. The fearful eyes that stared, round and unblinking. A woman's slanted eyes met his. The veil of her hat was a black web.

"You," John snapped, pointing the machine gun at a razor-mouthed man with a large Adam's apple. He stood outside a teller's window.

The man prepared to die.

"Pick it up. We don't want your money. Only the bank's."

The man had stepped back leaving four stacks of bills and

99

a small bag of coins on the counter. He hesitated, reluctant to expose his back to the lethal machine that John cradled. John motioned again. The man stepped gingerly across the open space. He gathered up his money as if he were a thief.

A noise drew John's attention to the front door. A cop walked in. His steps echoed in the quiet. His face was red with the cold, his navy blue coat fastened with two rows of brass buttons. His officer's cap had flaps that folded down over his ears. He wore gray leather gloves.

"We're doing everything real slow today, officer," John said.

"What the hell?"

"We're making a withdrawal. You keep calm. You don't want anyone to be hurt. Not over a few bucks. We know what we're doing here."

John raised the machine gun from his side. The patrolman swiveled his head, half-smiling, as if he'd mistakenly walked into a lunatic asylum. John positioned him beside the vice president.

John noticed faces staring in from the cold. A man wearing a gray overcoat started to enter. Looked. Retreated. As he moved out of sight he was pulling a gun from beneath his coat.

Steam clanked in a radiator. John motioned to Red, who had just emerged from the vault. He was carrying a cotton sack that bulged deliciously.

"It's heating up quick," John told him. "Let's take these two."

They lined up the vice president and the cop in front and pushed them toward the door. John's chest nearly pressed against the cop's thick back. He could smell the wet wool, the man's pomade.

The air outside was breathless. White. People were lined up on either side, a curious honor guard.

Someone shouted. The cop wrenched. Free of John's grip,

he stooped, threw his hands up near his ears, and scurried along the sidewalk without looking back.

The cold cracked twice. A bullet slammed into John's gut. Another punched him in the chest. He grunted. It was like being jabbed hard with a nightstick.

The man in the gray overcoat must have been a plainclothes cop. He pointed a big Irish face at John, a face as white as the sky, small-eyed, locked in an intense, almost infantile expression.

What is the sensation of being shot while wearing a bulletproof vest? Does invulnerability make you feel like God? Does that feeling leak compassion into your excited mind?

John shot for the legs of the man who was shooting at him. John's machinegun went HAHAHA.

The cop's knee ripped. His face opened. His eyes rounded. His teeth bared. He fired at John again. Missed. The bullet sprayed granite.

John made the gun stutter once more, aiming low.

The cop's legs gave out. He sank. He dove right into the stream of bullets. One tore his coat, shattered his collarbone, exploded his heart.

John's feet stepped on a sidewalk of air. He turned. Red was down. Red's fist gripped no gun, only a handful of blood.

The car rested at the curb, puffs of smoke seeping from the exhaust, a haven. If the bank robber has a prayer, it is always: Don't let the wheelman lose his nerve.

More angry cracks. A scream. The car's chrome handle reflected the clock over the bank door, telling reverse time. John's hand covered it.

John laid the hot machine gun on the floor of the backseat. He turned. A force like a hammer blow punched into his chest.

He crossed toward Red, who lay on the concrete, propped up on his elbow.

101

He lifted Red's bulk, held him while Red's slippery feet gripped for the pavement. He stooped again for the money.

The wheelman unlatched the front door. John helped Red in, slammed it, dove in back himself.

They were flying. Red rolled his head on the seat. From behind, John tried to keep it still. He patted the clammy skin, smoothed over and over the hair from the wide brow.

They flew, leaving behind the first man John had killed, the only one he would ever kill.

Like maggots in a wound, time cleanses death. O'Malley was the name of the policeman who died that January afternoon. His wife was not ready for him never to come home. She kept listening, years after, for his step on the porch stair. His mother had not spent her worried nights over him to have him cut down by a mad dog. His three daughters would carry the bruise through their lives. Fifty years after John and Red and the rest of them were gone, O'Malley's kids, old ladies, still sometimes visited the shrine of their childhood grief. They still winced at the sound of a siren, remembering.

I don't know any more. Time cleanses death, leaves bones of memory. And those who recoil at a corpse find elegance in a bleached white bone.

Leave it to the orators to preach. Many died those years. Bankers sapped more hope and life than any robber. Call O'Malley a victim. Call him a sacrifice laid on the altar of luck and daring. It doesn't matter. The pain is the same.

O'Malley was dead. But time cleanses death. You go to the movies to forget, as John went to the movies that night to forget. And the movies get into your remembering. And you convince yourself that it was just a game being played. Just a game and death the prize. As death is always the prize.

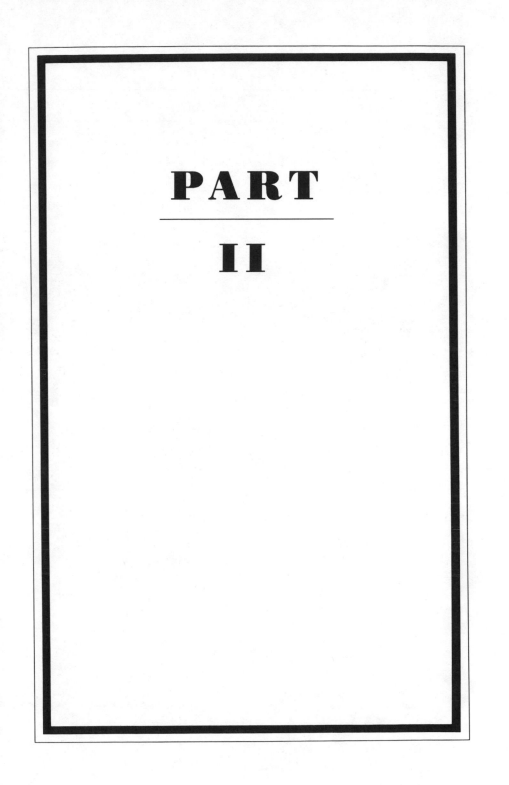

PART
II

10

EAST CHICAGO CHANGED JOHN. He read the papers the next day. He clipped the stories as usual. But the pleasant tingle the accounts produced took on a sweaty edge. Killing the cop, he'd stepped across a boundary he hadn't realized was there.

You put your life on the line. The cops and guards put their lives on the line. Somebody dies—it's part of the show, only part of the show. It's only an outcome of angles. Angles and reflexes, chance and ballistics. And yet—

And yet O'Malley's blood started in him a little boy's naughty apprehension. And made darkness seep into his eyes. And chilled him. And woke him at three in the morning breathless, soaked with sweat, the memory lacerating his sleep.

He couldn't stop thinking about it. He lived the scene over again and again in bizarre slow motion. The bullets would drift from the throbbing gun barrel and float through the air. O'Malley would stubbornly dive into their path, offering his flesh.

He was the one this time, the one who had killed a man. It was a confusing emotion, the bitterness of an awful responsibility flavored with the almost unbearable sweetness of being the one who had survived.

Red recovered. Red was a tough son of a bitch. A bullet

had found a seam in his armored jacket, but it only tore the flesh below his armpit. He insisted on lifting the bandage whenever John came to see him in the flat they'd rented. He showed the wound as a badge of his daring.

Billie arrived. She was sorry for Daytona. She never expected John to be sorry, but he was. His contrition overflowed into weeping.

"I couldn't stand to see him weep," she would tell me. "And yet I loved it. He was my baby."

John bought her a puppy.

They left Red behind to rest in Chicago. They headed out to meet the gang in Tucson.

"I'm okay long's I can keep moving," John told her. "I've got to stay ahead of myself."

Tucson in January was a city without weather. The temperature was tepid. An anemic sun shone some days, other days a thin sheet of gray covered the wide sky.

During a hotel fire they had to ask a fireman to dash inside and lug out the weighty suitcases that contained their arsenal. They tipped him too generously. He thought about it. No. He chuckled to himself. But later he took his suspicions to the cops.

They moved into tourist cabins. They lived quietly. In February the local police went out and arrested the most wanted men in America. Arrested them all, one by one, without a bit of fuss.

The Dillinger story was over, we thought. It had lasted nine months. The engine of justice would now settle the account. It would be written as a footnote to a terrible, desperate time.

They sent John back to Indiana by air—his first plane ride— to settle for O'Malley. The newsreels showed him shackled, downcast, a boy in his shirt and vest, a young Hoosier who had managed to leap into the spotlight of notoriety briefly, briefly.

Makley and Pete both went to Ohio. They'd killed a sheriff delivering John from jail there the previous autumn. It was now only four months since they themselves had broken out of prison. Makley asked them to shoot him in the head right there. He was sure he would never see freedom again. He never did.

The Indiana men drove John down to the county seat, Crown Point. As they swung into the lane that led behind the jail he saw a stack of sandbags, a heavy-caliber machine gun jutting out, half a dozen guardsmen in khaki standing around it. One of them waved.

John had taken prison with him when he'd walked out the gate of Michigan City. He now took freedom with him into Crown Point. The monotony of the cell was a kind of tonic, an odd homecoming. He didn't feel buried, because he was John Dillinger now. He was somebody.

He watched the world with amusement. Watched reporters scurrying to ask him questions, deferential, privileged to be in the presence of the hottest story in America. John knew that the churchgoers out there were avid to read of his latest evil exploit. He knew the guardsmen were thrilled to take time off from their tedious jobs. He looked at the glassy-eyed women and hoarse-throated men who looked at him. It was all strange and wondrous.

Politicians hurried to get close to him, eager to bask in the glow of his renown. They crowded their fat grinning faces into the frames of the photos, desperate for any shadow of immortality.

John smiled. He slung an arm over the shoulder of the prosecutor, smiling for the photographers. He shook hands with

Mrs. Holly, the sheriff, who had taken over for her dead husband.

He felt like Lindbergh. A curiosity. They wanted to photograph him. They asked him irrelevant questions. What did he think of the NRA? But they had no notion of what his life was like. Just as with Lindy they couldn't conceive of being alone over the Atlantic, alone at night a thousand miles from land, all alone. They wanted to glorify the adventurer. But if he told them how his adventure had shown him the clockwork behind their sorry world, they would stare without comprehending.

I remember the spate of newspaper headlines at the time. Then the nation reluctantly turned its attention toward the bleak future.

In Tucson Billie tried for several days to locate the puppy John had given her. No one knew what had happened to it. She finally made her way back from Arizona. She came to visit him once. She was his wife, she said. Mrs. Dillinger. The woman sheriff handled it personally. She told Billie to go into a windowless room.

"Take off everything. Put this on." A muslin smock.

Billie stood barefoot, shivering in the smock. Mrs. Holly came in. Looked at her closely. Picked up her clothes, her purse and took them out. Billie paced the empty room. The sheriff returned. Told her to remove the smock. Billie hesitated, blushed.

"If you want to see him."

She took it off.

"Turn around. Bend over."

This was a scene I would have liked to have included in my Dillinger Alive show. Of course it was impossible.

They let her in. She clutched John's fingers through a painted wire mesh. Two guards watched. She and John talked in codes they'd invented in Florida. They referred to people and places by number.

"I have a sense about this," he told her when it was time for her to go. "We're not done yet, you and me. I don't know how it will happen, but wait a little while. Okay? Wait for me."

She looked at him, at his eyes. She was mystified. It was utterly impossible that he could ever escape from this fortress. No one would rescue him now. Pete and Makley were locked up. Red Hamilton and Homer Van Meter were lonely, wanted men. The gang did not exist. John was dreaming.

Leaving the jail, Billie observed the bristle of guns, the drone of watching eyes. But she clutched his words in her mind. Not done yet. They became an incantation. Wait.

John became friendly with a Negro named Youngblood. Youngblood had lived his whole life outside of society. And he too had journeyed to the edge, out to the rim of the world, to the eerie twilight frontier from which the shining achievements of men are seen to be paltry, petty affairs. He too had killed a man.

John watched as rubes from the Farmers' Protective Society, a vigilante group, brought their double-barreled guns to join the squad of National Guardsmen in the alleys around the jail. Every night they would ignite large floodlights outside, casting an oblique rectangle of stripes on the ceiling of his cell.

But it was not a time of brooding or regret. He surprised the other felony inmates by talking easily with them about the events of the day, about the Cubs' prospects in the coming season, about the bleak weather, about how tough it was to make a living and try to keep straight. They knew he'd grabbed tens of thousands of dollars and had it stashed somewhere. Yet he could appreciate the concerns of somebody who had nothing. They laughed often when they were with him.

It was like I'd told Sparky. A gangster makes his money off the little guy. But an outlaw can appreciate the heartaches of the working man.

"Sure way to tell if a woman is interested in you," Youngblood said to John one evening. "See how her lip turn up here, right in the corner like this. She can't help that, she get that little turn-up there, you got her."

John told him about Billie.

"Oh, I know all about Indians," the Negro replied. "Gone with a yellow girl who was half Cherokee. You got to look out for Indian women. Friend of mine, he got stabbed in the back by a full-blooded Crow. And she twist that blade," he added. "That's one dangerous woman, twist a blade after she got it in."

Youngblood told him to memorize some gibberish that he said was a hex that worked against any and all women with Indian blood if they should turn bad on you. Liquor, they both agreed, was what caused that to happen.

"I never robbed a bank in my life," John told the inmates as they sat around a table in the small dining hall. "They got me mixed up with somebody else. I was in Florida in January."

"Must have been somebody who looked like you, John."

"I think you've hit it. There's gotta be a hundred guys around Chicago who are dead ringers for me."

"And they're all bank robbers."

"I bet that's it. They've got me robbing banks in Iowa and Kentucky the same morning. There's no other explanation. It's all these look-alikes, taking advantage of me."

"You're an innocent man, John."

"You said it."

Nights he whittled. Or he sat alone on his cot in a state of tense expectation. He would catch a glimpse of a moon out the high window and feel that the light was dissolving the walls of his cell.

He wrote his niece that he was sorry not to have taken her to the Century of Progress. But it would be on again this summer. It was said the fair would be bigger and better than ever. He would take her to see everything, all the shows, the laughter, the brilliant lights. They would walk up the avenue of flags with all those banners snap-snapping in the wind. They would ride an aquaplane—he knew all about flying now. They would see the great city as it should be seen, from heaven.

February ended. The days were growing longer. The familiar evening light, lost a century ago in November, returned. One morning he heard, very briefly, a bird's song.

March. The Dillinger story had long since faded to the back pages of the papers. The Dillinger gang was yesterday's news. There would be a trial, probably followed by executions.

John consulted with his lawyer. The special guards remained at their posts, settled into a routine of coffee, cigarettes and conversation. They began to tire of each other's stories and personalities, of the monotony.

John was above it all. He was living in history, while the rest of the world continued to plod through time. Destiny, John believed, had him within its grip.

He made no decision. Just as a suicide makes no decision to take the plunge, pull the trigger. The act itself has force. The act itself stalks you. The act itself looms in all its inevitability. Decision is irrelevant. The act completes itself.

He walked out of that fortress singing "I'm Headed for the Last Round-Up."

Crown Point was where the real magic began. Houdini was still fondly remembered in those days. Escape was on everybody's mind. So many wanted to escape from what their lives had become.

111

In the show I added a little speech to explain how easily he absconded from a solid prison secured by military force, like a hot knife through butter.

"Everyone says, what's the trick?" I'd intone, striding in my Dillinger costume. "The trick, if you call it a trick, is knowing you're going to die. No one wants to give up his life to the sea of possibility—call it what you will, God or fate. But I did. I said, I'm going to die. I don't know when. Now or later. It's not my choice. This thing is given to me to do. I'll die right now. It's not my choice. Let the cards fall. And accepting death, I was able to calmly reach out and grasp freedom."

Billie was waiting in Chicago, as he'd told her to. She hadn't much money. She'd hocked her mink. She'd asked around about a job as a waitress. To save money she ate in diners where seventy-five cents would buy a chop with mashed and string beans.

The weather was icy. Chicago was dirty, the snow congealed into blackened pyramids of ice. Soot and spit and garbage were frozen to the pavement.

Without a drink now she felt the cold sinking in too deep. She sometimes let men buy her cocktails in bars.

One afternoon she sat in a Belmont Avenue ice cream parlor off of Broadway. She knew that she should be making plans. Johnnie had told her plans were good, even if you don't follow them. But she couldn't. How could she plan for not being with him?

She was lost, separated from herself. The city was full of bad omens. She was like everyone else now. She wasn't part of the headlines. She was being slowly ground up by economics and heartlessness.

She was eating a Mexican sundae: vanilla ice cream with

hot fudge and salty spanish peanuts. It was one of the luxuries she permitted herself. She picked up tiny scoops with her spoon and let the ice cream melt on her tongue. They had a musical program on the radio. All the love songs were about her, the sugar lyrics knives in her heart.

Steam condensed on the plate windows in front, turned them translucent, and ran down in rivulets. The figures passing outside were ghosts.

An instrumental of "How Deep Is the Ocean" stopped abruptly in the second chorus. The announcer's voice came on, charged with exhilaration. He said something. Then he was done and the music started again. Was she dreaming?

Her first sensation was not relief or excitement, but a terrible giddy feeling, as if the floor had just dropped from below her feet. It seemed too much like a play, a show, like events following a script. She even thought that the radio might be lying. Or, she imagined suddenly that the sentimental tear-jerker songs that poured from the speaker were genuine prayers, that if you opened your heart to them, some dream god would make them work magic.

But maybe someone was playing a joke. How could it be? You sit in a simple ice cream parlor, your heart twisting because your lover is gone forever. Suddenly a message comes over the radio that speaks directly to you. He's escaped. He's escaped and he's all right. He's all right and he's coming to you. He's coming because you cannot live without him.

She dropped some money for the check and left her sundae half finished. It was no longer bitter out. The sidewalks were no longer dirty. The air was full of life. The sky suddenly stretched from coast to coast, from the north pole to the south.

She shared a small place on Addison with her sister. She went there, played the radio and waited. She wanted him to come and she didn't want him to come. She went out three

113

times, finally returned with the afternoon paper that had the first details.

She paced. Her teeth hurt, her fingernails hurt. Her eyes were wet one minute, too dry to blink the next. She couldn't eat. She lay down in bed that night and stared at the ceiling. The tightness in her chest would not let her sleep. Her jaw ached with clenching.

She started thinking about him with her body. How sweet they would be with each other now. How precious each moment. Hot skin against hot skin. She had a shiver of pleasure. She was embarrassed.

Then suddenly she sank into a cataract of despair. What if he did not come? What if he thought it too dangerous to ever contact her? Or if he had another girl? Or if they caught him before he could reach her?

No, that was impossible. He knew she had no money. He knew she needed him. That was what made him take the desperate plunge. Nothing could stop him from getting to her.

She thought she hadn't slept—suddenly it was morning. She left egg and toast on her plate, drank a little coffee, paced.

The longest day of her life lay before her. The telephone was ready to explode with silence. She grew old by afternoon. Her hope departed with the light. She wept uncontrollably for a long time. She had no more tears. She stood at the window and watched the streetlights, the few hunched figures hurrying past. Where were they going? Where was there to go?

She read about the manhunt. The authorities were confident that Dillinger would be back behind bars shortly. There was nowhere for him to hide now.

Abruptly, without the least warning, the phone rang. Billie shrunk back as if she'd been slapped. Her sister answered. Just a moment, please.

Billie put the receiver to her ear and made a noise.

"You okay, honey?"

"Fine." It was all she could say.

"How about it, Billie? Ready to go places?"

"Yes!"

"Be packed, okay? I know where you are. I've got plans."

"I'll be waiting."

"Bye for now." The line clicked dead.

Again she was gripped by an eerie unreality. She couldn't control the expression on her face.

The car pulled up outside two hours later. She'd had her bag packed for two days. She didn't feel any steps descending. She stood staring in the car window, letting her belief catch up with her.

"Get in," he said. "Let's get out of here."

She climbed in beside him. The car began moving at once. He turned rapidly down a narrow back street, then another. She could see his eyes flicking quickly to the sides, the mirror.

They drove all night to St. Paul.

He said, "I wanted to go back. After we took off in the sheriff's Ford, I wanted to go back. Turn myself in. Let them lock me up. Do it again. Just to try my luck. Just for that feeling I had when I walked out. I wanted to go back and do it again."

11

I REMEMBER LAUGHING the morning I picked up the papers and read about Crown Point. The whole country laughed. Howled with laughter and with outrage.

Dillinger! His name was everywhere again. No jail could hold him. In Chicago, people said, they would kill him on sight. Officials considered a house-to-house search of the city. His picture went up in every bank in the country. Crowds in the Bronx came close to panic over two men in a car with Illinois plates. A squad of federal men was sent to the Middle West to track him down. In Massachusetts vigilantes burned him in effigy.

Dillinger! He was "The Killer." He was "Snake Eyes." He was "Mad Dog."

A gag sprang up in ten cities at once: A guy would be selling genuine photographs of John Dillinger, world's most famous outlaw. You'd open the envelope and inside would only be a note that said, "So he got away from you, too!"

A few pages back in the papers there was other news, stories that wouldn't mean much to us until later. Hitler had just taken over in Germany. Studebaker had brought out a model called The Dictator. It sold for $695. These Nazis said they knew how to handle criminals of Dillinger's ilk. Sterilize them.

John contacted Red Hamilton in Chicago. Three days after

116

the escape they had a gang together in St. Paul. Homer Van Meter—it was his home turf. Tommy Carroll—he'd been in the prize ring but still had a handsome Irish mug. He could handle a machine gun. Eddie Green—Homer vouched for him, steady when the noise started. And Lester Gillis.

Lester had grown up a half block from the slaughterhouses in Chicago. As a boy he used to go down to hug the fences and watch them unload the cars of steers and hogs. The animals would stampede down the ramps for hours, eyes bugged and rolling. The sound they made cut to the heart of terror, yet Lester loved to watch. He would wave a stick and pretend he was controlling the tons of hoofed flesh. Or he would join their bellows, close his eyes, hurl a scream that blotted out their relentless protest.

In his youth, blood ran down storm sewers. El-trains clawed the nights with their steel wheels. Flies clogged the summer air.

Lester was a small man. He was twenty-five, but his nose and chin were still soft and round, his voice raw like a boy's voice. When he angered he couldn't keep his eyes from watering.

Lester had a pretty blond wife and two children. He went by the name George Nelson. Some called him Big George. Baby Face, that was just a name used by the papers, by jokers behind his back.

"There's one way to do these things," Lester explained to the others. "Give them a taste right away, before anything else." He waved off a protest. "A gun is one thing. A gun going off is another. And a gun going off and opening somebody's gut is another altogether. They think: that could be me, I'm going to do what this guy tells me. I'm going to do it quick."

"No they don't. They think nothing," Homer argued. "They freeze up."

117

"You have to let them know who's in charge, that's all."

"Horseshit. You walk it. Walk in, walk out. That's how this gang works. We've never had any trouble we couldn't handle."

"That's in the past."

"Past, present and future, little man."

Lester slipped his hand into his pocket to touch the gun. "Who the hell you talking to, Homer?"

"John," Homer said, "how do we do things? You know the way Pete used to lay it out. No cowboy-and-Indian."

"You talk to me!" Lester had his fist around the grip now.

"Shove it," Homer said flatly.

"Lester," John said, "if I see iron, you're going home."

"Say I was to blow your brains against the wall," Lester snarled at Homer. "Wouldn't that wake you up?"

"You like to make a lot of noise, don't you?"

Red put in, "You shoot, people get hurt. We don't—that's not what we want, is it, John?"

"Let me explain something to you, Lester," John said. "It's known as science. Did you go to the fair? What was it all about? Science."

"This is science," he insisted, hefting the gun inside his pocket.

"That's horseshit," Homer said.

"You . . ." Lester was shaking with frustration. "You don't see. No cat and mouse. No playing. John's got the goddamn army after him. This is war! You kill in war. Get hurt? Of course they'll get hurt, they don't do what we say. This is war, the whole goddamn thing is a war. It's all war! You understand that?"

"Sure, it's a war, Lester," John said calmly. "The main thing in a war is not to lose your head. Shooting only works if it has a purpose."

"John was in the navy," Red added.

118

Lester slowly removed his pistol from his pocket, laid it on the table in front of him. His face was blotchy, beads of sweat standing on his nose.

"You ready now?" John asked him calmly.

"I'll try it your way," he said. "But I think certain guys better wise up. They're going to be coming at us. We better be ready for that."

"Right, Napoleon," Homer said.

"What?"

They laughed, Lester's fingers reached to stroke the rough grip of the pistol.

John and Red Hamilton went out to breathe the early spring air still scented with the metal of winter. The sun was bright behind the clouds. Once in a while it poked through like a spotlight.

St. Paul had been an open town during Prohibition. All the cops were on the take. Anybody could come into town, pay a visit to the commissioner of public safety, and stay as long as he liked without fear of being turned up. As long as he kept clean in the city itself. The town became a cooling-off spot for rum runners and killers and heist men from around the Middle West.

But times were changing. Homer told John they couldn't make any deal for somebody as hot as Dillinger. It was take your chances.

They walked along the empty street, under bare trees.

"Baby Face solid?" Red asked John later.

"He likes to hear the bang."

"Could cause a mess, I'm thinking. When we're inside."

"We might need to make some noise. These jobs are going to get harder, Red."

"You don't think we can do it Pete's way?" Red said.

"Oh, Pete knew. Pete was right. Science, planning, all that. But Pete's in the can. It's not science, Red, not really. That's just a way of talking."

"Yeah."

"Anyway, like Homer said, how many guys want to go in with me?"

"Lots, I think."

"Lots of cowboys. I'm poison now. I'm telling you that."

"Except for your luck."

"That's just it. I used up my luck. I'm walking on air."

They went into a warm coffee shop, sat at the counter, ordered pie and coffee.

A man wearing a serge suit with shiny elbows was sitting up the counter. He was talking to the counterman, who paid no attention: "What I can't see—the common man is getting et up. And yet the common man is not, will not do nothing about it. There should be a revolution going on in this country. You lose your job, they make out it's your own fault. It could be them tomorrow, but they don't care. You go to the relief, they treat you like you done something to be ashamed of. Even though you wanna work. It's a pitiful disgrace. Should be a revolution."

The counterman dropped his cigarette on the floor and mashed it with his foot. "You a communist?"

"I ain't no communist. The only thing about me red is my blood. No sir. I just am able to see with my two eyes." He turned to John. "Like you. You smoking a cigarette. The president of American Tobacco made two million last year. That's right. And paying his workers fifteen a week. Think on it. I ain't no red, but you think on that."

"Sure," John said. "The big men got the whole deal rigged. I'm with you."

"I heard of a man in New York, his kids going hungry, he

goes out and steals thirty-seven dollars. Know what they give him? Five years in Sing Sing. Five years."

"Now you're talking about breaking the law," the counterman said.

"I'm talking about desperation, pure and simple. Did you know they had artillery out in Washington for the inauguration last year? Did you know there are men setting forest fires just so they'll be hired to put them out?"

"Forest fires, huh?" The counterman picked at his teeth with the nail of his thumb. "That's not a bad idea."

"The mirth of the land is gone, the Bible says. The earth mourneth. You see these are men of paper. They are men with paper faces who rob by paper."

"Who you talking about?" the counterman asked him.

"All of them. The magnates, the Wall Street weasels, the Rockefellers, the Elks and the Oddfellows, the Chamber boys and the Masons."

"I'm a Mason."

"The Masons."

John and Red got up to leave. "All I know," John said, "is, you get dealt a hand of cards, you've gotta play it."

"The deck is stacked, my friend," the stranger said.

"That make a difference?"

Driving west the next morning they passed the site of a carnival on the outskirts of a hick town. The tent lay stretched on the ground like a deflated dream. It reminded John of a show he'd attended as a boy. It was always summer then. His sister had taken him.

He remembered his first elephant. How he whipped his fiery wooden horse on the carousel. How he watched the men banging and banging at the shooting gallery.

But most of all, he remembered the Wild West show. The tent was full of the smell of sawdust and beer. The bleachers were crowded with men. John and some of the other boys were told to sit on the ground in front.

First came Little Big Horn. Custer's death was a long and painful one, punctuated by flowery proclamations and tragic groans. John marveled at how war paint changed a face. Those Indians were straight out of a nightmare. Just when the boys were snickering at the man in the long blond wig one of the braves leapt off the stage to menace them with a tomahawk. They all cringed.

One of the Indian girls was the rope expert. When she came out, the boys elbowed each other. Her rawhide skirt came barely to her knees. She got the figure eight loop going. She moved her legs apart so the leather stretched taut across her thighs. She had fine brown legs that John thought about in bed at night months after.

John had hoped that the show would go on forever. Why should it end? Why couldn't life be a show?

A man in a sombrero and a fancy scroll shirt came out. Two guns were slung low on his hips, the handles facing forward. He crossed his arms to draw them. He spun both silver pistols up over his head, around behind. He put one back, passed the other, still spinning, beneath his leg.

All the time, a desperado all in black was sneaking up behind him. The boys yelled, pointed, kicked their feet in frustration.

At the last minute, the man in the sombrero turned, drew his other gun, and fired half a dozen times. His assailant staggered through an elaborate pirouette of death. The hero blew on the ends of his smoking pistols, snapped them into his holsters. The audience cheered.

But before the clapping stopped, four more attackers approached from all sides. The fancy shooter held his hands out from his sides and waited, waited. When one of the villains drew on him he flew into action, blasting without mercy, dropping one, another, another.

The loud blanks inside the tent made John shudder. But the sound thrilled him. The authoritative crack spoke to him.

Now came the part of the show they'd been waiting for. A small man walked onto the stage. The adults applauded, but the boys stared in silent wonder. Was this Frank James? Was this man with the withered neck the same who'd ridden with Quantrill's Raiders? Was this man in the cream Stetson hat and vest made from the hide of a pinto horse the same who'd held up the train in Council Bluffs? Had this old man robbed the First National in Northfield, Minnesota?

After Jesse was shot down in his own home by the coward Robert Ford, Frank had finagled a pardon. Now, years later, he was touring, cashing in on his page in the history books.

He pulled out his silver six-shooter, spun it, fanned three blanks at the audience, smiled as he greased it back into the black holster on his hip.

His voice was not old. The words, inflected with a soft drawl, flowed from beneath his mustache. You couldn't see him move his lips.

"I was the son of a Baptist minister," he said. "Born in Clay County, Missouri. That was the end of civilization those days. I fought in the War Between the States and I'm proud of it. It was a carnival of blood and devastation."

He told of the federals burning Cole Younger's mother out of her house. Of Quantrill and Bloody Bill Anderson and the bushwhacker wars. "We was men who learned to dare when there was no such word as quarter," he recited.

He told of robbing the bank in Liberty, Missouri. February of '66. First daylight bank robbery in the history of this great

123

land. Jesse jumped the counter and grabbed sixty dollars in cash. A snowstorm stopped the posse.

" 'Seventy-one we robbed the Ocobock Brothers Bank in Corydon, Iowa." He pronounced it Eye-oh-way. "Jesse and me, the Youngers, Clell Miller. After, we rode out to where they was having a town meeting, told them the bank'd been robbed."

When they robbed the train at Gads Hill Jesse wrote up the newspaper story himself, Frank said. He left it with the train men, told them to fill in the amount of the take.

"Any time we robbed a train, we looked at men's hands," he said. "If they had callous, we didn't take. Only plug-hat gentlemen we ever robbed from."

The Northfield job was where it all went wrong. It turned into nothing but shooting. Bill Stiles and Clell Miller were killed. Bob Younger was shot. Cole and Jim stayed behind with him and they were all captured.

"All you boys listen to me," he said, sweeping a gnarled finger across the row of little faces, stopping on John. "It's awful being hunted. It's awful when they put a price on your head. It's awful a man guns you in the back. A man is forced to do what he's forced to do. But once you are in it, you can never turn back. And it's an awful, awful thing."

The audience applauded wildly as Frank ended his remarks with a short paean to Church and civilization. Afterward he mingled with the crowd shaking hands, nodding his agreement to all remarks, signing autographs for a nickel.

The boys stared at the bullets tucked in the loops on his gun belt. They stared at the spikes of his silver spurs. They dove and punched to grab the cigar butt he tossed into the dirt.

Awful. Awful meant nothing to John. This man was Frank James. He'd done things. Everybody in the country knew who he was. He was an old man, yes, but people talked to him gentle because he was Frank James. People smiled at him and shook his hand. He was Frank James, the famous outlaw.

Frank's ghost whispered to him as he drove this March morning.

From a rise now, far in the west, he could see their destination, the little city hunkered on the plains, the steeple poking through the trees. A row of smokestacks. A grain elevator.

And beyond, as far as the horizon, loomed a wall. It was a soft, formless, yellow-brown wall that went up and up, past the sky.

"There she is," Lester said. "Yo-ho."

"What's that?" John asked Homer.

Van Meter squinted at the wall. The sun was now a mere stain in the jaundiced sky.

"Dust," he said.

12

WHEN I MET HER she was a grandmother.

"Oh, I remember," she told me. "The sun hit the yellow paper shade, first thing I did, reach downstairs and make sure I still had my drawers on. There were times, me and Dag would get pie-eyed, forget. Kids? I wanted kids. But no way in hell we could afford a baby in '34. Nobody was having babies back in '34."

I talked to a lot of them over the years, the ones who'd been there, who knew him, who had had the light of his fame touch them, scald them.

Gladys was one of the last. I sat in her suburban living room in 1973. Her cheeks were sagging, but her slender legs still suggested what a number she must have been, what a dancer. Like the others, she was able to recall the details of the morning with an eerie clarity.

"Whiskey-on-beer-never-fear is a crock, I can tell you. You'd better fear, boy. Course, you can bounce back pretty good when you're twenty. I rinsed my face and powdered under my arms, changed my dress, rouged my lips—I have a wide mouth so I always drew a little cupid bow in the middle of it. Then I went to empty Mother's night pan.

"I gave her a bowl of Wheateena. Mother had to have

126

Wheateena. Every morning Wheateena. That day she called me Katherine, who was a maid Grandpa Verner had before I was born.

"I put the coffee on and while I was spooning out Mother's cereal I smelled metal burning and knew I'd forgot to put water in the percolator. It hissed steam when I ran it under the faucet.

"Mother said the toast was burnt. I told her I didn't have time to make more. I was late. I said Dag would do it. She got the look she got whenever I mentioned Dag's name.

"Dag was snoring up a storm, one shoe still on, his pants around his knees. He must have been dreaming he was in a fight because when I woke him he growled and covered his face with his arm. I told him to look in on Mother, make her some light toast. I set the alarm clock to go off in fifteen minutes and put it right next to his ear.

"My headache was out the door before I was. It was up in the sky, a kind of hollow blue-black. And in the distance you could just make out the crest of a dust storm. It had blown up on the plains. It would hit us by noon, they said.

"We'd had a couple of those black blizzards the year before. Hung wet blankets over the doors, but you could still taste the grit in your mouth, dust fine as flour. The worst thing was, you would wake up at night thinking the most awful thoughts. Those yellow clouds of dust moving across the plains, it was like judgment.

"Dag was out of work. He'd been out of work for over a year, though he liked to say it was thirteen months or whatever. He'd tended a lathe at a big machine shop. Fall of '31 they went out on strike. Dag was afraid to go out. Afraid to go out and afraid to keep working. He comes to me and says, 'Gladys, God help me,' crying.

"So he stayed and scabbed. I wouldn't talk to him for a

month, I was so disgusted. And then the shop went belly-up anyways, they had no business.

"So Dag would just sit around the house or he'd go pow-wow with some of his pals who were laid off from the railroad. They used to sit by the tracks as if they were waiting for the Chicago Express. Every day I expected to find out that Dag had jumped a freight. I used to wish for it.

"The First Merchants opened up after the bank holiday, though two other banks in town never did. People who'd lost money in them would ask me, Gladys, how can this be? Like I knew anything about it. Just hard times, I'd tell them. Money's just gone.

"I thought maybe Dag could get on the WPA. But he hated the Democrats. I kept Roosevelt's picture up in the kitchen just to rile him. He said he'd never take government money no way in hell. I said that's fine but we have got to live, mister. He said we're living. I said oh yeah? Barely able to feed ourselves and I can't get my teeth fixed and Mother's doctor bills hanging over us?

"The bank was a twenty-minute walk. I had to hurry because today was the day Mrs. Petersen came in.

"There were already plenty of cars slanted around the town square. And the butter-and-egg men were hustling. And the sun shining, lighting this line of storm in the west, making it glow a kind of sick orange.

"Sure we drank. Those times, you had to put some fire in your life. My friend Libby come over and Burton her hubbie, as she called him. I told Dag to get some beer. He said we should have a bottle as they'd mixed us highballs after that Garbo movie we all went to. So I gave him three dollars more and he brought home this awful stuff you could taste right through the ginger.

"Burton was a janitor at the school. He hadn't been paid

in almost three months and now the city was turning around and threatening to auction their house for taxes. The nerve, Libby said.

"After a couple of ponies of that coffin varnish all four of us got on a laughing jag. Dag started on about how the depression was all the fault of the Jews and the communists, only he couldn't say Bolshevik and kept saying 'boll weevils' and 'blushing brides' and things. We'd heard it all a million times, his theory so-called, but we couldn't stop laughing. And Burton says how he's in love with Jessica Dragonnette, the singer you'd hear on the radio. He says, Her voice makes my toes curl.

"The Neville Moore band came on and they were playing 'Give Me Liberty or Give Me Love.' I adored that song. Libby did, too. She stood and hiked her skirt practically to her waist and was showing us some new dance step. I saw Dag looking, this silly grin on his face. Didn't I have to get up and bare my gams, too? And sing, How can you hi-de-hi when you feel so low-de-low.

"They laughed. We all laughed. We knew the happy songs were lies, but we had an appetite for lies those days. We giggled. We howled. We roared. I remember thinking, Christ the bottom's dropping out of the world and it's only one big black laugh. And it's a good thing Mother's deaf.

"After that I didn't remember much. Me and Libby were the Rockettes. We kicked so high we fell over backward, numb. The two men laughed till they were wiping tears. The next day I had a big bruise on my elbow.

"They had this clock with Roman numerals on the wall opposite my cage. All morning that morning it creeped. Three times I thought I was going to be ill. But I couldn't leave my cage, we were so busy. Farmers would be coming in to take out a couple of dollars or to try and get a carryover till harvest

129

on their mortgages. Those boobs could never learn to fill out the slips right. It sure was a headache.

"Everybody that came in said, You should see it outside. The west was dark as anything. It was the dust coming, they said. I was beginning to get worried Mrs. Petersen wouldn't show."

She told me the next part as if it were a secret, but a secret she was used to airing, the way we sometimes like to air our vices. She was proud of her sins because they were hers.

Mr. Petersen, she told me, had been a hard-faced man who ran the local grain elevator. Had connections, it was said, in the pits in Chicago. Knew futures.

But Mr. Petersen's wealth was a churning kind of wealth. When his estate settled down, his widow wondered at how little was left—after the Crash only the house. She survived on an annuity that she had purchased herself from her household money.

Mrs. Petersen was pitiful, but in those days, sympathies had to be reined in. There was a glut of sadness. Gladys had received two notices from the electric company that she'd been afraid to open. She was terrified of returning home someday soon to darkness.

"So I was watching Mrs. Petersen when it happened. I didn't even notice them come in. Mrs. Petersen was showing the signs. I'd seen it with Mother—the palsy, the away look in the eyes.

"See, she didn't count her cash. Every other week she received a draft on a bank in Chicago. Not a lot, but in those days enough.

"I would rehearse what I would say to Mr. Lansing, in case. I'm afraid she is not all there, poor thing, I would say. Like my mother, I would say. The way they get. I would touch my temple and smile an innocent smile.

"Actually, it had started by accident. I'd miscounted. I realized it right away, but Mrs. Petersen's shaky hand was already picking up the bills. She never looked, never said anything. So when I justified my drawer I was able to slip a ten out without anybody the wiser.

"Ashamed? I was young. I was taking care of Mother. I had a husband that wasn't working. I needed that money.

"Everybody, it seemed, those days, was stealing. Grab a bottle of milk. Fiddle with your gas meter. You had to be a coyote to get along, had to be a brave coward. Just to get along.

"But I would always get my nerves up when Mrs. Petersen joined the line in front of my cage. I couldn't draw a proper breath. I was feeling like that that morning. Only more so—the hangover, the way the sky was darkening and darkening.

"She was right up to me, her eyes the color of a baby's eyes, the tight skin across her cheeks translucent. She'd just put the draft on the counter when the commotion started.

"I thought it was the police, so help me. They'd found me out, brung the police for me.

"I'm still counting Mrs. Petersen's cash, but Mrs. Petersen is turning. She's confused. A man comes along and shouts at her. There's something in his hand, but I don't realize at first what it is. He's a short man. His eyes are jumping all around. He gives Mrs. Petersen a tiny shove, the way you'd nudge someone to wake them. She falls.

"Another man in a gray suit helps Mrs. Petersen up. He speaks to the first man, but I can't hear. He points Mrs. Petersen toward the end of the lobby. His hand, I just catch a glimpse of it, is wrapped around the butt of a big revolver. His eyes are gray. They aren't jumping. He looks at me. Looks at me, do you understand? Looks, just looks. I felt naked clean through."

131

The bell started then. The alarm.

"I wanted to laugh, I really did. These men holding up the bank? They're dressed like Mr. Lansing, like businessmen. This is a movie. They're making a movie. It's all playacting.

"We sometimes talked what we'd do if we ever got held up. But when it happens, you're confused. You can't believe it. It's like entering a foreign land. You suddenly can't understand anything. And let me tell you, you're scared to death."

The short man ran around yelling he was going to kill the son of a bitch that set off that alarm. Then he jumped a railing, leapt onto a desk, fired a machine gun out the front window. The gold-painted glass cracked. One big section fell with a sound like the last judgment.

"Tear gas has a smell," she said, "that you can't ever forget. Imagine the smell of black pepper stripped bare and dense as lead. Your closed eyes itch. Open them, they scald themselves with white tears."

A guard had fired the grenade from a steel cage on the bank's balcony. One of the men sprayed the cage with slugs.

The shots never stopped. They echoed from the marble walls, rattled the windows, tore the air to pieces.

"I'm going to die. That was the first time I ever thought that in my life. Thought it was possible. I was on the floor, I didn't know what I was doing, just curled up on my side and pressed my fists to my eyes.

"Then a man came into my cage. I knew he was going to kill me right there. I wondered what it would feel like, being shot, would I even know it?

"I heard his feet by my head. I opened my eyes. They burned. He had on fine maroon oxfords, a gray suit. He had the gun in his hand.

" 'Sister,' he said to me. 'Take care you don't soil that pretty dress.' I was wearing a midnight-blue one with a tiny yellow flower print, a dress I liked a lot. I always remember him saying that.

"I heard him going into my drawer. I glanced up. I couldn't see his face, only the sack that he was putting the money into, one like the ones the bank used to hold coins.

"Then he opened the door at the back of my cage and started to go out. And stopped. I thought for a second he'd forgotten to kill me. But I dared to peek again quick. He was looking at my hand. I looked at it too. It was a little animal, completely independent of me. It had instinctively grabbed Mrs. Petersen's bills. It was wadding them into a ball, all on its own.

"He winked. I swear he did. My hand slipped over and tucked the bills down my dress, down the front. I didn't want it to, but it did.

"He told me to get up and come out with him. He didn't jab with the gun or anything, just asked me to. In the lobby they had nine or ten girls. It was a dream. I saw a patrolman— I didn't know his name but I'd seen him in town—lying on the floor. I thought he was dead, but he raised his head and looked. And all the time the alarm is ringing and we're coughing and they're shouting. And every once in a while, bang. Just like a dream."

Hundreds of spectators were waiting outside.

"They said, We're going out and you stay close around us. If you don't we'll kill you, the little one said. I was next to the one in the gray suit.

" 'Keep your hands up so they'll know you're hostages,' he told us.

"We walked outside. We were glad for the air. But the light—I'd never seen the town look that way. The sun was shining, but shining dark. The dust storm was almost on us, but the air was still. The little guy shot again, just shot for no reason. People yelled and laughed. It was noise, but it was so quiet, too. Some people crowded behind the meteorite in the square across from the bank—it's a memento to our boys that fought in the Civil War."

They walked the hostages around to the car, same routine as Racine four months earlier. Made them stand on the running boards. Two girls sat on the front mudguards. One they told to stand on the back bumper and hold on where the window would have been except they'd knocked it out.

There were eleven girls altogether. Girls in pressed-pleat skirts. Girls with flaming cheeks. Girls in sweetheart necklines, kumquat hairdos coming undone, burgundy nails clutching door handles. They were girls who spent their days at the dust-dry altar of commerce. Nothing ever happened to them. Now everything was.

"I was holding onto the door handle in back. The man who'd come into my cage got behind the wheel. They told me later he was Dillinger. But he was never Dillinger to me. Dillinger was somebody in the papers. This man was just a man.

"We started off. Slow. So slow. The dust storm loomed right over us. The sun was gone. It was quiet, then the wind blew a dry whisper and the air smelled of stale electric. The power company lit the streetlights—I saw them come on."

They left behind the bleeding—they had killed no one for all their trajectories. They left behind the terror-stricken who had soiled themselves, their garments turning cold.

They left behind ripples of innuendo, bullet holes for small boys to fit their fingers into, stories that would be told over and over, ghosts to haunt the town for decades.

Outside the village, a fine dust was already blowing. The sky turned a strange purple color. The car stopped. An eerie quiet overtook them.

"I couldn't let go," Gladys told me. "My fingers were knotted right around that handle. Then one of the men climbed out and told us all to get off. He had a bag of nails. He threw them in handfuls down the road behind. He was laughing, I don't know what about.

"The dust kept coming harder. They just left us standing there and took off and disappeared. We started to walk toward town. Some of the cars searching found us.

"They said that dust storm darkened the sky over New York two days later."

She shook her head, smiled, maybe thinking how long ago it all was.

"Funny thing," she told me. "Over the years those girls, those of us from the bank, used to tell each other about it a lot. At first, everybody else wanted to know, the newspapers, Dag asked me everything, Libby. But they grew tired of hearing it. And anyway, they never understood what it was like. They couldn't. So you'd go to somebody who had been there and tell them. They knew the weightlessness, like you were falling from a trapeze. They knew the coldness. They knew it could make a young girl think funny thoughts. They knew what it was like.

"Did it change me? It is the pivot of my life. Everything before that day I think of as my childhood. And as the years pass my childhood grows heavier—I suppose everyone's does. On this side my life since gets longer just in order to balance those early years. And right in the middle is that day.

"Because, I thought, if these men can do this, can just decide and walk in and do it, then anything is possible. It blasted my future wide open. Here I was, a lump of bank notes between my breasts. I'd robbed the bank. Me.

"It wasn't until two days later that it hit me full force. At first I was all bubbling and full of it. But it kept building and

I broke down. I cried my eyes out, I couldn't stop crying. I had chills."

Afterward she didn't want Dag. She never slept with him again. They divorced.

Her mother died that winter. Gladys moved to Chicago. When I talked to her she'd lived for years in one of the western suburbs, in a ranchstyle house with an immaculate lawn and pleated silk pillows on the couch.

Her second husband, an office equipment salesman, smiled his approval as she told me the tale. He knew that it was serious. It was one of the things that had happened to her. It was one of the things that connected her to her life.

I told her about my show, about how, long ago, I was the Man Who Looks Like Dillinger. She stared at me real hard. Then she laughed.

13

I WALKED INTO THE BANK. Baby Face entered behind me, a tommy gun under his coat, and slid up along the far wall. He would go wild, but not now, not just yet.

They had a guard with an old Buntline strapped to his hip. He would present no problem. He wasn't in our time. When the action started, we would simply brush him aside. He couldn't keep pace with us.

Half a dozen customers were scattered around the lobby. Three tellers waited behind steel grates. In the center of each, the steel was shaped into a sun.

"This is it!" I shouted. "Everybody down. Get down, now! On the floor!"

I leapt up over one of the windows and down into the cage of the first teller. She was a girl with blond blond curls all piled on her head so her long neck showed. As I reached around her into the drawer of money I stroked her round bottom. Nobody saw me do that. And gave her a little pinch.

"Better get down, sister," I said. "There's liable to be some shooting."

She kept her big hazel eyes on me as she squatted, went to her knees. What might have been a smile flickered across her lips.

One of the customers was still standing. I could see him

137

getting that hero look in his eye. I nodded to Baby Face. Baby Face fired his gun toward the ceiling, a little machine-gun soft shoe. The customer dropped.

I leapt up again and down into the next cage. Money. I grabbed the bills and stuffed them into a cloth sack. The money was the world saying yes to you. Yes, John. Yes, yes. Thousands of yeses. The bag began to take on a sweet weight.

The sound of shooting. A crowd was gathering outside the door. I could see the heads bobbing, people who wanted to see. An alarm bell began to sound.

"Take your time," I said to Red Hamilton. He was cleaning out the vault. "Get it all."

Baby Face yelled they had us covered. We were going to have to shoot our way out the front.

He started firing. Glass was breaking. Red and I came around with two big sacks of money. We shot. The sound of shooting just filled the place. Women screamed.

A whole phalanx of lawmen burst upon us. I mowed them down like bowling pins.

Red went down, wounded. I turned back, helped him to his feet. I heard clapping. I shot some more. Baby Face ratcheted another clip into the trench broom and let loose. The clapping got louder. We burst free and ran for the car.

They were stamping their feet on the bleachers when we came back for our bow. That was the stuff they paid their money to see. That was as close as they would come. That was the opportunity of a lifetime. They were seeing John Dillinger.

We pulled a curtain over the bank set and did the next number in front of it. Ivy went on as Billie. She paced up and down wringing her hands. She's worried about me, see. You could read it on her face, a big expression like they used to use in the silent movies. She's worried sick.

But then I come in. I have that bulging sack, the gun still

in my hand. I lay them down and open my arms to her. She's so glad to see me she can't move at first. Then she springs forward and embraces me, squeals. She makes a little move with her hips that somebody could read something into if they were watching.

Onstage, you're always a couple of seconds ahead of yourself, so you won't have to stop and think what to do or say next. Hesitation, so natural in life, takes the wind out of a drama.

But when I kissed Ivy, the show, the whole world stopped for a moment. It was only her pliant lips, the amber smell of her breath, her ribs under the silk, and those half-wild, half-sleepy eyes. Her fingers would paddle across my neck. Sometimes she would rake my scalp with her nails.

The crowd sensed that we were boring a hole through the make-believe. They felt the heat that seeped into that opening. They liked it.

Ivy grew into her role. To her, Billie Frechette was a queen. Billie was as magnificent as Ruby Keeler or Joan Blondell or Garbo. More so. A movie goddess depended on others, her fans, the studios, the alchemy that threw her face into giant patterns of shifting light. Billie faced the night alone, walked the tunnel of danger, sustained by her enormous love.

If Ivy's acting melted into lush melodrama, all the better. When you're putting on a show for hicks in a tent, you pour on the molasses and they just holler for more. At times her exaggerated anguish would bring tears to folks' eyes. Especially as they now knew that her fear would all too soon bear fruit, her man would be cut down.

She moved me, too, but not to tears. The shadow of an indentation that her skirt made as it curved down over her rump is what got me. The laugh she would laugh, like the gurgling of a stream; the way her lips would hang loose and her eyes drop when she was thinking; or the way she would dangle her shoe from her toe, arching her foot into a curve, as she sat reading a movie magazine in front of her trailer. These images filled my dreams. Weakened me.

Underneath my face, I was no John Dillinger. My blood ruled me. I was ready to do anything to win the sunshine of Ivy's favor. I played the cavalier, careless and crude, because I was afraid of how I felt and because I told myself that was the way the ladies liked a man. But when she would hurry off after the show, not even taking time to remove her make-up, so as to be sure she didn't miss Harry's act, then I would beg her.

"Just a second, Ivy. I need to talk to you."

"I can't. You know."

"Come here, honey."

"Stop that. Whataya think yer doin?"

"Billie!"

But she'd be off. She would stand in the aisle, by the band, and watch the wire flex, watch Harry step, step, spin around, lie down. She would hold her breath during the drumrolls, clasp her hands and grimace with each fake near-fall.

Those were our moments, those few minutes after a show, when she was still flushed with emotion and applause and my hands were still ringing with the blast of guns. Until Harry finished his walk we were at large. I could have eaten her up then, but she wouldn't let me. She had to watch him.

It pained me to hear the whine he brought out in her. He treated her like a chambermaid. Worse than that, like a whore. She told me. After their wedding night she couldn't bear to sleep with him again for three weeks. "Sometimes he uses me like a handkerchief like you'd blow your nose on," she confided. "Other times he tries and tries and can't bring himself off. He won't stop and it makes me so sore. And what's he thinking about, it ain't me."

Harry had a detestable completeness—his trim build, the

lithe strength of his arms and legs. I'd seen him climb a flight of stairs walking on his hands. His head was a little too big for his body, a head you'd find on a Roman bust, with a hard cleft chin and a nose wide at the bridge, topped by an august forehead and a neat wave of dark blond hair. He had a gentleman's silver-colored eyes, which seemed always attracted by some distant object.

Two months after I'd joined Sparky's show, I was sitting outside my trailer drinking warm rye after midnight. I'd awoke sweating with no sleep in sight. I went out looking for a breeze but the air hung humid and thick, heavy with insect drones and animal smells.

"Hot one."

I was startled. Harry nodded to me, then looked across the field that stretched a long way down from our site to a swamp that was full of the cadavers of maples.

I said, "Night like this you want to take off your flesh and sit around in your bones. Drink?"

I was surprised when he agreed to a glass of the liquor. Harry rarely drank. It bothered his nerves, he said. The glass he took that night affected him inordinately, as it does those who lack the habit. He was instantly drunk. He became talkative.

He talked about Gravelet, who'd been dead thirty years. The Great Blondin, he called himself. Just before the Civil War he'd crossed Niagara. Three hundred feet above the cataract on a five-eighths wire a thousand foot long.

"Walked Niagara," Harry said, awe in his voice. "Not just walked it, carried a chair out to the middle and sat down on it. Stood on it. Women fainted. He walked Niagara blindfolded. Walked it carrying a man on his back. On stilts. With baskets on his feet. Wheeling his daughter in a barrow. You understand? This happened. Niagara Falls."

"That is something," I said.

141

"Life now is a mess. It stinks."

"Yeah," I agreed.

"People stink, their lives."

"Times are hard."

"No, no. Not the times. People can't control their self-will. They're toys. Chance. And they try and make sense out of it, it's a mess. Unless they kid themselves. Most do. They kid, try and kid. But it's a mess. A mess."

"We had one of our biggest crowds ever today," I said. "They loved Ivy. Someday a movie producer's going to come along and take her away from you, Harry. To Hollywood."

He ignored me. "Up there. Up there it's clean. Opinions don't make a damn difference up there. All that matters, can you do it? Can you stay up? Do you have nerve?"

"I see what you mean."

"People are divided," he went on. "Me, myself and I. Body, soul. But up there—you are not divided. Don't watch yourself. Don't remember. Don't think what's ahead. You can't. Must be—home. You're clean."

"People eat up that act of yours, Harry."

"The crowd, those eyes, they hypnotize you. They want to see you risk it all. They lure you to the edge—that's where applause is, that's where the screams are. But you can only go so far. Because they want you to fall."

"No."

"They do. They don't want to see it, but—" He took a big swallow.

"Are you afraid of falling?"

He looked at me, away. "Yes. Of course I'm afraid. Of course."

During the silence that followed I imagined that Harry was the most self-reliant person I'd ever met.

He said, "You prove yourself every minute. That's the

142

secret. Never told anyone. Secret's you have to be ready. Understand? Have to be ready. You have to go at it smart all the time. Understand?"

"You can only be as smart as you are," I said.

He thought I was agreeing with him. A bullfrog let out a single mournful croak from somewhere quite close.

"Women," he said, when I'd refilled our glasses. "Same thing. I'll tell you another secret, a secret about women."

I was anxious to find out any secret about women.

"God's second mistake," I said, smiling to myself.

"You must have them young. Her, she was fourteen," he said. "That in itself."

It took me a second to realize who he was referring to. When I did, a hot flash swept up my back and I tasted acid.

"That in itself," he said, his eyes drifting. "A child. But you have a woman young, you can mold her. Keep ideas out of her head. Because mark my words. Mark my words. Women want to get ideas. A woman can make a fool of you so easy. They get you here." He pointed to his groin. "They know how to do that."

"So you take them young."

"Sure. That in itself. Sweet girl. Very smooth. Very smooth. What you think of Ivy?"

"She's nice."

"She worships me."

A faint breeze finally crawled up the hill from the swamp, bringing with it the fetid texture of air that's been breathed by salamanders.

Harry's discipline reasserted itself. He refused another glass of whiskey. He ground a laugh to extinction in his throat, slapped my back, and walked carefully toward his trailer.

I was glad he'd spoken that way about Ivy. I'd begun to like him.

I still couldn't sleep. Just before dawn it began to rain.

I wandered out, letting the showers cool my bare back. We'd rented a big hayfield from a farmer for the show. Up over the crest of a ridge a barn sat off by itself. I wandered down there and around to the other side of it to piss.

The rain increased and started to feel cold. I swung back the big door and stepped inside. It was half full of fermenting hay.

People talk about the joy of youth, the energy. But youth has its sadness, too. Later in life we suffer richer, more complex unhappiness, but we never endure heartaches as profound, as truly bottomless, as those that afflict us in life's summer. It's a delicious pain. You worry it. You prolong it because it makes you feel so flat-out human.

To hell with the show, I was thinking that morning. I didn't want to look like anybody but myself. I was tired of being behind the scenes. I was tired of living in a tin trailer and traveling around the countryside shooting blanks for hicks. I was tired of the people who couldn't understand anything unless you reduced it to sham and tinsel.

My life was wrecked. I watched the rain outside as Noah must have, waiting in secret bliss for the whole world to be washed away.

I never heard her footsteps. Ivy appeared in the door, wrapped in a pink silk dressing robe that barely covered her knees. The rain had plastered her blond hair down along her neck. When she stepped close I could see the beads of water on her nose and forehead. She looked like a teenager.

"He's sleepun," she murmured. She smiled.

I didn't care whether he was sleeping or standing behind me with a double-barreled shotgun. I licked the moisture from her upper lip and thrust my tongue into her small mouth.

The ladder up to the loft was made of tree branches with the bark stripped. I watched her hips move as she mounted it.

144

We weren't that high up, but there seemed to be enormous space above us and below. A swallow looped the air and pierced an upper door through the silhouette of the giant claw they used to hoist the hay

"You know when I think Billie was most scared?" she said. I pulled the knot loose on her belt. "When they'd go off to rob a place and she didn't know if they were going to be killed or come back with a lot of money."

I opened her robe. She was bare underneath. She crossed her arms in a way that bunched her breasts without covering them.

"And when Johnnie came she musta gone wild. Because it was him and the money and—just the glory of it. Of living. And of doing something. She musta gone wild."

"How about him?"

"Him, too. But he knew he was okay. She woulda been waiting and scared."

"They both went wild," I said.

"Yeah."

She reached her arms back. The damp robe slid off. She unbuckled my pants.

Naked, we started to climb the stack of hay, slipped, tumbled backward. She broke away. I tackled her from behind. We landed in a mattress of hay. Her squeal echoed from the cavernous roof and out the door overhead.

Soon we each wore a salty layer of hay and chaff. The hay itched and pricked. It got up our noses and dug into the crevices of our bodies.

She struggled. I held her. She pulled her greased wrist from my grasp. She made it to the top of the stack this time. She looked down at me, teeth pressed to her lower lip, eyes sparking.

I ascended the mound on all fours.

The rain had stopped. The clouds lifted a lid off the morning sun. Light stabbed through cracks and pinholes, illuminating rays of dust.

I wrapped my arms around her glistening waist. We swayed, fell. We clutched to hold our slippery bodies together. We tumbled. The barn somersaulted. Over and over.

Something slipped in us. We lost our names. Her whistling fingers shot through my hair and lacerated my back. Spontaneous combustion clutched our loins. She screamed. Our bones ignited. Melted.

There are a million kinds of love in the world. Some soothe, some fortify. Some titillate. Some take your breath away. Some your will. But some kinds grab you by the hair and hold your face to a crack in the world and make you taste and feel things you can never speak but that trouble you half a century later for reasons you can only guess at.

I decided to expand on one of the love scenes in the Dillinger Alive show. It was based on a real incident that had taken place in St. Paul. It wasn't John's last night with Billie, yet it was in a sense the climax of their short life together.

Sometimes, during this scene, Ivy would weep real tears that would make her mascara run down her cheeks in little black rivulets. The audience loved that. I would hear gasps, miniature sobs from ladies. I began to realize that the way I'd set it up, it pointed to something more than sexual heat. It was full of foreboding, full of the sweet tragedy of a brief love that ends in death.

That's what St. Paul was all about.

14

THE YEARS FLOW BY and you remember. You remember the criminals who painted giant hieroglyphics, in headlines and shooting, in fast cars and wild laughing escapades across state lines. You remember trying to figure what they meant. And maybe years later you decide it was this: that we were all desperate then, as the young are always desperate—in good times, too, but especially in bad. We were all desperate and we were all scared and we needed somebody to display our desperation just as we needed Crosby to croon our love and Garbo to act the sublime feelings we couldn't express ourselves.

In late March John was living with Billie in St. Paul. He had been out of Crown Point three weeks and had robbed two banks with the new gang. Every day the papers had another story about him. He'd been seen in Michigan. An Indiana carpenter come to Staten Island to work had been tailed by six police cars, the cops convinced they had Dillinger in their grasp.

A bank was held up in Ohio. A hardware wholesaler was robbed in Arkansas. Four men grabbed a payroll in Wisconsin. Each job was the work of the Dillinger gang. In one bank robbery in Kentucky witnesses claimed that each of the five men involved was Dillinger.

Winchell told the nation its children were playing Dillinger in disturbing numbers. Willow branches were turning into tommy guns. Dillinger stared from every police bulletin board, from the rotogravure section of every Sunday supplement.

John continued to clip articles dutifully from the papers. In one a European psychiatrist tried to explain John's rampage with references to incidents that were then known about his childhood—his mother's early death, his father's severity. John was mystified that an educated man could be so flatly wrong.

He took Billie to the movies. The spring air held a chill, but held it with soft hands, not with the iron grip of winter. Snow still covered the ground, but it seemed to carry the expectation of turning to water, of gurgling down the black streams of spring.

She wanted to see *Little Miss Marker*. Baby Shirley's curly optimism and dimpled cheeks cheered them both. They held hands in the dark buttered air of the theater. Billie poked him and clicked her tongue when the little girl cracked the hard hearts of the horseplayers.

"As thousands of federal agents, local police and deputized citizens scour countryside and city alike in the greatest man-hunt this nation has ever known, one man hopes that the search for John Dillinger will *not* succeed. That's the outlaw's father, John Dillinger, Senior, a dirt farmer in Mooresville, Indiana."

John shifted in his seat as the newsreel rolled.

" 'Mr. Dillinger, it must be hard knowing that your boy is on the run with orders out to shoot to kill.'

" 'Yes. I hope and pray always that John is safe.'

" 'Do you think it's justified, the charges that have been made against your son?'

" 'No, I do not. I don't believe he's ever killed any man. He told me he didn't and I believe him. He's robbed a few banks, but—' "

John made a small noise in his throat. Billie looked to see him grin.

" 'Do you think John will receive a fair trial if he's caught?'

" 'I don't think he will be caught.'

" 'You don't think the law can catch up to him?'

" 'If they do, they'll kill him.'

"And so the lonely vigil goes on for the father of the number-one outlaw in the nation."

Billie was startled when she looked over and saw the man on the screen sitting beside her. John's features had assumed his father's narrow-eyed, wooden expression.

"It was funny to see him," he told her afterward. "It made me think. Dad isn't getting any younger. Christ, he looked old there. I should get down and visit him."

He would take Billie with him, he told her. She was glad. She wanted to meet the people he always talked about, his friends, his nieces, his half brother. She wanted to look at those gullies and ponds and streams where he'd fished and hunted. She imagined that by some magic she would be able to see John there as a boy, before the bitterness, see him splashing naked in a quarry, the sun bright on his bare arms and legs.

After they watched Astaire and Rogers in *The Gay Divorcee* Billie gave John dancing lessons in the apartment. She bought a book that contained a supply of black-paper shoe soles to guide their steps. John picked up the foxtrot and the waltz quickly. In a week he was directing her around the living room with authority. She would squeal when he lifted her in a big overhead swing doing the lindy hop.

Pete and Makley were both convicted that month of murdering the sheriff when they broke John out of jail in Lima. John had passed on a portion of his take from the last couple of jobs to cover their lawyers' fees. But the case was open and shut and the jury came back with no recommendation for mercy.

"They're waiting for me to spring them," John said. He was bluer than Billie had ever seen him.

"No, they aren't, John," Red Hamilton told him. "The papers say that. They just want to trick you to get caught yourself."

The sentence came down before the month was out. Death in the electric chair for both. John sat all day with a faraway look in his eyes.

Nobody understood him except Billie. Oh, we knew him, the public. Everyone knew him. After the Crown Point escape there was not a person in the country who didn't know who John Dillinger was. They talked about him in barbershops.

But the more the yellow press twisted his life into legend, the closer he clung to her. She began to share his eyes. They saw through things together. She traced for him the strange sad Indian myths she'd learned as a girl.

The money, the high life, John and Billie were too young and too old to care much about those. What mattered was to move forward on this road together. To survive. The simplest events, cooking food or looking together at the glowing photos of stars in the movie magazines, took on the feel of a mission.

"Do you know why I sometimes call you Jack Harris?" Billie said, using the name he'd given her when they first met. "Because that's your protection. When Johnnie becomes too hot, you can be Jack Harris. You can be innocent and they can't touch you because you're not you. See?"

She would smile at his smile. He said they should get married. They would spend their honeymoon in Vera Cruz.

In the quiet moments, Billie told John stories.

"Two sisters were looking at the stars and the older one

said she'd like to have a young, bright star for a husband. The other said she didn't care, she'd be happy with a weak, old star. So they fell asleep and two stars came down to take them up above the sky, where stars are men."

"Like movie stars."

"No. You know."

"Douglas Fairbanks."

"And the younger one had a star husband who was sleek and bright as the sun, because she was good. But the older one's husband was dim and blinked with age. She wanted too much."

That Good Friday in St. Paul a pall of low clouds hung over the city. At three in the afternoon the air became deathly still and Billie heard a high-pitched sound that was like the sound of something about to happen. It scared her.

Red Hamilton came over that evening with a girl who said everybody told her she looked like Norma Shearer. Eddie Green and Tommy Carroll came with their wives. Later Homer Van Meter showed up alone. They all drank beers and ate popcorn and listened to phonograph records.

They looked at one of the new guns Tommy had gotten from a Texas gunsmith. They were based on a Colt .45-caliber pistol, but had an elongated clip and could fire bursts on full automatic.

"It's like having a machine gun in your pocket," Tommy said. "But it shakes your arm to pieces when you shoot it."

They all wanted to take it out somewhere and practice firing it.

Red finally brought up the subject that everybody had been avoiding: Pete and Makley. "I think about them having to sit inside a cell alone and face that," he said. His eyes filled with tears. "All alone and knowing you're going to die."

"Man tells you you're going to die," Homer said, "what's he telling you?"

"It's just damn sad to think about." Red pressed his lips together and hid his eyes.

John came over and rested a hand on the back of Red's neck. He said, "You know Pete's ready for it. He's always ready. And Mac can get a laugh out of anything. I bet they laughed about it. They're men."

Billie and Tommy's wife Jean prepared a big dinner of veal cutlets, German meatballs, boiled beets in sour cream, mushrooms stuffed with clams, potato pancakes, and for dessert raspberry pie and rice pudding with whipped cream. The men lit cigars and drifted, as they always did, into reminiscing.

Someone would remember how, when Lester fired at the ceiling in that bank, specks of plaster sifted down as if it were snowing. Somebody would mention the look on a girl's face as she clutched the side of the car, a hostage for a getaway. Like she was getting her ashes hauled. Or how this teller had a gold tooth. Or in that bank the window was a stained-glass scene of Indians shaking hands with white men.

Each robbery would leave behind it years of memories, a childhood of memories. The impressions and fleeting glimpses would be tangled like the dumped contents of a jewelry box, and in these sessions they would sort the gold and gems into delicious details.

They played cards, euchre and pinochle. The girl who came with Red said she'd been bitten by a dog when she was little and still had a scar on her leg. She pulled her skirt up to show the other girls. The men looked.

John dropped out of the game and went to stand by the window. He peeked through the curtains at the black, blustery weather. He said goodnight to the others and took Billie into the bedroom.

More than ever, she was his refuge. Beneath the warm covers her voice glowed in the dark, thick and salty as farm butter.

"Do you know what Indians do when they're courting, Johnnie? When a boy is interested in a girl they go to bed together."

"Oh boy."

"No, I mean with their clothes on. They lie all night and feel each other's heat."

"Not a bad idea."

"It's not dirty."

"I like it."

They wore the gold silk pajamas he'd bought for both of them. She sat with her legs curled, propped across him. He unbuttoned her top. She had round, plump breasts, but was self-conscious about them. Smiling, she crossed her arms. He tugged on the fabric to widen the gap.

"You're the Trickster," she said.

"I am?"

"The Indians say the Trickster made himself into a rabbit. The wind blew him across the lake. And when a girl saw him and cuddled him he stole the fire from her village and took it back to his people."

She knew how to gently resist. He slowly pulled the drawstring of her pants. The knot came undone.

"The Trickster fights a battle every year with the ugly cannibal who comes in winter to eat children."

"Who wins?" he said. She'd told him this before.

She shifted, letting the silk slip. Her hand dropped down to cover herself.

"They kill each other. Every year. Forever."

"And they rise from the dead."

As if by accident her downy forearm brushed the silk tent below his waist.

153

"Death is not forever," she said. "After death, the Indians say, a person wanders until he comes to a stream of water that shines like bright silver. He leans over. The water tastes like the sweetest nectar. He tries to drink and falls in. He's swept along this stream and that's being born."

"He comes out here."

"Don't."

She twisted. Her pajama fell open. Fell down off her round shoulder. She lifted her round arms to undo her hair. Her nipples were large, almost black.

She said, "That's right, though. Death isn't forever. You and me, there can't be any end to us, can there, honey?"

She looked at him over her raised shoulder, her eyes naked.

"And if it is forever," he said, "what difference does it make?"

She shook her head so that her black hair fell down her neck and across her face. But when he lifted his hand to reach for her, she drew back.

A voice sang an ancient tune in her blood.

It was time. She leaned to let her hair brush his face. She drew her ebony hair down his chest. He arched so that she could pull the pants from under his hips.

She became a bride. She knelt over him on the bed. A heart beat in her belly.

His desperate eyes saw through her, saw her lovely bones. Kissed her pretty legs.

Night was in her hair. All the fugitive grief was in his groaning voice.

When it happens, he once told her, it happens with a beautiful rush that is like a torrent, a waterfall. You can't stop that surge. You feel it all through you. It's in your body and it takes over your mind. The world is standing still and this—something is pouring through you. He was talking about what it was like to rob a bank. But this, too. This was like that.

They lay together afterward, their wet wounds cooling, her small body inside the comfort of his arms. Beyond the door they heard a strand of laughter, a woman singing on the radio. A gust rattled one of the windows. In some distant city men were knocking warily on the door of a house where somebody said John Dillinger was hiding.

"How come you feel the pain of a deer that's hurt?" she murmured, her lips close to his. "The Indians say, because you are a deer. They think everybody is an animal or a thing, a stone or a tree. That's how we know the world."

"And what are you?"

"Mink," she said, shyly.

He looked. She giggled lazily. He stroked her hair. They slept.

None of that got into our show. It was what came next that people wanted to see.

"Who the hell is that?" John lifted his unshaven chin above the blanket, scraped his tongue along his teeth, and frowned. A persistent rap, rap, rap came from the living room.

Heavy drapes kept the room dark, but two fingers of sunlight squeezed through cracks and illuminated lines of dusty air.

Billie rubbed grains of sleep from her eyes.

"I'll see. It's probably—who? I'll go."

"What time is it?"

"Ten."

She pulled her robe on. The living room had a foreign feel. On the table a cigarette butt floated in an inch of beer in the bottom of a glass. One empty bottle lay on its side. A bowl with hard kernels of popcorn. A deck of cards, the queen of clubs turned up. The fringed shade of the standing lamp was askew. Wrapping her robe, she crossed to straighten it.

The rapping came again. Not insistent, regular, six knocks, a pause, six more.

Her slippers scuffed the oriental carpet.

She hesitated, pulling the forest-green satin lapels of her robe across each other. The rapping began again.

She put the door on the chain and opened it six inches.

"Mrs. Hellman?"

A salesman, she thought. He was holding his hand and wiggling the fingers, as if the knocking had injured his knuckles.

"I'm— What do you want?"

"Are you Mrs. Hellman?"

"No. Yes. Who—?"

"Don't you know?"

"I said, what do you want?" She twisted the last word without meaning to.

"Your husband home?" He reached behind himself, under his coat, and hitched his pants with a quick jerk. Tight muscles drew his mouth back at the corners. He was not a salesman, she was sure of that.

"I don't understand. What—?"

"Carl Hellman, is he here?"

No. This was not happening. She did not want this to be happening. This could not be. Not now. Not this way. It was all wrong.

"No, he's not home. Who are you?"

"Police department. Mind if we come in?"

Another one was standing just out of sight. She tilted her head and saw him. His eyes were hidden under the brim of his hat.

"I'm taking a bath. I'm sorry."

"Are you Mrs. Hellman or aren't you? We were told this flat had been rented to—"

"I can't— I told you, I'm taking a bath. I'm not dressed. Please come back later. Please."

"We'd like to talk to your husband, Mrs. Hellman. Could you tell—"

She did not mean to slam the door, but her hand closed it with a crack. Suddenly every noise was amplified, as if someone had turned the volume the wrong way on a radio set.

The rapping began again. Slowly. Without urgency. Six knocks, a pause.

She ran. She saw herself running. Her legs were hampered by cobwebs of air.

"Johnnie!"

With a violent rustling of the bedclothes he was up, naked. She was struck by the pallor of his skin. It was translucent, laced with blue veins. He looked terribly vulnerable. Her cheeks swelled with a sob.

"Tell me," he said calmly. He was slipping his pants on, was tying his shoes.

"Police! Johnnie, police. I couldn't think of the name, my name. Mrs. Hellman, they said. They wanted Carl Hellman. They're still there."

"How many?"

"Two. I saw two. They wanted to come in. I wouldn't let them."

"You did good, baby." He had his shirt on, his vest. "Pack your things quick. We're getting out of here."

"Johnnie, I don't want this to happen."

"Only take what you can fit in the leather bag."

He knelt by the dresser and scooped some stacks of bank notes, three guns, and two boxes of ammunition into the bag. He tossed it onto the bed.

"What are we— Johnnie, we can't! I want this to stop."

"Simmer down. Get dressed now."

He started to go out. She stood with her fingertips to her lips. He stepped over to her, took one of her hands in his, and stroked the line of her jaw.

157

"Make it stop," she pleaded.

"Don't worry." His voice was soothing. He gave her a little push toward the dresser.

She heard the knocking again. It was too loud. It marched right into the bedroom, made her cringe.

She rushed to the closet. To select dresses was an absurdity. The complicated array of fabric flustered her. She grabbed three, four of them. Their metal hangers tangled. She stuffed them into the bag. Ran to the dresser. Grabbed at stockings and brassieres. The silk squirmed and slipped from her grip. The drawer, too far out, crashed to the floor. The noise made her jump.

Now she threw off her robe and pajamas. The chill made gooseflesh rise on her arms and legs. She dressed. Her fingers, as if frostbitten, worked the buttons stiffly.

John was waiting in the living room. He was calmly smoking a cigarette. She felt a moment of relief. The policemen must have gone away.

But the knocking resumed. Another pattern. Not the knuckle this time. A fist. The whole room shook.

John crushed out the smoke. "Ready, honey?"

She heard a metallic click that was louder than any noise she'd ever heard. He cradled a machine gun. Its canister bulged like the sides of a pregnant fish.

"Oh God, no! Johnnie, don't. Don't!"

"What are you talking about? We're here."

"Don't shoot! Don't shoot, don't shoot. You go. I'll stay behind. I'll let them take me. You go. Only don't shoot. Please, Johnnie!"

"Be yourself," he said calmly. "We're getting out of here."

For a second everything went dead quiet. Billie heard a robin outside the window. It was the first one she'd heard this spring. Its voice sounded strange, too loud.

An explosion blasted three splintered holes into the door. The noise was painful.

"Stay right behind me," John told her.

Numbed, her ears stoppered with the shots, she stepped mechanically. She held the suitcase in her hand.

John swung the door open. The hallway was carpeted with mauve roses. He fired a burst. Through the crack, Billie saw a flaming tongue, like that of a snake, lick from the gun.

"Come on," John said to her through the ringing. For a second he smiled.

She stepped out. It was cold in the hall. It was like stepping into icy water at the beach. You don't want to go any further. The water laps around your privates and you don't want to go on. You want to return to the warm shore. But you must go on.

Halfway along, the air cracked. The police were shooting. Billie's face curled. She tensed for the impact of the bullets. Electricity prickled her skin.

John made his gun scream.

They backed quickly down the hallway. They turned into the haven of the back stairs. John set off a final buzz saw of shots. They ran down the steps.

At the bottom he told her to go for the car.

"Walk," he said. "It's just everyday."

"They'll be waiting," she pleaded.

"Back it around here, take your time."

"You're crazy."

"Calm down. I'll be behind you."

"Johnnie, please!"

"Right now."

The sky was full of menace, the air poison. Piles of dirty snow still clung to the shadows. Her heels clicked on the brick alleyway. Prison could not be worse than this feeling. The electric chair, even. At least you would know what was going to happen.

Behind her John walked crabstyle, his eyes scanning the back of the apartment building, the Thompson cradled casually under his arm. He stood at the rear fender, the gun ready, as she backed out. He climbed into the back seat.

"Go on."

The car jumped forward.

"Easy! You're in no hurry."

They cleared the alley and turned onto the street. She couldn't believe there were no cars waiting for them.

"You did good, sweetheart," John said. "You did real good. That was a close scrape."

The peaceful Saturday morning city immediately began to turn what had happened into a dream. But when John climbed over into the front seat, she saw that his leg was wet with blood.

"They hit me right above the knee," he said.

15

WHEN THE SEASON wound up that first autumn I found myself in the agreeable position of being twenty-two hundred dollars to the good. To make that kind of money just on the basis of your looks, it's a feeling like the one you get when you win at the races.

Everybody thinks they know the value of a dollar. But back then, before welfare and all, I swear having money was holy. That was one link I had with him, one area in which I knew just how Dillinger felt. Money lands in your hands, you feel you're God's chosen one, you're blessed. You know it isn't true, but can't help feeling it.

I wanted to continue over the winter, get together a tour of theaters. I envisioned a shortened version of the show as an opener for the big movie houses. I was eager to cash in while the Dillinger idea gripped people. But most of the circus people had other plans for the winter. Faced with the time and cost of putting together a new cast, I decided to see what I could do on my own.

I gave some talks for small fees in Masonic halls down around Daytona Beach. I saw the house the gang lived in there, talked to a couple of people who'd seen them in town, on the beach.

I never liked the sun much. After New Year's my feet got

itchy and I headed west. I spent Mardi Gras in New Orleans. While I was there I won three hundred dollars off a couple of local card sharks. They held me up on the way out of the place and indicated with a knife they didn't like losing. They were surprised when I came out with the .32 automatic. In the middle of it I couldn't remember if I'd changed the blanks for real bullets after the show. It didn't much matter.

I rented a tourist cabin in Tucson. I worked part-time the next month selling cars for a Ford dealer. Off-hours I would drive into the desert and explore the scenery. I caught the wide-open-spaces bug and began to think this was what America was all about, the way most dudes do when they first hit the West. I tried riding a horse, but you sit too damn high off the ground when you're in the saddle. And they have these teeth.

Omaha won the Triple Crown that spring and I began to hear war talk. Not much, but the Germans were making noise in Europe and people began to say it was only a matter of time and would we get into it? Some said a war would be a good thing. A little war would be good for the stock market.

I missed Ivy. The few moments we'd had together left plenty of room for my imagination to go wild. The memory of our stage kisses burned in my chest.

Harry had gotten off-season work with a carnival in California. I thought of going on out there, actually considered it.

They were late arriving back in Cleveland to get ready for the '35 season. Sparky started talking about finding another act if Harry didn't show. There were plenty of good people available, he said. He knew of a woman who did a rope-of-death act that knocked them out.

I was worried. I could recruit another Billie easily enough, but my mind was concentrated on the prospect of seeing Ivy again. I told myself that the way I felt about her gave our act

162

an authenticity that it wouldn't have had otherwise. It was important for the show.

They finally arrived.

"He had this cow in Salinas," she complained to me right away. "A cow, she could have been his mother. He walked around with her in broad daylight. Her hips bulged ten ways from Sunday, I think she was a Mex. I coulda killed him."

She twisted her little mouth up and shot daggers in the direction of their trailer with her eyes.

" 'Who the damnation is that?' I asked him.

" 'She reads palms.'

" 'You don't believe in that stuff.'

" 'Sure I do,' he says. 'I've got a short lifeline, Ivy.' Like I'm supposed to cry crocodile tears or something.

"I said, 'You don't know how short, boy-o.' He slaps my face and I hit him right back. Hit him right here." She pointed to her chest. "And it hurt him. I'm strong when I want to be."

She was cockier than she'd been before. In rehearsal she put even more brass into her role, languid Gloria Swanson gestures, and cute hip bumps.

Offstage she became more open with her affections. She would lean over me while I was putting my makeup on and nibble on my ear. She liked to stand beside me while I was giving directions to somebody in the show, push a soft breast against me to distract me.

Her presence inflamed me. I had to catch my breath sometimes when she would casually run her hand up my neck.

She'd bobbed her hair over the winter. It was darker gold than I remembered. When she parted it, she looked like a boy. I've always been attracted by short hair on a woman.

"Harry loathes me like this," she told me mischievously. "He wants me to grow it down to my ass but I won't ever."

Still, she seemed in no hurry to arrange a rendezvous with

me. The closest we got happened on a robin's-egg Saturday afternoon while Harry was practicing. I found Ivy ironing in their trailer. Out the window we could see Harry balancing on a wire strung between two trees a yard off the ground. If he started across the field, I could hotfoot it out the back.

"Miss me?" I said. I watched the way her thin arm moved the iron up and down.

"Don't you know?"

"Tell me."

"I missed being Billie. I missed the shooting."

"How about the kissing?" I wrapped my arms around her waist, found the gap between her blouse and skirt.

"I'm afraid of him now. He's crazy."

"He hurts you?"

"Yes. It's scary because he don't drink. If a guy changes when he drinks, at least you know it's coming. Harry, he's going queer, is all."

"Leave him." I ran my fingers along her warm flesh.

"He'd kill me. Anyways, what would I do?"

"Come with me."

She laughed. I thought I meant it, but maybe she knew different. Knew I wasn't ready for her.

I laughed. She wasn't wearing a brassiere. I was nuzzling the short blond hair behind her ear when I heard her gasp. Harry was halfway back.

I canceled rehearsals and took off two days before we were scheduled to go on the road. Sparky didn't like it. He'd made me a kind of assistant manager and depended on me to look to some of the details of mounting the big show as well as my Dillinger Alive revue. I didn't care whether he liked it.

I'd found out that Billie Frechette was touring in a Crime-

Does-Not-Pay show of her own, along with John Dillinger's father. They were playing Fort Wayne that night, which was about a seven-hour drive. An amber sun was rising behind me when I set out, but the air quickly turned murky. Before I was halfway to Toledo black pillars were holding up all four corners of the sky.

From a crest I saw the rain coming, a bright wall of water. Big drops thumped the roof of my Chevy. Within minutes I was driving blind. A gush of water streamed down my windscreen; the lone wiper couldn't keep up with it. I hunched over the wheel and kept on, feeling for the shoulder with my right tires.

Wet, those gravel roads slowed you right down. Somewhere near Napoleon, Ohio, a crack of thunder almost knocked my car into the ditch. It rained so hard I really couldn't see and had to pull over.

I sat there thinking of Billie and how she would react if I got in to see her. Her mouth would fall open. Her eyes would blink and sparkle. Maybe she would scream. Maybe she would faint to see her dead lover in the flesh. Maybe she would smother me with kisses.

I imagined opening my arms to her, just as John would have. I imagined taking her on my arm and walking down the high street, the crowds parting to stare at us. We would trade secret looks. I would squire her to the fanciest nightclub in down. Better, to a palatial movie theater. We would sit holding hands in the dark and watch the romances of swank men and jeweled women.

The rain let up enough so that I could see the sheets of water rushing into the roadside ditches. A bolt of lightning exploded somewhere close behind me. I rubbed the fog from the glass and started again.

INDIANA WELCOMES YOU, the sign said. I hadn't gone a

quarter mile into the Hoosier state when I felt my steering wheel start to pull. As I was removing the jack from the trunk another shower swept by. My oilskin failed to keep the wet from seeping down my neck. My pants were soaked. When I got the right front off I found a roofing nail in it. I saved it as an omen, a relic. I have it to this day, I don't know where.

The car's heater didn't work. I shivered, but not just from the cold. I wanted to see Billie bad, but I was anxious about it. This wasn't some flouncy circus wife. This was John Dillinger's woman. This was the woman whose picture had been in all the papers. This was the doll who had faced police guns in St. Paul. This was the ravishing, raven-haired Billie Frechette. Alive.

It was a day, you didn't know when dusk came. It was dark all afternoon, and at some point it became completely dark. The rain continued, cold and steady now, not in showers. The lights were smeared all over Washington Boulevard. The dancing bulbs around the Lyric Theater sign lit the drops on my windscreen, but I knew I was too late for the show. A few people still stood in ragged groups under the marquee.

I got out and turned down a brick alley. A fixture over the stage door cast a pool of light onto the wet pavement, illuminating nothing.

I walked inside. Some stairs led to another door lit by a red light. Beyond that I made my way through dim stacks of scenery, oversized electrical connections, coiled ropes and boxes of props until I came to a row of doors that I figured for dressing rooms.

Three girls with the pinned-up hair of dancers passed me. I smiled but they didn't look.

Then two men approached. I walked toward them with authority.

"Gentlemen," I said.

"Night," the younger one murmured.

The other was silent. I recognized him. He was John Dillinger's father. He had a hard, tentative face and sharp eyes. I took the earnest young man with him to be Hubert, Johnnie's half brother.

I felt cold, fought an urge to sneeze. I knocked at an unmarked door, waited for nothing. The next was open a few inches. Behind it I heard someone humming "Orchids in the Moonlight." My hand was trembling as I raised it to knock.

The door swung open at my touch. She was sitting in a blue satin dress, her foot propped on a wastebasket, applying blood-red polish to her toenails.

"Yes? What do you want?"

I straightened, threw back my shoulders. I drew my mouth to one side and folded it up into a half smile. I put the look in my eyes. I waited.

"Well?" she said. She lifted a cigarette from an ashtray and dragged on it. Her eyes bore no glimmer of recognition.

"Miss Frechette—" For all my anticipation, I hadn't planned anything to say. Did I look like Dillinger or didn't I? I'd been arrested. Hicks crowded my show and went away convinced they'd seen the closest thing to John Dillinger they ever would see.

I said, "Let me just say, if you were—if to be with you were the reward, then they've got it wrong. Crime would pay."

She laughed. "You're soaked."

"I drove a long way. I wanted to be here for the performance. My car broke down. Tire," I explained lamely.

"That right?" She inhaled on her cigarette and crushed it.

"I'm the Man Who Looks Like Dillinger."

Her face questioned me.

I explained briefly about the show. I said I'd gotten the idea when I was arrested for being Dillinger.

167

She looked at me closely. "How much time did you do?"

"No time," I said.

She nodded. She'd served more than a year in a Minnesota penitentiary for harboring a wanted man.

"I feel funny," I said, "making a living off of John's reputation. But the times—you know."

"Sure I know. You'd be a fool not to grab the chance. John would have liked the idea. Anyway, look at me."

"But you lived it."

"Yeah." She reached for a nearly empty glass. I noticed a slight tremor in her hand. "Sit down. You want a drink?"

I nodded. She was sitting at a crowded make-up table. Among the jars of lotions and cold cream she found an empty glass. She poured an inch of rye into it, added the same to hers. I welcomed the burn of the liquor.

"They don't let you drink in prison," she said.

I began to think I was over my head. As I've said, I always wanted to consider myself an insider. But to her—to her I was a mark, one of the hundred million rubes in the country who read the papers and dreamed. I didn't know what it was like to kill a man. I didn't know what it was like to face real gunfire. It wasn't my face that had been printed large in every newspaper in the country. Not really. It wasn't my name on every tongue.

I swallowed another mouthful of rye. It brought me down to earth. With a disarming naturalness she went back to painting her toes. Every now and then she glanced at me curiously, as if searching my face for her lover.

It gave me a chance to look at her. She was small, smaller than Ivy even. Her succulent curves suggested the ripeness of a woman about to go to fat. Her hair was startlingly black, the shiny ebony that whispers wildness.

I nursed my drink for a few minutes. I felt foolish. I had a thousand questions for her, but I couldn't think of a single one. I drained my glass and got up to go. She stopped me.

"Have another. Dry off. Tell me about this show."

I described the robberies and escapes we depicted. I explained that I'd tried to keep it as close as I could to what had happened, if not to the facts, to the spirit.

"Not to glorify him," I said. "But I think people should know who he was, what he was."

"Of course they should. Everybody should."

"I've been trying to learn about him, what he was really like."

"Prison wasn't so hard for me," she said. "I can take it. Understand? That wasn't what was hard."

"No?"

She looked at me. "What was hard—I never saw him again. The second they grabbed me, I knew. I knew what was coming. I said in my heart, I'll never see him again."

Her voice was not musical. She didn't talk with the clearwater tones I imagined, nor with Ivy's girlish quaver. Her earthy timbre, though, appealed to me. It was raw and carnal and made me feel warm the way the booze did.

She told me a little about her show. John's father recited a monologue about his son's childhood. Drink and bad companions led the boy into crime, he claimed. The long sentence John had received for his first offense had soured him on the world.

"He was civil to me when John was alive," she said. "Now he stands off."

They had pretend cops come on to lecture about police efforts to contain crime. They would give a sharpshooting demonstration and show how they took fingerprints.

Her toes were dry now. I suggested we go somewhere for supper. She agreed.

"Wait though," she said. She sat me down and combed my

169

hair for me, slicked it straight back. The touch of her fingers was electric. I thought, she did the same thing for him. She's adding the touch that will turn me into him.

When she was done she stepped back and squinted, looking for resemblance. But finally she wrinkled her nose and shook her head. I laughed. She let out a small laugh herself, like a bird call.

The rain was still coming in showery gusts, great back-handed slaps. She took my arm. Her head barely reached my shoulder. She had on a small black feathered hat with a veil. The wind was shaking the streetlamps, making the shadows waver along the deserted street.

We went to a crowded, smoky grill. In the lounge a bored piano player was accompanying a girl singer. Her voice was like a leftover cocktail diluted with melted ice.

We took a table in back. I ordered steak and eggs with home fries. Billie wanted roast chicken. We both had rye Old Fashioneds.

"They've got a long song-and-dance section," she told me about her show. "It's supposed to show how Johnnie lived it up in Chicago. The band plays tunes that weren't even written then. Anyway, we didn't do much of that. Mostly we went to the movies."

The finale of their show was a G-man extravaganza that had Dillinger killing four or five lawmen before the federals came in and put an end to his "reign of terror," as the handbill called it.

Billie took the stage last. The emcee would introduce her as "Mrs. John Dillinger." She would deliver a short speech describing her love for Johnnie. She still loved him, she would conclude. And in her heart she would always grieve that he had done wrong.

"But he paid the price," she said. "That's what they have me say. He paid the price."

She leaned over and spit on the floor.

She said, "Know what they ask me? Where's the money? Where's the goddamn money? Think I'd be answering your stupid questions if I had money? Huh?"

I felt small. I'd asked her questions myself.

She laughed a mirthless laugh.

"I can't tell them about the love," she went on. "John had this love, and I moved into it. It was there before me. It was something powerful that shined out of him. Too powerful. Too powerful."

Our food came, more drinks with it. Billie picked at her half chicken with a fork for a few minutes. Then she lifted it up and began to tear meat off with her teeth. She threw me a little smile.

"He needed," she said, wiping her mouth with her hand. "The way he needed, it was like one of those giant lights they shine into the sky in Hollywood."

"Searchlights."

"You don't know what it feels like, for a woman, to step into that kind of light. Course, after I went into prison the light shined somewhere else."

I knew what she meant. He hired a lawyer for her. Naturally he couldn't visit her. Soon he was going out with Polly, his last girl. His need switched to her. His accelerated life left no time for heartbreak.

We ate slowly, replenishing our drinks twice during the meal. She talked. She described the color of a dress she wore one day when John took her to the Lincoln Park Zoo. She'd never seen a giraffe before, even a picture of one, and was fascinated by the creature. She explained a finger game that she had learned as a girl and that she used to play with John when they were living in St. Paul. She recited, half-singing, an Indian song that she'd sung in one of her sister's church theatricals in Milwaukee.

I told her about me and Ivy—I don't know why but I felt compelled to reveal it. Billie asked me what Ivy was like.

"It's good you like her," she said. "It's just like me and John."

Her glass, nearly empty, slipped from her greasy fingers. She tried to grab it, but it rolled off and smashed on the floor. She extracted a cigarette from her pack and signaled for the waiter to bring another cocktail.

Broken glasses attracted no attention in that place. The patrons all seemed hell-bent on finding the quickest route to intoxication. The haze of cigar smoke was so thick you couldn't see across the room.

"These people," Billie said, "ask me, what did I feel when they came and told me he was dead? When they came and told me the cops had shot him down like a dog in the street. When I was in prison and they told me, it's him and he's dead. What did I feel? Huh? How did I feel? Huh?"

Her dark eyes pleaded with me. I nodded as if I understood.

She sat lost in thought for a few minutes. Then she jerked her hand abruptly. Her cigarette had burned down and scorched her fingers. She dropped it onto the tablecloth and tried awkwardly to brush it away. I picked it up and crushed it.

"We had so much fun," she said abruptly. She giggled. It was a girlish giggle and it made me realize how young she was—only twenty-five at the time. She'd been born with a woman's face. Fatigue made her look older.

I took some money from my pocket to pay the tab. I'd deliberately brought a hefty wad of bills—I guess to complete my Dillinger costume. She eyed it. Saw me watching her look at it. Laughed.

She wheeled as she stood. I put an arm around her. We navigated into the night.

172

"Sometimes, he scared me," she said. I waited, but she didn't amplify.

The lobby of her hotel was deserted except for a salesman snoring over a wrinkled evening paper. The elevator boy let us off on the third floor.

We entered her room. She removed her hat, which she'd worn all through dinner.

"Another thing they always ask, did John believe in God?" She was pouring us two straight whiskeys. "Of course he did. Just, he didn't understand—how come God. You know?"

I knew, I said. We clicked glasses.

I felt awkward, being there. She had two Morris chairs and a small table by the wall, but the bed dominated the room.

"You know," she said. She was very close to me now. "I could join up with you, play myself. That would—wouldn't that be something?"

I tried to put my woozy brain to calculating the implications of such a setup.

I was distracted, though, by her ebony hair. Disheveled, it suggested a wildness beyond my imagination. With the electric glare, I could see the smallpox scars that dotted her face under her make-up. She still had chicken grease around her mouth and her lipstick was smeared.

I stared into her liquid eyes. I saw them look upward, then close as she lifted her glass to her lips and drained it.

She breathed liquor fumes into my face. "I try to dream about him. Can't."

She laughed at this. Laughed as she stepped over to the table for a refill.

"You love that girl?" she said. She had to grab one of the chairs as she swung back toward me. "You love that girl that's me?"

"I think so."

173

"You fuck her?"

I nodded.

"Good. It's the only thing. Loving and fucking. Everything gone, you've got love. Money in the world doesn't mean a damn. Find somebody. Most don't. Most of 'em. You have to be lucky. Luck that's—"

She fumbled a cigarette out of the package. I lit it for her. She stepped to the window and looked at her reflection in the black glass.

When she turned back to me, her eyes were old.

"All my life nothing ever happened me. Nothing, nothing, nothing. Nothing. I can't think of anything happened me when I's little. Life was just—hard. And nothing's ever gonna happen to me. Never again. Never ever."

She stared at me. I don't know if she was finally detecting a resemblance, or whether she was just having trouble focusing. She was so small.

"Only one thing ever happened, my whole life," she said. "And that was Johnnie."

We both knew it was time for me to leave. She closed the door behind me.

16

IT WAS BILLIE who told me the story of their visit to John's home.

"That was early in April," she said. "Just after the shooting in St. Paul. When he'd gotten his knee patched up, John started to thinking he'd like to go home."

Mooresville lies not far to the southwest of Indianapolis but really hasn't much to do with the city. The flat farmland that extends two hundred miles from the north without a breath begins to wrinkle there. Not into hills exactly, but ridges and mounds and gullies.

That spring of '34 John and Billie drove all day. Over the newly plowed fields she could see mounds of cumulus clouds so far off they looked like tiny puffs of white smoke.

The close humming of the engine, the long blur of roadside grass made her sleepy. The road rose up in her eyes, floated. Fatigue grabbed her and lifted her into a droning sleep.

Must have lifted him, too. For she awoke with a blast of bumps, a violent jolt. The horizon tipped. She slid beneath the dash, knocked hard against the door.

In the sudden quiet she looked at John. He was stretching, fists by his ears, elbows back. He gave her a tight smile. They got out.

The car had come to rest just shy of a stream that had overflowed its banks. In the plowed field pools of sky filled the long spaces between furrows. Dark grass waved like hair. Water surged through the culvert.

"Well," John said. "Just have to wait."

Small things can change it all, Billie knew. It was the small things she was afraid of: A wrong word. Somebody looks too close. What you do with your eyes when you pass a cop on the street. A knock on the door on a Saturday morning. Or maybe you slip off the road in the middle of the Indiana farmland and—

"I felt exposed as hell," she said. The open space made her think about school in South Dakota. The sky weighed on her. Nowhere to hide. A broken car full of guns. The hollow moan of wind.

A curtain of clouds ascended the west, obscured the sun. John sat on the angled running board smoking a cigarette. Half an hour later a farmer's truck came into sight and slowly grew in size as it approached. John waved, spoke to the man in such a twang that Billie could hardly make out the words. He had the farmer laughing in a minute. Together they tied a rope to the Hudson and dragged it back onto the roadway. John offered money. The farmer protested but his hand reached to take the bills.

"Much obliged, mister."

"Likewise."

Night descended. As they moved on Billie could sense the black water, rushing with low music through the crevices of earth.

They drove past the house slowly. A silver crescent of moon was shining. The farm looked peaceful. A faint yellow light was glowing from deep inside the house. John doubled back. He turned into the driveway, stopped by the back door.

176

They climbed out, closed the doors quietly, and waited. John slipped a hand around Billie's waist for a second. He pointed silently to an old rain barrel, the barn, an elm tree growing beside the yard, a broken corn picker clogged with last year's burdock. A thin light came on over the back porch. He let her go and stepped forward, limping.

For most, the phases of life are cushioned by time. Youth fades reluctantly, old age seeps unnoticed into the blood. But it had been less than a year since John had emerged, his cocky green youth preserved nine years in prison. In those months he'd grown to a sudden middle age where for the first time he could contemplate the landscape of his life.

"Hello, Dad! Thought you might need an extra hand for the spring chores."

In spite of his wounded leg, John bounded up onto the porch.

"Aw," his father said softly. "Aw, Johnnie."

They embraced.

John later told Billie he was struck by his father's decline. The old man had aged with unnatural suddenness. It wasn't the nightshirt, the spindly legs and slippers. Something in the voice, a helplessness—the voice he remembered so stern with command. Fragility was crystallizing his father's limbs. He embraced John tentatively, as you would a ghost.

John motioned Billie into the moth-swirling light. A scarf was gathered around her neck, a setting for her dark beauty. She greeted John's father with her respectful politeness and easy intimacy.

"Why don't we go inside, Dad?" John said. "Is anyone around?"

The question brought a look of alarm to his father's face.

"Why did you come here?" he said gruffly. "Why do you want to take the risk?"

177

"What risk?" John said, laughing. "Tell the truth, Dad, I wanted to see you, see all the folks once more."

Their eyes met. The "once more" meant that there was to be no mincing. Both men knew things they hadn't known last spring when John returned home from prison. The father, his second wife dead, now often turned his face forward to squint into the darkness of his future. John had found death in the noon sun. He felt its pulse everywhere.

Upstairs John cocked his gun and laid it on the nightstand. Billie undressed quickly, slipped on her cool silk nightgown, and curled up under the unfamiliar blankets. She watched John at the window. He lit a cigarette and looked out into the dark yard.

She drifted toward sleep, still feeling the hum of the car's motor. Often now John would stare into empty space, as he was staring into that Indiana night, stare very hard and very carefully as if he were watching a drama unfold on the edge of the world.

The air next morning was spanking fresh. John and Billie came down at nine. His father had already fed the horse, milked the cows, and collected the eggs from the henhouse. John stood on the back porch, stretching, breathing the aromatic air, listening to the slow bawk of the chickens.

Billie wanted to help, but the two girls, Johnnie's half sisters, insisted on making breakfast for her and Johnnie themselves. He hadn't had eggs and bacon this good in a thousand years, Johnnie said. The corn muffins Frances made were heavenly.

"You have to give me the recipe so I can cook Johnnie a taste of home sometimes," Billie said. Frances ran to get a card and began copying the ingredients in neat block letters.

John read the comics to the girls as he used to, though

they were teenagers now and had outgrown Dixie Dugan and Bringing Up Father.

He took Billie down to show her where he used to fish for bullheads in the pond. Frances came along. The warm sun prompted her to leave her shoes behind. She chattered about her school subjects and neighborhood gossip.

"The kids are jealous, Johnnie," Frances said. "Because my brother is more famous than anybody. I told them you know all the movie stars. You've met movie stars, haven't you? You musta."

"Sure. But you know something, Frannie? You don't even recognize them. In real life, they aren't as pretty as you."

"But everybody recognizes you. When we saw you in the theater they all cheered. You couldn't hear what the man was saying. I went back six times."

They came to the pond. Frances dipped her foot in. She pronounced it icy. She scampered along the bank, disturbing frogs.

Seeing the loose-limbed Frances made Billie realize the gulf that separated her from her own girlhood. She too had walked barefoot in spring. Squatted at the edge of ponds. Pried into the secrets of forests. But now her eyes had changed. She had glimpsed the menace, the urgency, the sadness that lurked behind the shallow surface of the world.

She knew the day was wonderful. She was so happy for Johnnie to be among his people. But she was afraid to take a deep breath, afraid of disturbing the bright air.

The girls judged Billie's blue dress the smartest one they'd seen ever. When they returned, she tied an apron over it and helped them prepare dinner.

John was reading a copy of *Popular Mechanics* when Audrey arrived with her husband Emmett and their son Fred. She'd been in bed with a bad cold and back pains. The strain showed on her face. Billie had known Johnnie's sister was older than him. But she was surprised to discover in Audrey a matronly woman who looked fifty.

Audrey hugged John again and again and wept. She hugged Billie and looked deep into the younger woman's eyes. Billie felt a warm pleasure and had to fight back the tears.

Audrey tried to take over in the kitchen, but they all insisted she rest.

"Come on in and sit down, Sis," John said. "You and me have some catching up."

John told Billie about the conversation later.

"I can't believe it," Audrey said.

Their mother had died when John was three and Audrey was nineteen. She and Emmett moved into the Dillinger home so that she could help raise her little brother.

John said, "I told Dad I had to come back and see the folks, didn't I? Being on the move, it gives you a taste for home. How have you been? How's Emmett?"

"He's good. We're doing fine, well as anybody these days. Things seem to be picking up, you know, in the country a little. I hope, for the young people's sake."

John asked about some of his friends in town. She told him what she knew. They talked about Frances and Doris, how their father was getting on since losing his wife.

Finally Audrey said, "What's this about, Johnnie? Where is it going with you? We read the papers, of course. But—"

"Sis, I'm not going to kid you, I signed on for something. I never dreamed it would be like this, but once you've signed on, you have to stick. It's a one-way road."

"People want to get you a pardon, Johnnie. There's a lot of talk around here about that. They want you to get off. You haven't hurt anybody, have you?"

"I swear to you I never killed anybody," he lied. "These stories—"

"We know the papers print a lot of hogwash."

"They want to pin stuff on me I had nothing to do with. I'm the scapegoat. They'll never swallow a pardon."

"But where does it end? Tell me that, Johnnie."

"I've learned about danger, Sis. I've been through it. I'm out the other side. Me and Billie."

"She's an Indian, they say."

"Only half. She brings me luck. We're married. I mean I'm going to marry her, real soon. She doesn't hold back on me, see?"

"I understand, Johnnie. I hope you'll be happy."

"I'm going to live till doomsday, Sis. I can feel it."

His laugh went against the current of everything in her and she laughed. He took her arm on the way in to dinner.

A boy who steals a car cannot return to a family dinner and brag of it. An adolescent who bungles a petty robbery— who batters unsuccessfully on the head of a local grocer—has to endure domestic disgrace. But a man who robs banks of cold cash worth more than his father's lifetime earnings, who flashes his face on newsreels, who strolls from impregnable jails with an arrogance that leaves the nation breathless, and who sets fire to imaginations as far away as Europe, that man can return home and sit down to Sunday dinner a hero. Hunted, he can depend on his family to insulate him. This was his father's attitude, it was the attitude of the rest of the family.

John had killed no man. He assured everyone of that. What it said in the papers, that was all lies. He'd been in Florida the January day when the cop was shot down in East Chicago. People down there would swear to it.

"Why, they're trying to pin so many robberies on me, I would have to be ten men to have done all of them."

"You eat like ten men," Hubert said, to general laughter.

John smiled and speared another slab of roast from the pink-brown juice of the platter. "I am ten men, Bud."

Billie sensed that John had become the father of the clan now. He was the one who had traveled. He knew the streets of Chicago, the landscape beyond the Indiana plains. He was the only one of them to have gazed on the Atlantic Ocean. He spoke with assurance. He could handle all emergencies.

In most families this transition takes place over years. Sons grow and marry. They have sons of their own. They learn what their fathers know. Through natural vigor they supersede them. But the elder Dillinger found his place usurped all at once. During a single Sunday meal he partook the pride of fathers and the desolation of fathers, satisfaction in a son's noontime glory and disquiet in his own lengthening shadow.

His name had been commandeered by history—he too was John. And though young John had no children of his own, the progeny of the Dillinger family would identify themselves forever as descendants of the famous outlaw.

John entertained his people with a cartoon account of the shootout in St. Paul. He made Billie demonstrate how she'd screamed, "Don't shoot! Don't shoot!"

They asked him about the Racine robbery and about the Sioux City job and about the getaway in the dust storm. They laughed over how he'd stopped the police with a handful of roofing nails.

What they really wanted to ask him, they couldn't put into words. How could he go out and become this giant, this John Dillinger that they read about, and still come back and talk and laugh like the Johnnie they'd always known? And what did it mean?

Of course, they wanted to know about Crown Point, how in the world he'd managed to escape.

"A gun is no use," John explained. "What can I do with a

gun? If I pull the trigger I'm kaput. I'm in a jail with a whole company of National Guard outside. How can I shoot? What I needed was an imaginary gun. Or, the notion of a gun. That's what scares people. It's like mass hypnotism. Do you see a gun there? Yes, I see a gun, do you see a gun? Of course I do. And what was it?"

He grasped his cigarette between smiling lips and reached into his pocket. He drew out an object wrapped in newspaper. It was the wooden gun, black with shoe polish. Hubert squeezed tears from his eyes and punched himself hard in the thigh, he was laughing so hard. John shut one eye and pointed the toy at Frances, who screamed with pleasure.

After a minute John gave into the girls' pleading and handed over the weapon. He said, "How's about another piece of pie, Sis?" Audrey reached for his plate.

"How many men you figure they got looking for you this minute, Johnnie?" Hubert asked.

"I don't know. Thousands, I suppose. They hate me because I stood up to them. That's what they hate, a person stands up to them."

When the last coffee cup had been drained, the last finger wiped over a pie plate and licked, Hubert said, "Get that Gatling gun, Johnnie. We'll put the Kodak to work."

The sun battered the clapboard house. Hubert snapped John and Billie together. He took Billie alone, her hands in the pockets of her coat. In spite of the brightness she felt a chill. For a second she wasn't sure where she was, who these people were.

"Say 'raspberries,' " John told her.

Hubert and John and lined up for a shot on either side of Audrey. They were all squinting into the sun. Each had the same pinpoint Dillinger eyes and lean Dillinger face and somber Dillinger mouth.

During the afternoon other relatives and family friends came by, quietly, in small groups. John spent hours in the parlor visiting.

Later John and his father walked together through the orchards of blossoming pear trees, the honeysuckle and hackberry. They passed into the woods. The trees had barely opened their leaves and the ground was dappled with light.

A rabbit crouched in their path, hunkered and sniffing. John pulled his pistol from his pocket, laid it across his arm, and sighted.

"Bam!" he said. "Dad, I would have had that one."

His father hesitated, said, "Are you married to that woman, Son?"

John turned to look at his father.

"Reason I ask," the old man continued.

"We've got plans. We're going to tie the knot real soon. Hey, remember that twelve-pointer we shot down there in the hollow? Fired at the same time and argued for four days over whose shot hit where. You gutshot the thing and tried to blame it on me."

"Hell I did. It was you—"

John was laughing. He wrapped his arms around his father. They stood embracing for a long minute. John could feel the other man's breath come in gasps.

The father pulled back. A breeze stirred the branches, flickering light over his face.

"There's something I need to know," he said. "Only there's no way I can think to ask it."

"About Billie?"

"You want her to—?"

"Don't worry, Dad. Billie understands. I'm crazy about her, but she's not family. Anything happens to me, I want to be buried by Mother. That's what's right. I want us to be together."

"You see how a father can't bring himself to imagine it."

"Sure. You know they've got me in a position now, with no way out. I'll probably end up living down in South America with native girls to bring me cherries in a silver bowl. That's the way I see it happening. But who are we kidding, huh Dad? I'm just glad I was able to get back to see you."

"You're my son. Remember that. Remember it."

"I was not made for happiness. I wanted it, but—"

They walked back a much shorter distance than they'd come. At the house, Billie had their bags packed.

The good-byes came quickly. Everyone felt the press of time. The girls gave Billie wildflowers to take with her. John grinned and said he would be back soon. He couldn't stay away from Sis's raspberry pie too long.

When they pulled out of the driveway it was as if they were on their way to another country. They were explorers, compelled to venture further and further into the interior, the unknown. They could not tell others the nature of the landscape through which they traveled, its pathways were too strange.

Except that the others felt in themselves the stifled urge to venture, too, beyond the worn limits of their daily lives. And they took comfort in knowing that it could be done. John had proven that it was within the scope of their own lives. All it took was to dare.

A week later John was supposed to meet a friend of Homer Van Meter in a Chicago tavern. He and Billie pulled up in front of the place.

"Wait," she told him.

"What?"

"I have a feeling."

"You."

"Really. Let me go in. I'll see. Make sure."

"If you want to."

"I'll be back, two seconds."

Inside, the Chicago police arrested her. John took off. She never saw him again.

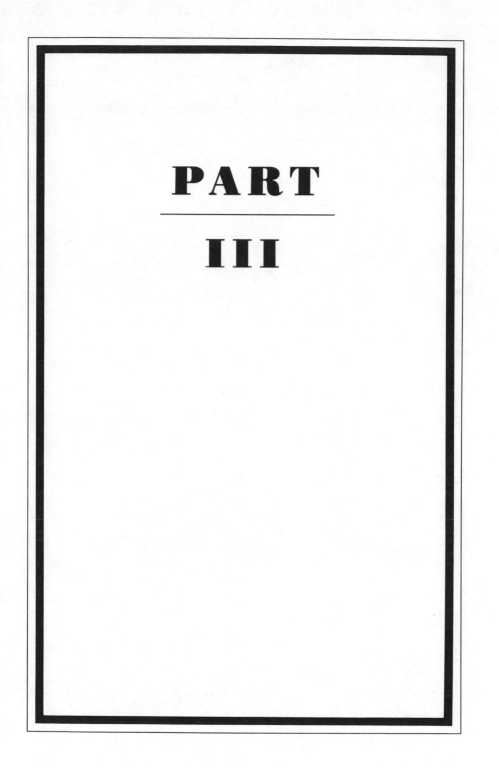

PART

III

17

AFTER CROWN POINT, Will Rogers and a lot of them made jokes about Dillinger. After the Little Bohemia shoot-out, which I'm going to tell you about now, people didn't laugh so much. They started thinking in the backs of their minds maybe the government was losing its grip on the country.

All the members of the new gang took their women up to northern Wisconsin with them, all but John. Homer had a girl. Red brought his new darling, a sparkling little Italian. Tommy's wife Jean was an amiable woman who knew when to keep quiet. Lester was married to a blond Polish girl named Helen.

It was all log cabins up there. Deep woods. Dark icy water. Lonely wind. The air smelled of pine and cedar. At night the prehistoric silence would blend with the soft sighs of the boughs.

The first night Red stayed up with John in the bar after the others had gone to bed. They nursed warm beers and listened to the tinkle of a piano coming over the radio.

"How's it look?" John asked him.

"Lester's got big ideas."

"Oh yeah?"

"We go out west. California. Jugs crack easy there. After a couple jobs, we all buy ranches. Spread the grease and they don't bother you. You don't have to run anymore."

"He's just talking," John said. "He's afraid of the dark."

"We need him?"

"Yeah. Now."

"If we had Pete here—"

John said, "Go farther. That's what Pete would say. Wherever you've got to, keep going. Don't waste your time wishing you were somewhere else. All you can do is go farther."

"Yeah," Red said. "Except Pete's got no farther to go." His eyes softened. John told a familiar story about when they were all together in the Michigan City joint to cheer him up.

John lay awake that night thinking of Billie's hair. He had the feeling he'd gotten in prison, when faces of women haunted him. Her image became more vivid than in real life: a little movement she often made to toss the hair away from her eye, the lustrous black tangle of it splayed on a pillow, the silken hairs on her nape that he would brush with his fingers to make her shiver. Blue-eyed women were fine, he thought. And brown-eyed and hazel-eyed women. But Billie's eyes were a deep indescribable Indian color, the color of moss and deep water. He sweated over them now.

The first day none of them knew what to do. They sat over cups of coffee after breakfast reading the papers. They walked down to the lake. Mounds of dirty snow still clung to the shadows. They passed each other on the way to the lake or returning. They took naps.

Two of the women drove into town to buy hairpins. Red's girl, Marie, decided she needed to see a doctor. She'd suffered a rash for a week. A Chicago kid by the name of Reilly, an errand boy who'd ridden up with Red, drove with her to St. Paul. Homer gave him instructions to pick up cash from some people there.

Wanatka, the owner of the lodge, was a thick European who had run a Chicago speakeasy during prohibition. They didn't clue him in, but they figured if he tumbled he knew to play straight.

He tumbled.

After dinner he called John into the kitchen. John noticed the knives and cleavers scattered over a long butcher block.

"I don't want any trouble," Wanatka told him.

"You won't get any. We're staying a couple of days, then we'll be gone. You can spend the rest of your life telling people about it. But remember, if word gets out, there's bound to be shooting—or worse."

"Just go. I won't say nothing."

"We'll go when we're ready. We're paying."

"I have a boy."

"Sure. Everybody's got a kid. Take it easy."

Lester saw them talking. He grabbed Wanatka when John was out of sight.

"You listen. Whatever he told you, I give the orders here. Understand?"

"Sure."

"I'm the one you talk to."

"Okay."

"Don't get the bug, fella. Hear me? Hear me?"

"Don't get the bug."

"That's right."

The next day, walking down the upstairs corridor toward the strong coffee smell that drifted from the dining room, John passed a maid, an Indian woman. The woman's calm eyes and broad cheeks and thick black hair made him wonder if she wasn't related to Billie. Billie had grown up less than a hundred miles from here. She had played among these pines, swum in the breathless water of these brooks, and had dreamed of him under these skies.

After breakfast, John played ball with Wanatka's son.

"Did you play in the big leagues?" the boy asked.

"No. I could have, but I was too busy. Sometimes you get too busy, kid. That's what happens."

John showed him how to grip the curve ball.

They went down to the lake that afternoon to shoot. All except Van Meter, who was sleeping in his room. Homer slept a lot.

Wanatka was being pretty friendly, Lester told them. Hell, what kind of business would he have if it weren't for them? They were the only ones staying over and they were spreading the green thick.

Wanatka lent them his .30–.30 deer rifle. They took turns plinking cans. Needles of ice jutted into the lake from the shore. The sounds of the shots ricocheted from the gray water.

Lester insisted they put money on it. They agreed, a three-shot match, everybody would chip in five dollars to the kitty. Wanatka set up half a dozen beer bottles down the shore, two hundred yards.

Hamilton and Tommy Carroll both missed all their shots. John shattered a bottle on his first shot, missed the next two. Lester, who had rarely handled a rifle, took his time lining up the long barrel. He pulled the trigger once, twice more quickly.

"Sights are off," he said.

Wanatka aimed carefully, broke two of three bottles.

"He knows the gun," Lester said.

They set up the bottles closer and shot .45 auto pistols. Lester fired the entire clip, his arm bouncing on the recoil. Wanatka handled the gun as if his life were in the balance. He moved in slow motion. He won the second pot, too. He stood under the overcast sky fingering the bills.

John slapped him on the back. Lester turned silently and walked back toward the lodge.

The men stood breathing the lake air, talking of Chicago.

"I was in a speak one time," Wanatka told them. "A place on State Street where some Capone people drank. That night three O'Bannion men came in. There was this buzz, like a nest of hornets before they swarm out. This one Irish hood didn't like being looked at. He pulled a big revolver from his jacket. The bartender came up with a sawed-off ten-gauge. Both the other torpedos drew. I saw a Sicilian over here with a snub-nose out under the table. Somebody poked a carbine from the back room.

"For ten hours—or maybe it was ten seconds—you were in the quietest drinking establishment you ever been in. You didn't want to breathe. I had a terrible itch up here on my temple. I didn't dare scratch it. Like somebody driving a ten-penny nail into my scalp. I got to wishing they'd let loose just so I could raise my hand. But they slowly, slowly put the guns down. The O'Bannion boys walked out backward. Did business pick up then? Oh, boy."

They all laughed. Red told about a shooting contest he was in with a loudmouthed Pollack. "He unloaded six shots at a target, then claimed that he'd put every one of the bullets through the same hole."

"Wait a minute here," John said.

Red looked. Lester was coming down the slope, a satchel in his hand.

Red said, "We have to put up with this, John? Tommy, talk to this guy."

Tommy shrugged.

When the little man reached them, John said, "Not here, Lester. Not a good idea."

Lester was opening the satchel on the ground.

"Why not?" he said. "The guy's wise. I need some practice."

"It makes a noise is why. I'm telling you."

"Yeah?" Lester's eyebrows rode up at their outer corners as he stood up with the machine gun. "Well, *I'm* telling *you.* Set up those bottles, Annie Oakley."

"What is this?" Wanatka asked John. "You said—"

"I said set 'em up!" Lester screamed.

"Do what he says."

Wanatka, watching over his shoulder, walked down by the lake and arranged some beer bottles on a log.

"We're here to rest," John said. "There's no point in this."

"We're leaving tomorrow, right? What difference does it make?" To Wanatka he yelled, "Clear the hell out!"

As the proprietor ran, Lester unloosed the gun, firing half the canister in one burst. Two of the bottles shattered. Fountains sprang in the water. The ripples they left spread serenely, intersecting in diminuendo patterns.

Red snorted.

"Something funny?" Lester said. He fired another clack of shots into the water without looking.

Wanatka was walking quickly back toward the lodge. John trotted to intercept him.

"I'll tell you what it is," Lester told Red and Tommy. "These people are getting the bug. Because of John. They want to be front page. They get the bug. They think, it's the big man. John Dillinger, it's John Dillinger. All they think about is Dillinger. Not even their own selves. I'm telling you it's going to be chaos. Too many bugs."

"And I suppose you're the one who's calming things down," Red said.

Lester's mouth dropped open. He looked at Tommy, back to Red.

"You see who's on top of it when it's bedlam," Lester said, thumping himself on the chest.

"Where's the bedlam?" Red answered. "You're the lunatic around here."

194

Lester stroked his mustache. It was a wispy mustache, the kind young men grow. They're trying to make themselves look older, but of course the effect is to emphasize their youth. "I'm telling you that bastard deliberately set those sights wrong on the rifle. If you're going to play—am I right, Tommy?—play straight."

"You missed three bottles with the spray gun," Red said, smirking.

Lester hefted the gun, aimed carefully, smashed the remaining bottles quickly, and drew a perforated line clear across the lake with the remaining ammunition.

That afternoon Wanatka's wife, convinced that her family would be killed when the desperados left, passed word to her brother that the Dillinger gang was at the lodge. Let the federal men know, she said.

"A man discovered the color of wind," Homer was saying after supper.

"Let's play cards," Lester said. "I feel lucky."

"They are, they're real Indians," Tommy's wife said.

"He went outside and found it blew," Homer concluded.

Helen went, "Woo-woo-woo," patting her lips with her fingertips.

The women went to bed, the men played cards. Saturday night and the bar was crowded. Men came in from the logging camps. They talked loud, lifted shot glasses of rye to their lips with oversized fingers, moved their arms and legs as if they could barely control them.

Homer got up from the table three times to check the parking lot out front. It was too early for tourists that far north. Some of the locals squinted at them.

Lester was cackling over winning eighty-five dollars at Michigan rummy.

195

"A man who doesn't gamble is as bad as one who does," Homer said solemnly. "Know why?"

"Why?" Red asked.

"Because he's no better."

John crossed through the crowd toward the lavatory.

"Hey, Jasper," one of the lumberjacks called to him. "C'mere."

John walked over to the bar.

"This is my friend Jasper," the man said to another man. They both wore coarse wool shirts. They smelled of sweat and tobacco. "Where you from, Jasper?"

John smiled. "Chicago."

"Yeah? Have a drink with me, it's on me."

"No thanks."

" 'Smatter?"

"I don't drink."

"You don't drink? You drink. You drink with me, mug."

"Sorry."

"My heart is broken," he crooned to his pal. "Jasper, have a drink with me. I ask you, have a drink with me."

John smiled at him. He glanced quickly over to his table. Red was stirring uneasily, watching. John shook his head minutely.

"Because you don't drink with me," the man continued, "I'm gonna take the bottle and kick it up your rumble seat."

Wanatka was around from behind the bar. "Judd, relax. This guy is a friend of mine, a personal friend. Don't start."

"He's a friend of mine too, Emil. Aren't you, Jasper?"

"Sure," John said. "I'm everybody's friend. Set us up, Emil."

Wanatka poured the shots. As he raised the glass to his lips, John kept his eyes on Judd. Judd smirked, but looked away at the last minute.

196

"Emil, hit the whole bar, put it on my tab. Judd, been a pleasure, man like you."

"Watch yourself, Jasper," Judd said.

"I'll do that." John leaned close to him. "You know, you're a pretty tough character. I can tell by looking at you. Just by looking, exactly how tough you are."

The Sunday morning sky was cold and leaden. In Chicago federal agents were starting on a rickety air flight north.

At the lodge they were tense during breakfast. Lester complained that his eggs were "rubber" and shoved his plate aside, overturning a glass of orange juice. The glass rolled out of his reach, fell to the floor, broke.

John talked to Homer Van Meter, who was sitting at a table with his young girlfriend. He came over to the others.

"We'll leave this afternoon," he said. "Soon as Reilly and Marie get back."

"Oh, Judas," Tommy's wife said with a sigh.

"Why wait?" Lester said. "Gonna go, go."

"We have a plan."

"Everybody's got plans."

"Relax."

A few customers were already arriving for the special seventy-five-cent Sunday dinner. The radio was playing enamel dance music that pulled at John's nerves. He put his coat on and went outside.

The forest was dead calm. Walking to the lake he heard a blue jay squawk, its voice lighting up the tops of the trees. Little Star Lake made him think of the girls who took star husbands. He climbed into one of Wanatka's boats and rowed onto the iron water.

Another bird called, a warning voice that echoed. It made

197

John tense. You have to be alert all the time. Okay. But you can't start spooking. You have to read signs others miss, but you also have to sort out which omens are true. Otherwise the whole world turns into an alarm.

He returned to his room and studied road maps.

Lester stayed around the lodge all day, keeping a close eye on every movement, on the scrubbed, church-smelling families who arrived for the dinner.

John settled with Wanatka for the bill. He told the proprietor they wanted to eat around four, then they'd be off.

"Smile, Emil. You're making money. And you'll have something to tell your grandchildren."

"We don't want trouble."

"No, we don't want trouble either. Take my advice: relax, you'll live longer."

By dusk Reilly still hadn't returned. Homer telephoned his people in St. Paul. Reilley had left on time. They decided to give him until midnight.

"I'm gonna go pack," Lester said to the others. "This waiting is a fool's game. What are we waiting for?"

"Good idea, get packed," John told him.

Lester and Helen went to their cabin, which was just to the side of the main lodge.

In the dining room, the last of the Sunday patrons had finished their chicken, potatoes, turnips and gravy-soaked biscuits. A few boys from the Civilian Conservation Corps camp down the highway were drinking in the bar. The clatter of dish washing sounded from the kitchen.

Outside, fifteen federal men were taking up positions in the darkness around the lodge.

18

THE MILKY ELECTRIC GLOBES on either side of the mirror had specks of flies in them. Lester ran the comb through his wave, smoothed it with the heel of his hand, ran the comb through, dipped his head to see. He whipped out his fist, forefinger pointing, thumb cocked. But the image in the mirror had him covered. He and the image fired simultaneously. The bullets met halfway, fused to become a drop of condensation that ran down the glass in a crooked rivulet.

"Lester," Helen said to him as he entered the bedroom, "do you think Arlene could get into the movies? She's a lot cuter than Baby Leroy. Do you know how much that kid makes?"

Her pale-green slip rippled as she walked.

He said, "I wouldn't put my kid on a stage."

"She can sing. She's got a cute voice, not like that little Shirley Temple, you want to stick your fingers in your ears. And she's prettier. She's a doll. She'll be famous."

"Those movie people are all on dope. Here, I've got that pain again."

He stretched on the floor in his shorts and undershirt.

"Know what I read in the paper today?" she asked. She stepped carefully onto the small of his back with her bare feet.

199

"Lupe Velez and that Tarzan fella are splits again. That guy never knew what he was getting into when he married Whoopie Lupe. He's a simple Simon."

"Aaw—aw-aw-aaw." Lester imitated the call of the jungle.

Helen moved her feet in tiny steps up his spine.

"What it is," Lester said, "she fell for her own gag. They blow a guy up on the screen, make out like he's a big man. Some hick. Yeah, right there."

She walked slowly in place.

"When are we going to get going, do you think?" she said.

"How do I know? These people got the bug. Understand? The bug."

"What?"

"The bug, I'm telling you. Can't you listen? Dillinger, Dillinger, Dillinger. That's all I hear. They got the bug."

"I hate driving in the dark. I like to see things."

"You can sleep."

"Why don't we go by ourselves, Lester? Drive up in the morning, you and me. We can meet the others there."

"You giving orders now, too? Right there, that's the spot."

"I'm not giving orders. Here?"

"That's good, get off."

"Just, what kind of a vacation is this? God, it's almost May and it's like winter here."

"Cold? I'll cold you."

He rolled as she was stepping off. She stumbled, squealed. He grabbed her ankle, but she pulled away. She scrambled across the bed. He grabbed.

Helen giggled, kicked at him. He slapped her bare knees. Her skirt rode up to her waist, a strap slipped from one shoulder. She thrust her fingers into her blond hair and looked at him, her tongue between her teeth. Her breasts pushed against the fabric.

He took hold of her ankles and twisted her back and forth. She reached over to the nightstand for a jar of cold cream. She kept her eyes locked on him. She scooped a gob with two fingers and applied it to her spread toes. With her other foot she dug up under his shirt for the elastic of his shorts.

She saw his head turn, his eyes come into narrow focus.

He pulled away and climbed into his pants.

"What's the matter?"

Without buttoning his shirt, he slipped on his jacket, dropped his .45 into the pocket. He snapped off the lamp by the bed.

Darkness swallowed the room. A volley of shots exploded outside. Helen screamed.

"Oh boy, here we go," Lester said. He held the machine gun in his hands as if it had materialized there. He cracked the door. The cold air filled his lungs like pure oxygen.

The shooting ceased abruptly. The lodge had gone dark. He could see several figures moving behind cars.

Glass broke. From an upstairs window of the lodge came four quick muzzle flashes, four cracks.

A disorderly staccato of shots answered from the parking lot. Each shot had a deadly, final sound, like that of a bone breaking.

"Get on the floor!" Lester commanded in a loud whisper. Then louder, but almost to himself, "See you in hell, babe."

The gun jumped. The crash of sound punched six times against his eardrums. He heard more glass break as he dragged the spitting barrel across the parked cars.

Another machine gun opened up from the roof of the lodge. It fired a burst, then a steady pulse of single shots.

Shots blasted out an upstairs window. The flame from the barrel lighted the room like sparks.

Lester wanted to make his gun talk. He was saying some-

201

thing that moment that he'd always wanted to say. He was expressing in precise terms a secret he'd never told anyone before. He'd found his voice. He wanted to utter everything out the barrel of that gun.

His hands shook. The roar of sound exploded colors behind his eyes. His lips peeled back. His teeth, grinding together, turned to sugar. His knees went electric.

The storm of noise ceased abruptly. The gun calmed. The ratchet spring made a buzzing sound as it continued to unwind in the empty canister.

For the first time since he'd been in the woods, Lester saw the stars. Above the pines, through a break in the clouds, a spray of weak stars was glimmering at his face.

Three shots rang from the parking lot. He heard a click that marked the trajectory of one of the bullets through the trees.

He dropped the machine gun and walked into the woods. He was sweating.

The shooting from in front of the lodge was sporadic now, like the crackling of a hot brushfire.

Lester hurried down toward the lake. He wondered how many of the bastards he'd gotten. Sons of bitches. You don't wait around. Goddamn Dillinger bug. You don't wait. You move.

Red and yellow lights zinged along his nerves, fending off the darkness that was wrapping around him. He glowed.

When he met the others he would laugh in their faces. See? See? They've got the bug. They're puppets. You can't let them. You gotta. Show 'em. That's it. Show 'em.

He reached the water. A slice of moon halfway up the sky broke through clouds to illuminate the outline of the lake. It left a ghostly sheen on the water. Lester's throat stung like a hot gun barrel. He squatted by the shore and dipped one hand in. The cold bit his fingers. The water tasted of slate. He scooped more with both hands. When he stopped drinking he was panting. Water dripped from his chin. The darkness pressed against his back. He shivered.

Where were they? Meet by the lake, they said. Meet by the lake. In case.

He heard shots from the lodge, hairline fractures in the air. Without thinking, he moved off along the edge of the water.

He quickly came to where the shore turned. From there he would have to angle to the road, a half mile away. There was supposed to be a path. He couldn't find it.

He had to do the thing he didn't want to do. His face tensed. He squinted, ground his teeth.

The woods loomed black before him. An open mouth. Waiting.

He began to move forward like a sleepwalker, groping in front with both hands. The brush clawed at him. He felt for an opening. He took hold of a branch, twisted it out of his way. Each step was a step off the edge of the world.

A hand grabbed hold of his leg. He pulled. It wouldn't let go. He kicked at it. Fell backward into a slimy bed of leaves.

He clutched at his beating heart, which threatened to burst his chest open, explode in the dark. Dampness seeped through his pants.

He stood. He folded his arms over his face, leaned forward, walked quickly ahead. He stumbled. He crashed on through the underbrush. A twig lashed his eye. He fell again.

He stood. Which way was the lake now? It hurt his eyes to peer into the dark.

He pushed forward in the direction he was facing. He'd told them, he'd told them, he'd told them. You're going to go, go. A guy tumbles, ace him or blow. People get the Dillinger bug. You can't trust them. What in hell do you have to lose? Kill them all.

203

He lurched down into a depression. Cold seeped into both of his shoes. He sloshed on, his wet socks slipping at each step, his pant legs clinging.

This was like no dream. He pulled the pistol from his pocket. He pushed the catch and felt the pleasant weight of the magazine sliding into his hand. He pushed it back. The metallic click reassured him.

He stopped trying to move in a straight line. He simply followed the path of least resistance.

Then over the top of a rise he saw a yellow glow. He climbed, saw a house, a smear of light from over the side door, a lamp showing in a window.

A Model A Ford sat in front. The light caught one of its spoked wheels and splayed a spidery shadow out behind. Lester felt buoyant crossing the open yard. He checked the car for keys.

He climbed the porch steps. Turned the knob. The door swung open with a creak. He slipped his pistol from his pocket.

He was in a hot, dark kitchen. He could see a lighted parlor down a short hallway. A clock ticked loudly near the window. A radio was playing in the other room.

A sound. Lester flattened himself against the wall. An old man shuffled down the short hall and switched on an orange overhead light.

"What? What in thunder? Who—?"

"Slow down, Pop. No lip. That your car?"

The man was looking at the gun.

"Listen, son."

"Is that your car? Yes or no?"

He nodded.

"Get me the keys. Who else is here?"

"Nobody."

"Who's in there?"

"Nobody's in there!" He was shouting.

Lester went into the parlor, shoving the old man before him. A gray-haired woman wearing spectacles with lenses the size of dimes had been knitting in a rocker. She had put down her yarn and was starting to get up. A comedy program must have been on the radio, a hiss of laughter was pouring from the speaker.

"We're going for a little ride. People get old quick. You want to die right here, you die."

The man, who wore suspenders and sleeve garters, did not move. A vein snaked along his bulging forehead.

"You think I'm kidding?" Flames crackled in the fireplace, scouring the oxygen from the room. Lester was sweating.

The man drove, the old lady sat in back. The roads up here were just strips of gravel through the woods. The headlights illuminated walls of brush on both sides.

Suddenly the road disappeared. Blackness.

"What the hell are you doing?" Lester screamed.

"I've been having trouble with the headlamp circuit," the man explained. "I thought I had it fixed."

They rolled to a halt in the pitch dark.

Lester could see a flutter of light up ahead through the trees. He ordered the man to drive forward slowly. The old lady was murmuring in the back seat.

"Shut up!" Lester yelled.

"She's praying."

"I said, Shut your trap!"

Her voice creaked, ceased.

A figure appeared in the front door as they drove into the driveway.

"George," the man called. "What's the matter? Did you hear about the shooting at Emil's? Gosh darn, they got federal men up there and the whole caboose. They're saying it's Dillinger."

The sight of Lester's pistol silenced him. Lester hurried the old couple up the steps and pushed them all inside.

"Oh no," the second man said. "Mother!"

In an instant, Lester had him by the collar and was jamming the gun barrel into his neck. "Keep your mouth shut! You think we're playing Parcheesi?"

A woman in a pink bathrobe entered. Her hair was in wire curlers. Her face was curled. Her fingers curled at her cheeks. Her lower lip curled. A bleat curled from between her yellow teeth.

"You have a car?" Lester asked the stocky man.

They all began to talk at once. Words with no meaning.

A crystal chandelier hung down over the table. It was dangling parallelograms of glass that broke the light into colored slivers. On four arms were cardboard fixtures—candles, complete with dripping wax. Each held a small unfrosted light bulb. The filaments of the bulbs gave off light, then inhaled the illumination. Glowed, darkened.

Lester worked his cotton tongue around in his mouth.

"Don't talk back!" he screamed. "Brainy goddamn puppets. Get the bugs outa ya! You're growing old. I heard you. Shut up!"

Four gray faces stared at him. The air burned.

On the opposite wall Jesus wore a crown of thorns. One of those picture where, if you look at it long enough, the eyes open. Lester stared. He couldn't stop himself. The dry heat was driving thorns into his own scalp. He stared, but the eyes would not open.

A sound nudged him from behind. He spun. Wanatka, the clown that ran the lodge. What the hell? One of the bartenders. How had they?

He ordered them all against the wall. They mouthed at him. He told them he would kill them—that was what he wanted to say.

"Were you the sap who called the bulls?" Lester growled at Wanatka, menacing him with the gun.

"What are you, crazy? You think I'd want them to shoot up my own place? I didn't call them."

"We're getting out of here. You're coming. And you." He waved the gun at Wanatka, at the man who owned the car.

A woman's wail colored the air. The chandelier lights were panting.

He pushed the hostages out the front door. The night air turned his sweat to chill.

He ordered Wanatka behind the wheel, the chubby man in back. He climbed into the front passenger seat himself. Wanatka stepped on the starter. The engine turned over without catching.

"You son of a bitch!"

Lights flared behind them. A car turned into the driveway and pulled up nearly alongside them.

Lester looked. Three men in the front seat. They all wore ties and snap-brim hats.

The air was singing as Lester opened the door. The idling motor of the car chugged with a menacing beat.

The driver of the other car opened his door and stepped onto the running board. The light from the house reflected on the flat lenses of his glasses, hiding his eyes. He was saying something. The immense dark of the forest absorbed his words.

Wanatka and the other man were scrambling out. Wanatka yelled to the newcomers. Lester heard the words as he raised his pistol toward the face in front of him.

"Watch it! That's Baby Face Nelson!"

207

19

"WE'RE GETTING out of here. You're coming. And you."

On stage we'd have Marty, as Lester, putting the hostages in a mock-up of an Olds when the federal men arrived. Marty had practiced a very elegant move, a kind of arabesque turn, that brought him face-to-face with his unwitting pursuers. He would fire.

The first G-man represented a Mormon lay preacher by the name of Jay Newman. J. Edgar Hoover was then consolidating the force that would become the FBI. He liked Mormons. They didn't drink and their piety suggested a moral armor.

Our man would throw a hand to his head. I had him palm a little sack of red glycerin. The effect of blood spraying between his fingers and running down his arm would drop somebody in the audience into a dead faint about every other show. In the actual event, Lester's bullet only grazed Newman. The government man got off a few shots as Baby Face fled.

Next Marty would aim at Carter Baum, a second federal agent. Hit in the neck, Baum was to die of his wound.

Finally he would empty his gun at the local constable, Carl Christensen, who was along for the ride. In life, Christensen lived to describe his encounter with the Dillinger gang to his grandkids.

"They had guns," Marty told me once, referring to the lawmen. "You're a hunted animal, what are you going to do? Somebody had to die. That was the chemistry of the thing. Baby Face had the quickest nerves."

Marty had no liking for authority when I met him. Playing Baby Face Nelson fueled his animosity. Lester became a hero to him, a man who stood five four and three-quarters and spit in the eye of the federal government. A man who went the limit.

"Dillinger played games," Marty would tell me. "Nelson was wild clean through."

"Sanity," I answered. "Brains. Gentleness. Just pure wildness I can't appreciate."

"I can," he said.

"What happened up there," I told him, "the car that had belonged to the CCC boys sat there all night, the body of this poor kid in it, lights on, radio playing. The federals were afraid to go near it."

The whole gang escaped without a scratch. Planning did it. They each fired a single burst of bullets from inside, then hauled out the back. Tasting blood, the federals had started firing before they completely surrounded the place.

By the day after, just about everybody in the country knew about Little Bohemia Lodge. Hoover, a publicity-hungry young man, had alerted the press that his men had Dillinger surrounded. But before the ink was dry on the extras, new headlines were proclaiming that the desperado had evaded yet another trap. And federal men had shot three innocent CCC boys, killing one. And they'd lost one of their own men in the process. History wavered in the balance as people screamed for Hoover to resign.

We played up Little Bohemia in the show because it was

pure war. There was no money involved, it was no bank robbery. Survival was the only issue. Man against man. Or rather,
man against authority. Man against order, against decency,
against regimentation. It depended on how you looked at it.
It was an American scene: armed men face-to-face shooting it
out, one walking away unscathed.

After Little Bohemia, Dillinger was known around the
world. Transatlantic ships were searched at Southampton and
Le Havre. A sighting of the Dillinger Gang in England turned
out to be a group of American students on scholarship at
Oxford—their accents raised the alarm. The Nazis scoffed at
the Americans' failure to capture the outlaw.

We were now in our second summer with the show. As we
traveled, I found that the audiences wanted more mayhem and
more bombast. Reacting to the applause and cheers, we fired
more blanks, shed more fake blood, turned our dialogue to
rant. It became a whirlwind of violence.

We couldn't keep up with the movies.

Accuracy? Forget it. I gave my Dillinger a swagger. I turned
him into a braggart, which the real Dillinger never was. I made
him fast on the trigger, because patience doesn't play on stage.
Hokum is what plays. And hokum, believe you me Bob, is
what pays.

His legend was growing and I shaped the show to keep up
with it. I killed more men and added phony money to the loot
I stole in mock holdups.

Same with the love element. I found myself bouncing my
eyebrows at the audience and hitching up my pants too often.
I had Ivy wearing a tight slit-skirt dress with a deep V neck
that showed the tops of her breasts. I spiced her dialogue with
double entendre lines and added a string of risqué jokes for
myself. I told her to wiggle her fanny and flash her pretty
legs—she thought it was fun. When we'd kiss now we made

some thrusting motions with our hips that had the farmers howling. And Ivy would let out a sigh that she twisted into a moan of pleasure.

I didn't give a damn. It was show business.

"They're paying," Sparky always told me.

That's right. If they want cruelty and orgies, they're paying. And I figured, well, they need to forget. Because everywhere you went those days you saw children dressed in burlap feed sacks, staring men broken in midlife, people who'd had their hope taken away from them by force.

Offstage Ivy was still driving me crazy. Harry was watching her more closely now, she said. "He suspects somethin."

We could hardly ever find a chance to get together. But her kisses were as ardent as ever during the show. The situation left me a perpetual satyr.

She was genuinely afraid of her husband. He wasn't beyond beating her.

"For not fixin his eggs runny like he likes em. I had it, so I said, I'll crack an egg over your noggin. Half-jokin like. But Harry went through the roof."

He hit her. In my dressing room she pulled her skirt down to show me the bruises on her hips and sides. I was going to put some live ammo in my gun and go have it out with him. I let her talk me out of it.

My urge began to find other outlets. After the show I would hang around for a little while selling the photos of myself, the bloodstained swatches. In nearly every town there would be a woman who would take my arm and press against me. Or one who would hold my eyes and bite her lip just so. We would talk. She would always have a lot of questions about Dillinger, but wouldn't be too interested in the answers.

Sometimes, especially at first, I'd drive her into town—to the next town over, more like, I wasn't a total fool—and buy her a drink. We'd get a hotel room and she would have the privilege of being laid by the Man Who Looks Like Dillinger.

Later I began to trim the preliminaries. I'd take the ladies straight to my trailer, pour them a drink and proceed. Most were in their twenties. For some reason, telephone girls seemed to be the randiest.

One time Sparky took me aside for a Dutch uncle talk. "You're playing with fire, all these town women. Canvas and a calliope make them hot to trot. I've seen it. But the next day they can turn. Or the locals find out you're witching their women, they go nasty fast. Anyway, they ain't worth it. You're better off taking the pick of the local cat shop. You never wear out your welcome there."

"I see your point, Sparky."

I did. And I was glad he never said anything about Ivy. I figured he knew, but Sparky was never one to waste words on the obvious. If I was walking into trouble with my eyes open, that was my business.

Around that time a rumor was getting going that Dillinger was generously endowed below the belt. It was a rumor I spread as fast as I could and that I made veiled references to in the show. It's a rumor that continues to this day. I understand they still get people calling up the Smithsonian to ask if they've got Dillinger's penis pickled there.

Fine. But these broads I was going with, they invariably made some joke about the subject. It bothered me. I'd see a calculating look in their eyes sometimes that just took the wind out of me.

They weren't interested in me really. Celebrity, even the watered-down replica of celebrity that I represented, was the lure. They spread their legs for a headline. It left me feeling lonely and used up.

That summer I indulged in the luxury of discarding scruples.

I didn't care. I entered a dangerous, unfettered period of my life when I was perfectly willing to spit in any man's eye or take a pinch of any woman's fanny.

I began to detect a coolness in Ivy's manner. She refused to surrender to our stage kisses the way she usually did. She spoke her lines without enthusiasm.

It bothered me. I started leaning on the crutch. Got so I was taking a couple of shots of rye before every performance to loosen my creativity. They always left me with a giant thirst afterward, which I'd kill with a half bottle or more.

Ivy came into my dressing room still in her costume. She sniffed a few times and rubbed her knuckle against her nose, which meant she was upset.

"He almost fell last night," she said.

"Harry?"

"I can tell. I know when he always stumbles to make it look hard. He left those out. But then he was doing the thing where he sits down and rolls back on his shoulders and he just about slipped off the wire."

"Maybe he fooled you."

"Know how many times I've watched him? He slipped, I'm tellinya."

"So better luck next time," I said, taking a swallow of the rye.

"Wha-at?"

"Maybe tonight he'll break his neck. Does he have life insurance? I don't suppose he can get it."

"What are you saying?"

"It would leave Sparky without a headliner. But maybe I could take his place. Yeah, I can see it. Dillinger on the high wire. The desperado in tights. Firing a Thompson on a thread of steel. I'll be a sensation."

I'd never seen her make her mouth so small.

213

I continued. "You put on your slippers and we'll do the beast with two backs out on the cord. We'll make headlines."

I didn't see her hand coming. It struck the glass I was holding and slammed it back into my chin. The tumbler broke. Liquor fumes burst in my face. The gash under my jaw began to drip.

I hit back. In the funny way your mind can work, despite my rage I was careful not to bruise her face or arms. I was thinking of the show. I slapped at her. She fought back with her small fists.

It was over in a minute.

"He's a person," she sobbed. "He's my husband."

"Leave him."

"I can't. Anyways, who do you think you are? You aren't Dillinger. You got me goin on this."

I was holding a handkerchief under my chin. I took a swig from the bottle.

"Didn't take much gettin."

"I'm worried aboutum. Can't I say that? With you and me it's somethin different. I'm married to Harry."

"That's your problem."

She marched out. I knew she had to get over to the main tent to watch Harry's act. I sat there getting to know a kind of bone tiredness that I've felt many times since. I was tired of Ivy's moods. I was tired of the rubes who came to gawk at an ersatz Dillinger. The only thing I wasn't tired of was the money they paid for the privilege. It wasn't a fortune, but in those days I was damn glad to have it. It kept me in whiskey.

I wasn't Dillinger? That was what she said. That was supposed to hurt. But she was wrong. I was Dillinger, all right. Because Dillinger wasn't a person any more. It was just a state of mind, a myth. And I was building the myth just as much as John ever did. More.

I thought our encounter would cure Ivy of talking about her husband, but he became her number-one subject.

"Somethin's eatin him," she would tell me. "He's thinkin too much. He can't think when he's up there."

I learned to sympathize. I assured her that Harry's distraction had nothing to do with her. The man had an artistic temperament. Hadn't she told me so?

She warmed to me again quickly.

One night I'd had a couple more than usual before the show. During a kiss I let my hand slip down over the curve of her hip. She responded by pressing her pelvis against me. I put the other hand down there and jerked her onto her tiptoes.

Feet had begun a regular stomp on the bleachers before I realized what I was doing. I glanced at the audience. I actually saw one woman blushing.

I flashed my Dillinger grin as if it were all part of the act. I drew my pistol, pointed it at a leering face in the third row, fired. The crowd loved it.

Yeah, I'd have to add this to the act regular. Bring in a couple of cooch dancers to spin tassels on their tits. Add a matinee for the schoolkids. This was educational. This was history.

Ivy scolded me afterward. We had to be extra careful, she told me. She was afraid of what might happen if Harry caught on. Even as she was warning me her little hand was sliding provocatively down the midnight-blue silk that wrapped her belly.

It was about a week after this we were playing outside of Springfield. I was making one of my regular attempts to cut down on the sauce. As a result I felt scalded and vulnerable. One hot summer morning I wandered over to the trailer Ivy and Harry lived in. I can't remember why—I don't know if I had a reason.

215

I knocked lightly on the screen door. Without thinking, I opened it and stepped up inside.

Ivy was still in bed. She slept ten or eleven hours nearly every night, sometimes more. She lay on the bed totally nude. She must have been thrashing, the sheets were tangled, twisted around one ankle.

But at that moment her posture was one of perfect repose. Her face was virginal, childlike. Her cheek was pressed against a small fist.

I felt a desperation behind my eyes. Time was pressing against my back. Dillinger was dead. My show, where I kissed this disguised child in front of greedy-eyed spectators, would soon dissolve. I would move on. Maybe she and Harry would have kids. A few years and she wouldn't be quite so fresh. Everything seemed poised in an awful, delicate way.

I didn't articulate it to myself then. I just felt a confusion and regret that was like a bottomless well.

A sound made me turn. Harry was standing behind me in the doorway.

20

"A HOT BATH," Red Hamilton was saying. "That's the first thing for me. I'm gonna soak in there for about nine hours."

Just before noon, Homer Van Meter was driving a big Ford along the Mississippi River just south of St. Paul. John was in the seat opposite him. Red sat in the middle, a handkerchief tied around his head to protect where glass had nicked his forehead back at the Little Bohemia Lodge.

They'd made a circle in the stolen car in order to enter the city from the south.

"You figure the girls are okay?" Red said.

"What could they hold them for?" John answered him. "They weren't breaking any law."

"Wanatka set us up," Homer said. "The son of a bitch suckered us. Think he won't hear from people? There's people in Chicago know him. He'll hear about it plenty."

"Forget him," John said. "We haven't time to settle scores. We haven't any time at all."

"Maybe if we went out west," Red offered.

John said, "You've been listening to Lester."

"The hell with that bantam," Homer put in.

"We don't want to go somewhere where we don't know anybody, don't know the country. Pick up money, guns, a clean car and we're on to Chicago. We're safest when we're closest to them."

It could have been another car backfiring. Homer squinted into the mirror.

"They're on us," he said.

John scrambled into the back seat, a pistol clutched in his fist. Homer stepped on the gas. John banged out the oval back window.

The police car swept down on them. The bumping and heaving threw off John's aim. He could see the elbow of the cop on the passenger side, the head, the rifle stock. The sound of the shots barely caught up to them. But the bullets did.

Red took a slug in the back.

Homer found driving room and gained a quarter mile on the other car. Rounding a bend he pulled into a dirt road to the side. He slowed immediately so as not to raise dust. Red was gasping. John kept his squinted eye at the pistol.

They watched the police speed by.

Red's face was blanched. John climbed out. He had Red lean forward onto the running board. He laid his folded handkerchief over the wound. A crimson spot quickly soaked through.

"He's going to need a doctor. How's it feel, Red?"

"Lousy. Like it's in there. It's burning."

"You'll be okay."

"John," Homer said. "They got a tire."

Red groaned. "Will I, Johnnie?"

"We'll have to grab something and get out of here," Homer said. "Haul it for Chicago."

"Think you can make it, Red?"

"I don't want to die, Johnnie. I don't want to die alone."

Homer steered the car back onto the highway. He idled on the shoulder, waiting.

218

A new blue Ford approached from behind. They pulled out. The deflated tire hissed and flapped. Homer crowded behind the car and flashed his headlights. When they failed to pull over he steered into the opposite lane, gunned his engine.

The blare of a horn sounded as he nudged toward the side of the road. Both cars stopped amid the smell of burning rubber.

John got out and walked around to the other car, a smile on his face, his hand on the gun in his pocket.

"Sorry," he said, in answer to the protest of the young man who was driving. "We're going to have to use your car. Sorry."

The man started to say something. Stopped. He stared, as a person stares at some utterly unfamiliar object. The next breath of air he took was not the same air he'd breathed all his life. He slowly shook his head.

"You can just climb in back there. And you, missus. Don't worry about the baby. What is it, a boy? We've just got a flat tire. We need to borrow your car. Understand? No harm."

When the man hesitated John removed the still-hot pistol and looked down at it, a man checking his watch.

A minute later John was driving the new car. Red's blood was slowly oozing into the front seat. Homer rode in the back with the couple and their infant.

"You're John Dillinger," the wife said. She was a slender, fine-boned woman.

"I just look like him," John answered pleasantly.

Responding to her husband's nudge, she said no more.

Red was licking his lips painfully.

"Thirsty, Red?" John asked. "We need gas, anyway."

He pulled up at a filling station. While a man in overalls was pumping fuel, John went inside and bought a couple of Nehi's. He gave Red one and passed one back.

219

"For the baby," he said.

"He's just eaten," the mother said. "He doesn't want it."

Homer gulped from the bottle. John waited while the attendant brought him two cents change.

Five minutes later John pulled over and let out the family along a deserted stretch of road.

"Good luck," he said.

Homer took over driving. He knew the back roads that cut through the Minnesota forests. He drove the western bank of the Mississippi, following gravel farm roads instead of Route 61.

By nightfall they were down onto the Iowa plains. John tried to make Red comfortable in the back seat. They had nothing, no luggage, no clean clothes. Red hugged himself, shivering. He rode stoically, but when he fell asleep he began to groan. Once he slipped onto the floor. He woke up thrashing. He didn't know where he was.

They crossed the bridge at Prairie du Chien at two in the morning. The Mississippi water moved beneath them in a flat black sheet. Long rippled Vs marked the pilings and reflected the lights that lined the roadway.

Red, who had been snoring wetly, roused. He lifted his head and said, "Where are we?"

John's hand was on his shoulder.

"Almost home, buddy."

"Where the hell are we, Johnnie?"

"We're in Wisconsin, honey. We'll be down to Chicago in no time."

"Where? Where?" He emitted a childish sob.

They wound their way east along the Illinois border. John drove through the night. He eased to a stop in front of a closed general store. A cone of light bathed a red Mobilgas pump. A sign said Chesterfields Satisfy.

John got out to examine the map. He sat down on the steps

of the store and smoked, staring into the darkness of the spring night.

They should have rules for this kind of thing. In war they let you tend to your wounded. They don't treat enemy soldiers like dogs. No reason there shouldn't be rules on both sides. The cops could care for one who'd fallen.

His stub sparked as he flung it into the dirt. He crossed back to the car.

Back on the road, Red punctuated every bump with a groan. Homer slept with his hat over his face.

They were down on the Illinois flats when the sun first lit the horizon. It dragged itself up to stare John square in the face. The night's mist slowly lifted. It became low wisps of three-dimensional clouds that vanished in a breath. The concrete highway before them was a quavering ribbon of light. The brightness washed Red's ashen lips. His eyes flickered.

Nearing Chicago, they stopped for breakfast at a diner on the outskirts of De Kalb. The farmers in overalls and mud shoes squinted at their city duds. One old man smiled at them, folding his toothless, white-bristled cheeks.

Homer ate a ham steak and four fried eggs. They asked the counterman to pack a liverwurst sandwich, a doughnut, and a cup of coffee for their friend in the car.

Red couldn't eat. He sipped the coffee as if it were medicine. "Johnnie, don't leave me, okay?"

"We aren't going to leave you, Red. We'll have you to a doctor in a couple of hours."

"You need your girl," Homer said. "A couple of weeks of breakfast in bed."

"Where is she? She never came back. Where is Marie, Johnnie?"

"Reilly must have picked up the ambush and hightailed it. She's probably waiting for you in the city."

221

"Waiting to love you up, Red."

"Just don't leave me. Okay? Don't leave me alone."

"I stick by my pals, you know that," John said sharply. "What do you think, I'm going to run out on you? We're all on the same road, Red."

Red smiled. He hummed, "On the road to who-knows-where—"

"That's it."

"How'd we do?"

"Did good, Red," Homer said.

"A good take?"

"All we need," John assured him.

"See that guy? God. I says, Gimme the big bills." A gurgling chuckle rose in Red's throat. "The big bills, Johnnie. Good take. God."

They decided not to enter Chicago immediately. They veered south and contacted a friend of Van Meter's in Aurora. Homer talked to him for an hour while John waited with Red in the car. Finally the man sent them to an empty house on the bank of the Fox River.

The clapboards were silver-gray, a few chips of paint clinging around the trim. The windows were washed with sediment from the cement factory to the north.

The place was perched on a steep grade that dropped to the dirty water below. A scaffold of six-by-sixes propped up the rear corner where the foundation had slipped toward the river. Below a burned automobile lay on its back, half in the water.

The closed house smelled of urine. Yellowed newspapers were scattered around the bare floors.

They had Red lie on a soiled cot. John eased Red's jacket off, ripped his crimson shirt. The wound began to bleed again. Homer poured Mercurochrome onto the small ragged hole between Red's shoulder blades. Red said, "Hss!"

Homer went out to look for a doctor.

In the house, the sun beat against the yellow shades exciting files. John ran out of cigarettes. He paced.

Homer didn't return until almost dark. He brought a doctor with a black bag and a long olive cigar. The man's eyes surveyed the room. His thick lenses magnified his pupils.

He asked Red to sit up. Red's flesh was frog-belly white. The doctor pressed his stethoscope to Red's chest and listened, frowning as if the sounds he heard irritated his ears. He probed the laceration with a small scalpel.

Red emitted a helpless, falling sigh. But the examination seemed more painful for the doctor, who scowled and ground his teeth throughout. He removed a gauze compress from his little alligator bag and taped it over the wound. Homer helped Red put on the new shirt he'd bought for him, a blue and red plaid flannel.

"What do you say, Doc?" John asked in the other room.

The doctor spent some time relighting his cigar, making kissing sounds as he sucked at the match flame.

"It's bad. One lung's collapsed. He's got a fever, probably septicemia setting in. Maybe internal bleeding, depending on where that slug ended up. I can't tell that without an X ray."

"So take an X ray."

"He needs a hospital. He needs it right away."

"What can you do for him here?"

"Nothing." His lips formed a small smile, as if he had just extricated himself from a dilemma.

"What do you mean, nothing? What do you think we brought you here for?"

His tongue was visible behind his lips as he drew the cigar out.

"Take him to a hospital, that's my advice. You think I'm a miracle worker? Huh? Think I can change wine into water? I'm risking my neck coming over here. Maybe he'll live, I can't

223

tell. People walk around with one lung, with half a dozen bullets in them."

"That's all you've got to say?"

"All I can say. He may live, he may die. You're rolling craps with the man's life."

He gave John a pill bottle with no label. They were morphine, he said. Red might need them later.

The doctor left. As night fell, Homer drove into Chicago to ditch the bloodstained car. He planned to get hold of an apartment and clothes, draw on the money and guns they had stashed with friends on the North Side.

The electricity was shut off at the house. While Red slept in the dark front room John sat on the porch that ran across the rear of the building.

He watched the river below. Late at night he saw flashes that might have been the northern lights, or only the headlamps of cars turning on the other side.

It was only seven months since Red and the others had broken out of Michigan City. Was that possible?

Red had fallen for a girl usher in a South Side movie theater. He saw *Flying Down to Rio* eight times. Always he would stop in back returning from the concession and ask her questions in a whisper. Favorites were his standby. What's your favorite color? Who's your favorite movie star? Your favorite day of the week? Favorite fruit, car, dance band, comic strip? Favorite character on *Amos 'n Andy*? Favorite kind of fur? He could go on for hours asking. He would show his deadpan interest in every arbitrary answer, mull it over, indicate his approval.

In every category he had a favorite of his own and a reason for his choice. His favorite dog was a police dog—they were loyal and good with children. Favorite car, the Ford Coupe—for acceleration and ride. He had spent the empty hours of incarceration ordering his world into comfortable choices. Favorite pistol a Colt auto with pearl grips.

The usherette brought Red home to meet her mother. The old lady responded to his politeness with inexplicable hostility. The romance cooled.

Red met Elaine in a bakery shop where she was a waitress. He spent hours eating eclairs and throwing her boyish looks. She paid so much attention to his table the owner fired her.

She moved in with him. They would double-date with John and Billie, often spending the evenings playing cards and listening to the radio. The four of them drove out to rural Illinois to attend confirmation ceremonies for Elaine's daughter, who was boarding with a family there. It was one of the few times John had seen Red really beam, his face flushed with ideas of an impossible future.

John tried to sleep on a davenport that had been left behind in the living room. The broken springs nudged and poked him. The fabric was as coarse as a wire brush.

The windows were graying when he was startled from a deep sleep. His hand went instinctively for the gun on the arm of the couch. Red was standing over him.

"Johnnie, we've got to get going." His shirttails hung outside his pants, but he had his hat on.

"What is it, Red?

"We're going to hit that place on LaSalle. Down off Michigan. By the bridge there. By the river. It's ripe. Eighty thousand. Why wait? Payroll. We can't wait. It's time. Let's go."

"We're not going anywhere," John said.

"You've got the plan, right?"

"Everything's planned. It's not today, though."

"Wheelman. You and me. All we need's a wheelman."

John led him back to the cot. "Nothing's on. We're just going to sit tight. I want you to relax now. Relax, you'll live longer."

"Get Pete. He knows the—where's Pete?"

"He's laying low. He's okay."

"Pete knows."

"Sure. Get some sleep."

The big man shook his head. As he lay back down he held up his hand, looked at it as if surprised to find only three fingers. Once he'd told John the story, how on a dare he'd tried to steer his sled between the wheels of the Northern Nekoosa 4:17 as the freight rolled toward the Sault Ste. Marie yards. He'd veered off at the last minute, the giant wheels only nipping him.

One of the things Red had often wondered about, he said, was that such an accident to a child could deprive a grown man of his fingers.

John waited until he was asleep. He went out to a delicatessen three blocks away to buy rolls and coffee and cigarettes. A light rain began to wash down the morning sky as he returned.

The rain continued all day. John watched it from the covered porch. It swept in sheets across the river water, pocking it with patterns of light.

When Red awoke he became agitated. John found him upstairs, slamming the doors of empty rooms. He tried to calm him, reassure him, but Red was hearing other voices.

Red paced, clutching his fist to his chest. John made him swallow two of the pills.

Red sat on the cot, holding himself and rocking. He would look to the right, then quickly to the left. Then back again, as if trying to catch a glimpse of something just out of the range of his vision.

John told a story about a trick they'd played on a guard named Fatty during dinner hour at Michigan City. Though they'd related the story among themselves many times, Red stared uncomprehending. He said he was hungry, but when John brought him a roll his mouth refused to taste it.

Red began to make a keening sound in his throat. The new

226

flannel shirt became soaked with sweat. John checked the bandage. It was oozing blood. He rested his hand for a long time on Red's burning forehead. The gesture seemed to comfort the big man. Red's eyes drifted closed. His breathing was the back and forth of a rasp.

John returned to the porch. It was afternoon, but the light from the overcast sky had not changed all day. He watched a bird trace a lazy loop over the river. Suddenly, as if shot, it plummeted into the water near the middle of the current and disappeared. The sight gave John a shudder of apprehension. But after many seconds it emerged with a fish squirming in its bill and flew off.

For an hour the house was as quiet as the tick of rainwater down the rusted drainpipe. A smoky evening was settling in.

Something in the air changed. John went inside to check on Red. He didn't hurry. He sensed there was no reason to hurry.

He knew from the first glance that his friend was dead. Red's eyelids were half open, showing the whites. His lips no longer formed a tight, deadpan line but lay slack, like an unmade bed. His skin was no longer suffused with a desperate pallor but had faded to a serene eggshell color.

John grasped the big hand with its three fingers. It was still unnaturally warm. He was surprised how loose it was, almost feminine in its suppleness. Red had always kept his fingernails well trimmed.

The dusty house was quiet. Outside, the rain fell with an almost imperceptible hiss. From far away, the sound of a siren drifted in on a current of air.

John pulled a cord from one of the ramshackled venetian blinds in the living room. He gently removed Red's pants, his shorts and shirt. He stared for a moment at the naked body, its flesh nearly translucent.

He lifted the bare legs, folded them at the knees and hips.

227

He passed the cord under the buttocks, up across the small of Red's back. He looped it, tied it tight to hold the legs in a squatting position. The posture gave the corpse a boyish look, as if Red were about to spring up and turn a somersault.

He made a slipknot, looped it over Red's wrist. Crossing the arms over the chest, he tied them together.

Homer returned at dusk.

"Red's gone," John told him. "We'll get out of here as soon as it's dark."

"You okay, Johnnie?"

"I'm fine."

"You look whipped. This getting to you?"

"What's it matter?"

"You want to stay here and rest tonight?"

"We've had our vacation. We're working now, remember? I trussed him like that because—"

"Huh?"

"In case rigor mortis sets in."

"Sure, so we can get him in the car. I know. That's perfect." John sighed.

Homer said, "Damn bit of luck, isn't it?"

"Yeah, well—I'm not doing my pals much good."

"That's not here nor there. We knew we were going off the deep end."

"One lousy bullet."

"It's not a bullet, Johnnie. It's the way the world's set up."

While there was daylight Homer stayed in the kitchen. He spread newspaper on the table, laid out tools and oil, disassembled and cleaned his pistol. John sat with the corpse, smoking, watching the dead man's mouth as if he were waiting for the lips to move.

When the house was lit only by the faint glow of a streetlight they wrapped Red in a gray blanket. They lifted him with an effort. His loosely hanging head made a bulge in the cloth at the bottom. As they reached the door Homer lost his awkward grip and let the load down with a dull thump.

It was still raining.

On their way out of town they pulled up at a neighborhood grocery. John went in. Commenting on the weather, a bald man behind the counter rang up the purchase. It was the most ordinary thing in the world—a hollow-eyed man in a business suit, needing a shave, comes in on a rainy evening and buys three cans of household lye.

They drove out of town for a long ways. They smelled a skunk that had been hit in the road. They bounced on through mud. Homer stopped the car at a disused gravel bank. The scooped-out hill formed a small amphitheater.

At the side was a hump of clay with wild onion and milkweed sprouting. They lifted the burden from the back seat of the Dodge Homer had acquired in Chicago. They carried it into the beams of the headlights.

Homer went back to fetch the shovel from the trunk. Earlier, when John had mentioned their need for one, Homer said he'd already picked it up.

They took turns digging, the blade of the tool ringing on the stones.

A fresh breeze swept from the east. It bore the sweet decay of last year's leaves as well as the even sweeter nectar of burgeoning spring, of pungent weeds. In the headlights, rainwater gleamed on the piles of colorless pebbles and soil.

John cut the cord that held Red's knees. The corpse unfolded only slightly. The skin now glowed with the luster of silver. John and Homer each pulled on one of Red's arthritic legs. The rain dripping on the bare flesh made John shiver.

They dragged the heavy blanket into the trench they'd dug.

229

John took the lye from the car. He turned Red's palms upward and poured half a can of the chemical on each supplicant hand. He emptied the remaining two containers onto Red's face. The crystals sparkled on his eyebrows, caught in his teeth and nostrils.

He gently folded the blanket over the corpse. The first scoops of dirt they sprinkled gently, awkwardly. As the body became covered they shoveled more quickly. In the end they heaped the soil almost frantically.

When they were finished they walked over the grave to pack it down.

"So long, pal," John said before he got into the car.

"We're right behind you," Homer added. His laugh soared into the black rain, the sound of a crow.

21

DILLINGER'S FACE was one you would see over and over in the Middle West. I wasn't the only one who was harassed while the outlaw was at large. A man in Bloomington, Illinois, was nearly shot when he tried to laugh off a pack of American Legion vigilantes.

You would see an auto mechanic wiping grease from the same cleft chin. An insurance salesman you would meet at the Rotary Thursday night would have Dillinger's thin-lipped mouth, a Kokomo tavern owner his who-you-trying-to-kid-pal expression. You could see Dillinger's flat forehead on a downstate bank officer, his weary eyes staring from the face of a foreman in a Hammond steel plant.

You'll see the face to this day. It's an American face, cocky, cavalier, insolent, a face that suggests the surprise of a youth who finds himself suddenly burdened with manhood.

A month after Little Bohemia, a month after they buried Red Hamilton, a doctor gave himself a shot of blue morphine to steady his nerves, then laid a scalpel to the landmarks of Dillinger's face.

The operation took place in an upstairs storeroom rented from a Chicago tavern owner. Cobwebs of ether hung in the air. The doctor traced an outline of blood around the mole in the middle of John's frown. His narcotic-cooled fingers worked the suture. He opened a crevice in front of Dillinger's ear, used a nickel-plated puller to stretch the skin tighter across the cheekbone. Next he sliced into John's dimpled chin. Tucking and rearranging flesh, he tried to produce a smooth line.

Blood began to ooze again from the line of stitches on the left side of John's face. The doctor coughed. A high tone sounded in his ears, a choir of sick angels. A fly, awakened by the licks of a warm spring, buzzed against the window. The doctor stanched the wound, added two more stitches.

John made a mistake here. You can't excise your personality by slicing open your face. The surgery left him with the same half smile, the same eyes. He dyed his hair black. On meeting a friend he would say, "Guess who?" They recognized him with no trouble. They thought he had the mumps. He dipped his fingers in acid to obliterate the prints. They burned for two weeks but vestiges of his whorls and arches remained. He took to wearing glasses.

That month the police shot the machine gunner Tommy Carroll in Iowa, killed him in front of his wife.

At the end of June, on Dillinger's thirty-first birthday, they named him America's Public Enemy Number One. This was a publicity gimmick dreamed up by Hoover, who'd been publicly humiliated by Dillinger. The celibate lawman was especially infuriated by Dillinger's reputation as a ladies' man, and by the persistent public support for this "enemy." The citizens of John's hometown had recently got together a petition asking that he be pardoned.

John was living openly in Chicago, in a rented apartment on Seminary Street off Lincoln Avenue. He had a new girl, Polly Hamilton, a waitress at a North Side restaurant. She hailed from Fargo, North Dakota, a windy woman of the plains.

Polly was twenty-six. She'd been married to a policeman in Gary, Indiana. All of John's women had been married, including Billie. I don't know what to make of that. Maybe a failed marriage removes the mist from a woman's eyes, tempers her nerves somehow.

Polly liked her husband's uniform. But every cop in the world has an attitude and it's an attitude that doesn't suit most women. She divorced him and moved to the city.

Anna Sage, who'd run a whorehouse in Indiana, introduced Dillinger to Polly. John didn't tell her who he was when they met. To her he was a bond clerk named Jimmy Lawrence. He spent money on her. He knew where to take her. He was always fun. But much more than that. The man had—what?—patience.

Time has a way of forever pushing us forward into our lives. We stumble, trying to keep on our feet, and we're three steps ahead into the future. What happened to the moments that brought us there? We cannot say. What counts is what is to come. The present tastes stale. This point of view is habitual and universal. We are expectant animals.

But John had broken himself of the urge to rush onward. Now more than ever he was learning to sit still. The holes he'd seen burn straight through time during his bank jobs had opened his eyes to something pivotal about his life. He was on the run, yet never in a hurry. His calm overflowed.

The way I figure it, he had no future. We always think it's the past that weighs us down. But the past is gone. It's the future that shackles us, the tangle of anticipation and dread.

John had no future then. And he knew it.

She was a woman at the peak of her beauty. She had a large face with the beauty of flagrant jewels. Her wide lush cheekbones were opal, her eyes emerald, her throat glistening marble. She was a product of wind—her hair always appeared whipped, her smiling mouth drawn tight against the swirl.

When he told her, she laughed. He told her again. Her eyes beamed. She pressed her smiling lips together to hide her slightly bucked teeth.

"Jimmy," she said to him.

"Look at me. Close. I wouldn't fool you."

"You most certainly would."

"Not about this. I'm that man."

"You're John Dillinger?"

"Correct."

"The bank robber, John Dillinger? That's— I don't believe you."

"Anna knows. I had to tell you. I don't like pretending with you. And I had to give you a chance. Before anything happens."

One of her hands went to her shoulder, one across her waist, wrapping herself as if she were naked. She was not smiling.

"You are completely serious."

"I don't work for Pierce's. The reason I carry the gun, it's not because I have to messenger negotiables. If you want you can call up the federal men. They'll give you ten grand and put your picture in the paper."

"Oh, Lord."

"I'll walk out of here and you'll never see me again. You just say one word."

"But Dillinger's a killer, a mad dog—I read it."

"That's just in the papers. I've never killed a soul."

"But the other—?"

"I robbed banks. I found myself on a road, Polly. I walked down it. I didn't draw the map. I didn't put up the signs. I've made mistakes, but I never wanted to hurt anybody. You know I'm not like that."

"I know."

"I have to have your answer now."

She blinked back a tear, giggled nervously, lifted her chin, let a smile grow on her lips. She opened her mouth to speak, said nothing. She felt the touch of his scarred fingertips on the back of her hand.

Both were as giddy as teenagers that day. To celebrate, he took her to the Century of Progress. The fair had proven such a success in '33 they held it over for another year, promising bigger and better attractions.

The wonders. A whole village populated by midgets. They rode on Bozo the dragon roller coaster, paid a nickel to gaze at a real two-headed baby in a bottle of oily liquid. Polly marveled at the sight of a scale model of Mount Vernon constructed from half a million dollars' worth of pearls. They saw a lion riding a motorcycle up the side of a barrel of death.

John visited a strip show. He waited for the naked flesh to set fire to his eyes as it had when he'd attended the fair the summer before. But the burleycue left him cold. He felt the sting of remorse for a pleasure gone stale.

They had this robot, Polly told him later, that would talk to you and operate an automatic carpet sweeper. She had to see that. She dragged him into the Hall of Science. He would have spent another hour at the General Motors building watching them put together Cadillacs. He loved machinery.

One exhibit stopped him.

"It makes me feel noodly," Polly said. "You can see right through her. It's like she was naked, only more."

It was the exhibit of the Chicago Roentgen Ray Society. Dr. Hollis Elmer Potter, the sign said, had created the first X-ray image of an entire human body. The model was a Rochester,

New York, girl who sometimes posed for Eastman Kodak advertisements.

"She was wearing a white dress," Polly read. "Those white lines are her bracelet and watch. She was wearing hairpins and metal stocking clasps. See?"

"That," John said, "is something. That is what science is all about."

"She's twenty," Polly continued. "A hundred and fifteen pounds."

"That is something."

Her bare skull, its fine teeth ranked in even rows, was balanced at an angle on her delicate vertebrae. A fog of gray flesh surrounded her white bones, webbed across her long fingers. Her slender belly glowed as if heated from within. Perched on high heels, the glossy shadows of her bones assembled themselves into an eerie architecture. John looked and looked.

Because, she wasn't just a skeleton. She was a living girl, stripped in a way that no cooch dancer ever dreamed of. And she caught the fascination of a man for whom the world now seemed exposed, naked.

"Come on," he told Polly abruptly. "We're gonna fly."

The night before, Homer Van Meter had come up to his apartment.

"It's perfection, Johnnie. South Bend, Merchant's National. They take the deposits from all the branch post offices there. It's all cash, no bonds, no bullshit. And dirty bills. Maybe a hundred grand."

"Where?"

"Right downtown. Wayne and Michigan."

"How about getting out?"

"Just gotta make a run for it. You know the lay of the land as well as I do."

"We'll need something with a lot of speed."

"It'll take five men, the layout."

"I'll get in touch with Lester."

"Johnnie, listen—"

"You have people? Nobody's willing to take the chance. We're dead men, especially me. Lester's crazy enough—"

Homer said, "He *wants* in. He *wants* to be part of the show. That's why he's no good if we're going to do it the right way, plan it."

"What choice do we have? Tell me that."

"If he goes cowboy, we're all going to die."

"I'll remind him."

"A week from Saturday," Homer said.

"A hundred grand."

"Hear you've got a new girl."

"No, Johnnie," Polly said. They were approaching the aquaplane dock. "Please."

"I want you to go up if it kills you. People have been walking the earth since—what? the days of the cavemen. Now, right now, finally, they have the chance to fly. You have to do it. You owe it to your grandmother—her grandmother. What if they'd had the chance?"

"I'll die."

"Hold my hand."

She kept saying no. He bought the tickets and waited for the next plane. They saw it circle in a lazy loop out over Lake Michigan, the sun flashing from its windows. It descended, took on size, and seemed to hover for a second over the lagoon before it splashed, slowed quickly.

The propeller made noise, a gigantic animal trying to sing. Polly clutched John's arm.

"We're going to see another world, sweetheart," he said to

comfort her. "Things you never dreamed of. Things as they really are. It's going to be beautiful."

The previous load of first-time aviators climbed from the belly of the plane. They all talked and laughed. Their faces were flushed. A man wobbled drunkenly. One girl squeezed her fists to her eyes and pounded her feet up and down on the dock.

John and Polly climbed inside the craft along with three other couples. The men joked and blustered. The women giggled. John said nothing. He clutched Polly's hand in his and patted it.

The door closed, the engine spit and growled. They floated, rocking and bouncing, across the water.

Without warning the pilot gunned the engine. A howl filled the plane, not a sound but a force. The plane moved forward, slowly at first, then faster and faster as if they were at the end of a giant, stretched rubber band.

Polly turned to him, her face a map of terror and pain. The machine was about to shake to pieces. Water sprayed. They were skimming. They bounced once, twice. Then they bounced and instead of smacking back down on the hard water they floated. Soared.

A woman behind them let loose an erotic sigh. The air was so soft. They were rising, rising, dipping and rising some more. They watched the glittering world of the fair recede. The Sky Ride. Christ, the Sky Ride, which had offered such a dizzying view, was now below them, two foreshortened towers, a tiny compartment strung between.

Just as they were looking, the lights came on. Big searchlights shot out their rays from the top of the towers.

The fair itself condensed. They could see the whole thing stretching along the river. The people looked like ants. The plane turned out over the water. It banked. They all gripped the arms of their seats. The blue of the water filled the windows on one side. Out the other they could see the twilight sky.

When they leveled, Chicago appeared. It was a city they'd never see before. The buildings of the Loop coalesced into a child's castle. The sun cast long sharp shadows, set fire to the glass of towering windows.

"There's the Allerton Hotel," a man said.

Someone said, "There's the Rialto."

But mostly they were silent. Past the buildings they saw the western suburbs, and beyond, in the misty brilliant light, the beginning of the plains. And they were still ascending.

They saw the curve of the earth. Somewhere way down the shore of the lake John thought he could make out the tiny walled world of Michigan City Prison.

He knew with certainty he would never be confined again. The air was filled with hope. South America was just over the bright southern horizon. He and Polly would go there soon, very soon. A hundred grand would take them there. They would fly there. They would spend whole days naked, sipping tropical juices and eating dates.

Polly, who'd been eagerly staring out the small round window, now turned to him. Her eyes were full of intimate wonder. He answered, a quick half smile.

22

IVY AWOKE. I was standing directly in front of her. Harry had just entered, back in the shadows.

If she'd moved to cover herself right then, if she'd showed embarrassment or chagrin, maybe the thing would have taken a different turn. Maybe I could have fumbled through, convinced Harry that what he was thinking was a mistake.

But she sat up and began to smile at me. Then, still squinting with sleep, she looked past me and her smile dissolved.

I turned to Harry.

"Listen. This—"

He wasn't paying any attention to me. I was inconsequential, a man in a mask. He was staring at her as if he'd never seen her before. I didn't want to look at her nudity again, but I did look.

"What the hell?" Ivy said.

"Ivy." Harry inhaled as he said it.

Ivy's body, fresh from sleep, was both boyish and womanly, the body of a radiant baby, complicated in its folds, sleek and utterly wanton. The sheets were immaculate—she'd told me Harry always made her boil them, bleach and blue them.

"Ivy," he repeated.

She stretched, raised her hand to the back of her head,

pulled her navel into a taut line along her belly. She made a little growling sound in her throat.

"Ivy." The word was becoming terrible.

I noticed the image of Jesus baring his Sacred Heart over the bed. Mounted on the other wall was a collection of butterflies behind glass, big lunas and monarchs and iridescent swallowtails.

"I just came in." Was that my voice? "I didn't think. I didn't know. I should have. Nothing. Happened. I mean."

Harry had lost all his flesh. His cheekbones burned through his face. His body was ribs and femurs, clavicles and skull and knuckles.

"I never loved you!" Ivy said it. But which of us was she talking to?

"You. Whore."

What made this unbearable was that Harry was drawing the right conclusion from the wrong evidence. Standing between them was intolerable.

In the moment of quiet that followed, I became aware of the dry ticking of probably a dozen watches that were scattered across the little table where Harry worked on them.

I tried again: "I didn't know she was in here. I didn't know she was sleeping. All I wanted was—"

I hated the sound of my voice.

"God damn it!" Ivy said. "Leave me alone! Leave me alone, willya?"

She preened. She moved her elbows toward the back of her ribs, making her breasts jut at us. She raised her chin. Her mouth formed a tight smile. Her eyes burned.

Suddenly the trailer was full of noise. Harry must have knocked over something as he rushed forward. He struck me hard with his forearm as he pushed past. I saw the thrust of his fist. Ivy's head snapped back.

The shot from my pistol froze all motion. Long after its reverberations settled down I heard the sound of the breaking glass. The wild bullet had crashed through the window.

Harry's hands were still clenched. He looked at me. I had the barrel pointed at his face. I was eager to shoot him. I wanted him to give me an excuse. I thought for a second I would need no excuse. I felt such an urge to pull that trigger.

Ivy's nose was dripping blood. Her little tongue came out and licked some of it. A drop rolled over her chin and fell onto her thigh. She started to laugh. But looking at me she swallowed the sound.

"Get dressed," I ordered.

Completely bare she retained a certain innocence. When she first held the slip to cover herself, her nakedness became flagrant. The movements she made as she wiggled into her clothes were recklessly carnal.

Harry wasn't mistaken after all, I thought. Watching her asleep, watching her naked, bathed in light, dreaming—that was a worse sin than what we might have done in some sweating hayloft.

I had shot a gun in jest before. But I'd never used the threat of death to control a situation. It was a heady feeling. Harry was shaking. Good. I had a sudden insight into murder, crimes of passion, bank robberies. A gun is so clean, so absolute. It ends confusion. Its speech is never ambiguous.

A gun makes a small man feel big.

I began to feel I was a bigger man than Harry. Had he really never suspected? Had he allowed another man to make love to his wife onstage in front of ten thousand hicks without an inkling of what was happening? To hell with him. To hell with any man who would crack a girl's nose, bruise her face. I was making the rules now.

"Get out," I told Ivy once she was dressed.

She was patting a bloody hanky against her nose. "Whata you going to do?"

"Go on."

She hesitated at the door, closed it behind her.

Left alone with Harry, I couldn't think of anything to say to him. He stared at me with the insolence of a victim.

I put the gun in my pocket. I said, "Be careful, Harry."

He didn't answer, didn't move. I left him there with his butterflies and watches.

I cleared out for the day. The show was back in Indiana, playing outside of Terre Haute, not all that far from Dillinger's home. I drove into town and spent the afternoon at a beer garden. I smiled at the waitress and she smiled back. We got quite a thing going, smiling at each other. I asked her when she got done work.

"I can be done right now," she told me, "for two dollars."

That quenched my fire a bit, but I paid my two. She took me into a storeroom that smelled of stale beer.

I had a headache by the time I got back for the evening show.

"Where've you been?" Ivy demanded. "I was afraid he was gonna croak me. He hasn't come out all day."

"He won't kill you."

"You don't knowum. He stews. He noodles everything to death. You never know what he's gonna do."

"I handled him, didn't I?"

"Why'd you wanna go and do that for, anyways?" she asked me.

"It was a mistake."

"Some mistake."

We went onstage. We had added a twist where Ivy, as Billie, lifted her skirt to stuff some bank notes in her garter. Only that night she really pulled it up, really gave them a show. She smiled at the catcalls.

We came to the South Bend robbery. I let rip with the blanks. I fired the tommy gun until my ears rang.

During the questions afterward I handed out a lot of smart-alecky answers.

"How many men you kill, John?"

"A lot. Too many to count."

"You feel bad about it?"

"Why should I? They was gonna die anyway."

"Why didn't you go straight when you had the chance?"

"Because I'm not a sucker like you are."

"Who's a sucker?"

"All of you. All of you. You want a playacting world to live in. I pull a gun, people die. It ain't playacting."

It was a humid, foggy night. Ivy was waiting for me in my dressing room, still wearing her make-up. She was drinking rye from a tumbler. Her cheeks were flushed red.

"Gimme a nail," she said. I threw her my pack of cigarettes. She lit one. She paced as I poured a drink for myself. She talked rapidly, almost hysterically. I didn't pay attention at first.

"We're gonna get outta here," she was saying. "Only place to go's California."

"How about South America," I said, thinking of Dillinger's dream.

"California," she said, dead serious. "The weather's always peachy there and if you're smart it's the nerts. I think we can get in movies, both of us. I'll have my picture in *Screen Magazine*. We'll live in a mansion. Huh? They grow oranges out there. D'you know? They growum on trees and you can walk out in your back yard and pickum. And we'll have kids. And a limousine with a driver."

"What about Harry?"

The cigarette had burned down without her noticing. It scorched her fingers. She snapped it away angrily.

"What aboutum?"

"You're married to him."

"So what?"

I'd never thought about having Ivy on a permanent basis before. That evening was the first time I considered the practicalities of life with her—marriage, children, a steady job. The idea didn't appeal to me.

"Maybe he won't give you a divorce."

She frowned at me. After a brief pause she said, "Killum."

"What?"

"You can. Getum mad. You seen how he can go off. Getum mad and be ready."

There was a noise behind her. Sparky came in. "Planning a new scene?" he said.

"Yeah," I answered. "Our third act's a little depressing, don't you think? The Biograph and all?"

"What did you have in mind?"

"Dillinger in heaven," I said. "A little fantasy thing. Up where all the vaults stand open, where the prison bars are licorice, and where the streets are lined with eager Indian maids."

"But that wouldn't be accurate," Sparky said. "Dillinger's in hell."

"We could make it up. We've made up everything else, practically."

"No. It wouldn't fit with the crime-doesn't-pay message. You mind, Ivy? We need to talk."

"Sure I mind." She nestled her buttocks into my lap.

"Wait outside, sweetheart," I said.

She didn't want to go. I got her onto her feet. She insisted

245

on a deep sucking kiss and ran my hand over her breast for Sparky's benefit. I reassured her once again and shut the door.

Sparky wore his ringmaster's outfit, red coat, cream jodhpurs, and patent leather boots. He was carrying his silk top hat and black bullwhip. I poured him a drink.

"So she wants you to kill Harry."

"Kid stuff, Sparky. She's got hot pants and big ideas."

"Time was, I'd have read the riot act to you for a play like that. Because sooner or later it costs me."

"Now you don't care?"

"The show's folding."

"What?"

"I'm broke. The banks are calling me. I thought I could finish the season. But this will be our last week."

"The hell with the banks," I said.

"Yeah, the hell with them. Another time, I would have fought it. But I'm coughing blood now. And every once in a while, at night, I feel like an elephant is sitting on my chest. It don't feel good."

"So that's it."

"I've sold most of the stock to Roberts Brothers. They wanted a few of the acts. Yours, you could take it on the road by yourself if you had the inclination. Run the state fair circuit. You'd have to jazz it up, though."

"Add a sword swallower?"

"Some more general-purpose gangster stuff. Dillinger's a good angle, but people aren't going to remember him, time goes by."

"I think you're wrong there, Sparky."

"I probably am."

"What about Harry?"

"He'll find a show easy enough. Acts like his are always in demand. Harry won't have any problem."

"And yourself?"

"I've got a house in Florida. Maybe I'll write my memoirs. Barnum did. I've got a few stories to tell."

We both heard the band start up in the main tent. The show was getting under way. Sparky had to go.

The whiskey was having no effect on me. I wandered out along the edge of the lot. Crickets were chewing up the heat. The roustabouts were already dismantling the sideshow tent. We'd be moving on to another town that night, setting up for another show—our last—in the morning.

There's a pleasant kind of relief you feel at the end of a thing—whether it's a circus season or a love affair. It's a deliverance, a realization that the end is a form of completion even if you felt you had a lot more to do, lot farther to go. You can breathe easy. It's a sensation that almost makes you imagine death won't be so bad. No matter what you leave undone, it'll be over. No regrets.

Maybe the whiskey was getting to me after all. Maybe all that time playing Dillinger I was starting to think like him. Or maybe I was just wising up.

I smoked a cigarette out there in the dark. Then I strolled back toward the blazing big top, toward the smell of popcorn and sweat.

Inside the three elephants were lumbering around the ring. Estelle, the girl who handled them, wore a tight costume covered with blue sequins. She had very slender legs, which contrasted nicely with the gray limbs of the beasts. Rama, the biggest bull, would curl her delicately in his trunk and rise on his back legs to loud applause.

Rama and Shakti both had that bored nonchalance that to me is always part of the appeal of the elephant act. As if they're putting one over on the suckers, performing stunts that to an elephant are the casual gestures of everyday life—and getting paid for it.

But Poppo, the smallest of the three, had a different attitude.

247

He seemed to make an effort at showmanship. He would swing his trunk rhythmically to the band music, shift from foot to foot in a kind of elephantine tap dance, and flash his little elephant eyes to reflect the fascination of the crowd. He was a ham. And as a reward, he was the one whose head Estelle straddled with her milky thighs.

The bulls came right past where I stood in the runway. Estelle stopped briefly and threw both her arms in the air to acknowledge the cheers. As she strode past she tapped me affectionately on the leg with the hooked stick she used to control the pachyderms.

The clowns put on a mock baseball game. They juggled and tumbled, swatted each other with rubber bats, blew up in a fake rhubarb. One in whiteface spilled the water from the ladle a sad sack was drinking from. So the sad sack picked up the bucket and chased his assailant around the ring. Finally he heaved the bucket onto the first three rows of spectators. Of course it was filled with confetti. The band began to blare.

Sparky came out to introduce Harry's act. While he went on about the crowned heads of Europe and about laughing at death, I looked for Ivy. She was there, all right, standing opposite me beside the bleachers. It was a habit, no matter what she might feel about him at the moment. She had to watch his act.

The band went into the brassy waltz they always played at the beginning of Harry's number. He pranced into the ring, handed his turquoise satin cape to Sparky, and proceeded to climb the rope ladder to his wire.

The folks in the stands tipped their heads back. They were farmers whose red faces stopped at a line across their foreheads that marked where the brim of their hats would sit. They were farm wives, with thick, bread-dough, Monday-washday hands and round jutting chins. They were people with teeth missing, with blackened fingernails, and with the eyes of children. All those eyes turned upward. Each mouth dropped open a bit. And they all looked at a man in tights step onto a taut half-inch cable.

"When you first step on the wire," Harry had explained to me once, "it shakes. You think it's shaking on purpose, that it's alive, that it wants to throw you off. Later you realize it's you who's shaking. You realize that you've been shaking all your life. Shaking inside. Restless. Troubled. Impatient. And it comes out in the trembling of the wire."

Walking the wire, he said, was a question of replacing the agitation each of us carries in his core with a stillness, a repose. It is that still point that you balance on, not on the wire. You balance on yourself.

When you step out high above the crowd that point inside you becomes a source of light and calm, he said, of an almost unbearable sweetness. You want nothing more than to glide forever along its equilibrium. Your life on the ground loses its interest. The only life for you is the life of poise and balance. The only time you are alive is the time you spend on the wire.

As Harry unfolded his act that night he seemed totally self-possessed. He turned a back somersault, he performed his handstand on the balance pole, he sat on a chair perched on two legs and pretended to read a newspaper. He leapt, he strode back and forth across the wire as if moving on air itself, as if suspended by his own breath.

The audience knew they were seeing a display of genius beyond the ordinary. They gasped, they moaned. Throughout there was the smattering that was not conventional applause but the spontaneous crack of delighted hands.

The sousaphone burped out an oompah rhythm, straining, as all the instruments were, to keep pace with Harry's antics. And in the curve of the big horn Harry's golden image danced in miniature.

He was dancing now, skittering across the wire in a way

I'd never seen him do before. And as a cloud's shadow is traced across a landscape, his fandango was reflected in the crowd. A woman clasped her hands. A man strained his neck back, bounced his Adam's apple. A girl laid her hands over her eyes and peeked through a lace of fingers. Breaths were inhaled through clenched teeth. Ribs were clutched. Hands reached up of their own accord.

Suddenly, in the midst of a routine transit, Harry stopped and began to reel backward. The audience gasped in unison. Harry tripped, spun around, grabbed for the wire with his hand. His balance pole performed an easy flip and thudded to the sawdust below. Harry swung, swung, thrust his legs through his arms, arched back onto the wire. His pole was handed back up to him. The crowd cheered.

I looked across at Ivy. She was watching him, frowning. Harry did include a number of practiced near falls in his act. But this wasn't one of them. I could see Ivy pressing her teeth into her lower lip.

The band reached the finale of its medley and stopped, leaving only the drummer to accompany Harry's climax. He would leap across the wire in three bounds that culminated in a flying front flip. But as he moved into position, he slipped.

He grabbed for the wire with his hand. Missed. Tangled his legs around it. Held for a second. Slipped again. And was left dangling by his toes. The audience burst into prolonged applause.

Ivy's head was bent, her fist pressed to her forehead.

The drummer improvised a staccato rhythm to cover. One of the ring crew pulled the rope ladder across to where Harry could take hold. He should have come down at that point. Called it a day. He'd already put on one of the best shows of his life.

He climbed back up. The drumroll started again. Harry

paced for a minute on the wire, back and forth, like a man searching for something that's dropped from his pocket.

I could see anguish on the faces in the crowd. They wanted it, and they didn't want it. Anyone who watches a wire walker wants the artist to fall. That's the thrill. That's what draws them. The quickening in the blood waiting for what you don't want to see, yet long to see.

They were waiting now. And Harry's recklessness had stripped away the pretense that it was just an evening at the circus. It was death they were waiting for. What they were watching was more real than their own lives. They didn't want to watch, but they couldn't turn away.

The drumroll continued, mounted toward a crescendo.

Harry walked across the wire with absolute assurance. He turned. He took two strides. He leapt. He missed the wire entirely and fell.

23

SATURDAY is special in America. A day of release. It's the day the barbershop reeks of smellum, the bakery overflows with the aroma of yeast bread and crullers, and rainbows form in the mist of lawn sprinklers. It's a day of expectation. It's a day when people wash their cars and plan picnics and stop to talk with each other at the market or the feed store.

Of all Saturdays, none can match a Saturday in June. Big maples and elms and chestnuts, resplendent in leaves, are weighed down by their own shade. Green lawns invite laziness. The sky aches with blue. The heat wafts on harmonies of cicadas. On those thick midsummer Saturdays life seems to detach itself from before and after and float, dreamlike, in a time of its own.

South Bend was enjoying such a Saturday in 1934. A heat wave that would maul the Middle West for the next two months was only beginning to bake the soil, which was still fertile from recent rains. That morning the air was vibrant, not wilted. The sun rolled down the city streets and lit up the chrome on all the cars and drew the scent from borders of grape hyacinth and lily of the valley.

At the corner of Wayne and Michigan autos jockeyed for position in heavy traffic. Trolley drivers clanged their bells trying to work their way uptown. A traffic cop in the intersection kept the vehicles moving with toots on his whistle and mild gestures of his white-gloved hands. Sweating under his tunic, he performed his duties with a good humor.

The patrolman's name was Harold Wagner. He liked to look at the pretty girls who passed. He was a shy man, but he sometimes ventured a wink or threw a fancy salute to a lady driver. He was pleased when they favored him with a smile. He was thirty-two years old.

Pretty girls were out in abundance that morning. They wore white middy blouses—which were to be a rage all summer—and pleated skirts and barefoot sandals and glazed baku hats with tight curls of pheasant feathers. Their heels clicked along the pavement, their calves flexed as they stepped onto the curb, their bright lipstick glistened. The men almost all wore straw boaters or panama hats. A few sported light linen suits, many were in shirtsleeves.

Just up from the corner the sun was pouring into Harry Berg's jewelry store. The light shattered on the display of diamonds in the window, breaking up into red and indigo shards. It illuminated a string of pearls so that each opalescent sphere seemed to contain its own sun within.

Inside, the proprietor was discussing topaz with the daughter of a wealthy Ironwood Drive family. He agreed with her that the earrings she was contemplating beautifully emphasized the blue of her eyes. He was happy to talk to her at length even though the shop was busy that morning. The bottom had dropped out of the precious stone market since the Crash. His trade in watches and plate silver made up most of his business now.

Across the street a few people were already lining up at the State Theater to see the first showing of *Stolen Sweets*. A newsboy passed Berg's store selling papers that told of the assassi-

JACK KELLY

nation of storm troop leaders ordered by German Chancellor Hitler.

A brown Hudson stopped near the corner, just short of Berg's store. Five men climbed out.

Across the street another car pulled up to let out a passenger. He was Jacob Solomon. He'd ridden downtown with his friend Sam Toth to pick up a watch he was having repaired at Berg's.

Homer Van Meter, wearing farmer's overalls and a straw hat, walked casually over to stand under the gigantic brogan that advertised the corner storefront, Nisley's Shoes. He carried a .351 hunting rifle. Passersby thought he was a clown preparing for some kind of advertisement.

Patrolman Wagner wiped his brow with his handkerchief, returned it to his pocket, held up his hand to stop the north-south traffic on Michigan.

John Dillinger and two men who were never identified walked into the Merchants National Bank next door to the shoe store.

A breeze stirred, bringing the smell of the farm fields that lay just beyond the city limits.

Lester Gillis, for whom the government was offering a five-thousand-dollar reward under the name Baby Face Nelson, stood defiantly on the corner. He carried a Thompson submachine gun slung under his right arm.

Mr. and Mrs. Louis Linder, tourists from Richmond Heights, Missouri, were searching for a place to park. Mr. Linder stopped his car in front of the bank to see if a car by the curb wasn't about to pull away. Mrs. Linder remarked that the afternoon was likely to become uncomfortably warm.

Inside the bank the vaulted room was full of noise. Thirty people waited in line. Dillinger announced the holdup. At first there was a moment of loud confusion.

Patrolman Wagner stopped east-west traffic and was waiting for the intersection to clear.

Jacob Solomon arranged with Toth where they would meet for lunch. He slammed the car door shut and began to cross the street.

One of the robbers inside the bank, in an attempt to control the patrons, let loose a rattle of machine-gun fire into the ceiling. Instead of quieting the room, this brought on panic. Screams echoed from the marble.

Wagner, curious about the commotion that he noticed brewing on the corner, now began to cut diagonally across the intersection. He still held his whistle between his teeth. Seeing Lester swing his gun around, the policeman began to reach for his own pistol.

Harry Berg saw several people outside his window turn quickly. One pointed.

Van Meter fired the rifle. The shot cracked the air and was gone. A brace of pigeons lifted from the cornice of a building down the block.

For Wagner a dead silence suddenly swallowed the world. Gravity deserted him. He struggled to keep his feet on the ground. He reeled. The sky turned a somersault.

He was lying on the roadway, but he couldn't feel the asphalt. He couldn't feel the blue steel of the trolley rail that his hand was resting on. He pushed against it. He felt himself rise as if filled with helium.

But as he took a step the sky reached down into that busy street to clutch his face. It flooded his eyes with cobalt. An auto flew past him. The curb slammed into the back of his head. The blue sky went black.

Lester, a delicious strangled feeling gripping his throat, yanked the trigger of his gun, spraying the street with bullets. One of them blasted a spiderweb in the windshield of the Linders' car. Horrified, the couple hunched down out of sight.

Harry Berg dashed onto the sidewalk holding the pistol that

he kept under his counter. He took a jeweler's aim at Lester's back. Fired.

Jacob Solomon, halfway across the street, began to call out to the shopkeeper.

Berg's shot thudded into the bulletproof vest Lester wore. Lester swung around. His gun chattered.

Berg dove back into his store. His plate glass storefront with its gold and black lettering dropped, shattered.

As Solomon was about to step onto the sidewalk one of the bullets ricocheted, tore up his leg and lodged in his abdomen. He fell.

Lester swept the gun back around. A last slug crashed through the windshield of Toth's car, tracing a line along the man's skull. Glass sprayed his face.

During this shooting, Van Meter had stepped inside the shoe store and ordered two girls outside to serve as a shield. He positioned their shaking bodies in front of him, held the rifle at the ready, and swiveled his head slowly back and forth.

A high school boy, Joe Pawlowski, left his car in front of the movie theater, crossed the street, and leapt onto Lester's back. Under the gunman's shirt he felt the stiffness of the vest. Lester whirled, cracked the boy's head against a storefront window. Pawlowski fell stunned to the sidewalk.

Less than ten minutes after they'd entered, the three robbers exited the bank. One carried a feed sack full of cash. Each gripped another man as a shield.

"People stared at us with mouths open as we went," Perry Stahley, one of the hostages, reported later. As he came out into the sunlight he was trying to dislodge the cigarette that was stuck to his lower lip. He held his hands high over his head. He was afraid the butt made him look like a criminal.

A short distance away two police detectives were eating

pork chop sandwiches in a restaurant. A radio report sent them scurrying to their car. Unable to make their way through the clogged traffic, one of them got out and ran between cars with a shotgun.

Two other policemen, approaching the sound of the shooting on foot, took cover from what would be described as the "death-dealing rattle" of Lester's tommy gun.

The street was now consumed by screams and shots and echoes of shots. Police bullets ripped the legs of Dillinger's hostage Delos Coen. The cashier dropped to the pavement unconscious.

A slug thumped into Stahley's side. Others tore his pant legs without touching him. The bandit dragged him toward the Hudson. He hung back. Leaving him behind, his captor hurried toward the car. But he then inexplicably turned, pointed a revolver at Stahley's head and fired. The bullet nicked Stahley's ear.

A round from one of the cops tore along the side of Van Meter's head. Blood streamed down his neck, hot then cold.

They were piling into the Hudson now. Police detective McCormick, out of breath, aimed the shotgun and fired into the back window of the car. A gun barrel emerged from the shattered glass and spit flame. He let loose with the second barrel, but the vehicle was already moving.

The Hudson narrowly missed a collision with a green Dodge driven by Maxene Mullenhour, a local dancing teacher. She swiveled her head to watch the robbers' car speed off.

For a moment silence gripped the street. Then came the slap of shoe leather against the pavement. It became a patter as men ran from all directions. Shouts. Hundreds of people surged down the sidewalks, crisscrossed the street, leapt onto the fenders of cars.

The first man into the bank found it empty. The employees

and customers had all sought refuge in the director's room in the back. This man whirled, tried to catch his breath, sprinted outside with no idea where he was going.

Patrolman Wagner's lips were white. He kept shaping the word "water" with them, but his voice was escaping before it reached his throat. At the edge of the sky the policeman could see a stranger standing on his tiptoes straining, straining to see something.

After being shot, Sam Toth had driven his car around the corner. He sat there now, his head resting on the seat. His face was a glistening mask of blood. Curious bystanders looked in from either side.

As the heat of the sun mounted, the crowd milled around the intersection. Each person related to strangers his fragment of the drama.

"I heard the shots."

"I saw the officer stumble. He held his chest."

"I was there when they got out of their car. One of them told me, 'You better scram.' "

"I went to call the police. I couldn't find a telephone."

"Was it Dillinger?"

"The sounds of the bullets ricocheting—I hugged the concrete, buddy."

"There's blood right over there—real blood."

"How much did they get?"

"Look at the hole in that Ford."

"Sure it was Dillinger."

"Just stepped out there to the corner and started shooting."

"A brown car, a Hudson, I think."

"They'll be talking about this."

"It was Dillinger."

*   *   *

The Hudson cruised through the brief suburbs and out toward the southwest. A cop on a motorcycle approached from behind. Dillinger, driving, fed the car more gas. The motor responded nicely. The acceleration pressed them back into their seats. The speedometer needle hit ninety and kept going. The cop suddenly fell back, smoke clouding from his machine.

Mounting a rise, the getaway car crashed into a swarm of butterflies. Black and yellow wings swirled around them, were plastered to the windshield, swept past.

They stopped. Lester climbed out of the back with a bag of roofing nails. He walked back fifty feet and began scattering them across the road.

The bullet-punctured car continued. On either side of the road corn stretched in knee-high rows. The fresh leaves waved like a mass of green pennants. They turned down an aisle of locust trees. The wind was raising the leaves, exposing the white undersides to the sun, making the branches sway.

John stopped the car at a railroad crossing. A freight train had just reached the grade. It rumbled by, car after car, gondolas of coal on the way to the mills in Gary and Hammond. Then flatbeds loaded with lumber. The wheels beat a steady chunk-click, chunk-click.

Then empty freight cars, doors open to frame the plain beyond. In some sat groups of hoboes, legs dangling. The faces stared, face after face. They became one face, a face with the expression of a man being carried toward his fate, or away from his fate. A face whose hope was not ahead or behind, but in movement itself. A young face with all the youth drained away.

That face looked out at five men in a brown Hudson. Noted the shattered glass. Waved. John waved back.

"Let's go, let's go," Homer said. He groaned, a bloody handkerchief pressed to his temple.

The others kept looking behind as they relieved their tension with the usual chatter. Lester snapped a new magazine into his gun.

"So, Mister Ten-Thousand-Dollar-Reward," Lester said to John. "We'll see now. We'll see now who held up a whole city. Ho ho."

"You're right, Lester. We'll see."

A hawk circled overhead.

They waited. I sometimes imagine what John would be thinking. So this is how it goes, maybe. How there was a kind of mathematics to it. The more they blast your face across the newspapers, the wilder the ride. Pete wouldn't have liked it, all the shooting. But how else were you going to crack a jug like that? And what's the use of being careful now?

You just walk in. You pick people who'll stand their ground and you walk in. One thing you could say for Lester, he stood his ground. What happens after, that's not up to you.

For an instant, glancing up at the porcelain blue sky, maybe he understood the complex ceremony in which he played the central role. He couldn't have said a word about the meaning of it, except that it was contained in just this: waiting at this graded crossing, on this warm Saturday, with these men, while alarms flashed across the country.

The last car whisked past. Quiet returned on a breeze.

John put the Hudson into gear. They bounced over the rails and kept going.

24

TODAY it's hard to comprehend the relentlessness of summer heat in the days before air-conditioning. It was a maddening, metaphysical heat.

During July of '34 the whole country was broiling under a merciless siege. More than four hundred people were dead from the heat. An Ohio farmer died in his kitchen and wasn't found for ten days. When they opened his house the smell caused retching a half mile away.

You couldn't fight that kind of heat. You could powder yourself with cornstarch and talc. But as soon as you went outside, your underwear began to cling and sweat tickled your spine. Your hands and neck would erupt with heat rash. You might suddenly develop the sensation that all the oxygen had been baked from the air. Black stars would appear. This was the prelude to heat exhaustion.

Big pillows of hot air that had been inflating all the way across the plains rolled onto Chicago to suffocate the city. It was a heat that had all the chaffing flare of the dry-grass flatlands. Add to that the oily, festering taste of the city. And the stockyards, which gave off their own bloody heat. And the haze of dust from the storms that were still grinding the soil in the Dakotas. The papers listed a death toll every morning. People walked the streets in a beer fog.

Thousands fainted on the elevated trains. The heat turned Lake Michigan to iron. People stood thigh-deep and watched across the stagnant gray water for relief. Millions tossed all night, or paced hot rooms, or climbed onto fire escapes, dreading the return of day, preparing to curse the sun.

Ivy came to me very late on the night Harry fell. She was already dressed in mourning. I never asked, but often wondered, how it was she'd been prepared like that. She wore a veil, and under it the black wig. She must have felt that hiding her sunny hair completed the effect. She was right. Her pale face shone with a milky beauty.

I was sitting outside my trailer drinking beer. I walked with her to the tent where we put on our show. We sat in the bleachers and looked at the empty stage where we'd so often kissed.

She gave me a widow's speech. She had loved Harry with all her heart. She didn't know how she could go on without him. It wasn't possible that he was dead. She'd never thought it could happen. No, somehow he would rise from his ice bath and return to her, his shattered spine and burst vitals healed. No man like Harry had ever walked the earth, not with his sensitivity, his insight, his tenderness.

I laughed in her face.

She protested. Harry had had his faults, yes. Who didn't? Death put them in perspective.

"I lovedum," she pleaded. "We had some rumpuses, but I really and truly lovedum."

A little girl's eyes looked at me through the veil.

"Now I've heard everything," I said. "What about me?"

"You were temptation. I shouldn'ta give in."

"No."

"Now I realize it."

"Sure." I ground my cigarette out. She let me lift her veil. But when I leaned to kiss her she stopped me. No, she said. Oh no.

And I thought how small she was and felt sorry for her.

That Sunday evening in July John rose on his elbow and blew a stream of cool air onto Polly's neck. She smiled. He shifted, blowing lightly onto her glistening chest, her moist belly. She sighed. He relaxed back onto the damp sheets of her bed. He watched her rise, the pattern of the streetlights on her flesh. She stepped to the window, switched on a little electric fan. It whirred quietly, stirring the sluggish air. She turned to lick some salt from his slippery body. He took her face in his hands and pressed his mouth to her full lips.

"It's so hot," she said. From out in the street came the sound of breaking glass.

John said, "Let's go to the movies."

They couldn't send Harry's body home, he had no home. Ivy declared that Harry had been a devout Catholic, which was the first I'd heard of that. The undertaker arranged with the local priest. A plot was to be had in consecrated ground for a price. They buried him a day and a half after he fell.

Ivy looked fine at the funeral. Widows, like brides, shine with a mysterious, solemn beauty. As she passed me she raised her liquid eyes. Her little mouth formed the most sorrowful of smiles. I nodded my condolences. I felt a genuine desire to comfort her, to kiss her sweet tears.

The priest sprinkled holy water, waved incense, droned Latin. In his eulogy he fashioned an allegory about tightrope walking. How the wire was the straight and narrow, was life. How Jesus was our balancing pole. How we had to struggle to maintain our precarious footing.

This was all wrong. Was he implying that Harry had fallen into sin? That the fires of hell were waiting below the artist? What did he know about balance? Did he have a wife who loved him and hated him? For better or worse, Harry had wrestled with spiritual conundrums this padre had probably taken the cloth to avoid. But a priest has to say something. You always have to say something. That's the problem.

We all followed the coffin up a hill to the graveyard. Some of the townies stared at us.

It was a fine plot. Pleasant view. A big elm tree cast shade. A gentle breeze carried the scent of sweet clover and sweet death.

They lowered him on ropes. The priest's surplice rippled in the breeze. He waved a sign of the cross. He spoke to Ivy briefly. He headed back toward the church with the look of someone late to lunch.

Sparky guided me toward the town tavern. Inside it was cooler, dark, with an air of beer and nicotine. We ordered two cold bottles of Carling and took a table near the window.

"He left her sitting pretty," he told me.

"He did?"

"Big insurance policy. And he had dough salted away. She don't have to worry. Not by a long shot."

"Great. I play it right, I might be able to dig into that stash."

"Do you want to?"

"Times like this?"

"Somebody's crying hard times all the time. That's nothing. What Ivy is to you, only you know. What I say, living on a dead man's money, your age, that's not good."

264

Sparky wasn't the type to give advice. Funerals bring out the pensive streak in a man.

"Thanks," I said. "What do you figure happened on that wire, anyway?"

"He slipped. Everybody, sooner or later, one way or another, is going to slip."

We had a movie marquee that swung out from the scenery. At first it was just two plain slabs of pasteboard that said BIOGRAPH. Later I got them to add yellow lights that flashed on and off. We installed a ticket booth and we were set for the final act of Dillinger Alive.

The night they buried Harry we were scheduled to perform our last show. Ivy would participate as usual. Sparky insisted on that. What had happened to her was personal. The crowds were coming to see a performance. They didn't care about personal. You went on. A dead husband or a killer hangover made no difference. You performed.

The show was ready to start. I went to her dressing room to check on her. She was wearing her make-up. She was looking at herself in the mirror, touching her face lightly with her fingers.

"You all right?" I asked.

"Do you think I look like her? Really? Like Billie?"

"More than ever."

"I feel like I know better now."

"Know what?"

"That the whole world is crying. It don't matter who you are or what you did. You gotta cry. And people gotta cry for you. That's where we're all connected. Tears."

"That's one way of looking at it."

"It's the truth."

265

"Yeah. You ready?"

There was a lot of applause as I took the stage. I fired my gun off a couple of times to give them something to think about. Dillinger had never been trigger-happy, but I was used to giving people what they paid for.

"This is a stickup, sweetheart!"

Our robberies had gradually turned into burlesques. We lined up the bank girls to serve as hostages, the way they had when they took the bank in Sioux Falls. But instead of cowering, they would pull up their skirts and kick their legs in unison. That's what played, the hell with reality.

I used my wooden gun to escape from Crown Point. Ivy spoke her lines like a trouper. If anything, she played it bigger than usual. I took her into my arms for the love scene, our first embrace since Harry. Her kiss was convincing but completely empty, a stage kiss. I wanted to hold her forever. My eyes watered.

The yahoos loved it. One of them shouted an off-color remark. I always had a comeback for that kind of thing. But on that night I couldn't think of one.

Marty was in top form as Baby Face Nelson. He jumped around, fired his machine gun, and ranted like a maniac. I saw doubt creep into the faces of several of the rambunctious farmhands in the audience—they were wondering if maybe he really had gone over the edge. The look on his face as he killed the federal agent was a masterpiece of abandon.

I didn't want to get to the Biograph. Not that night, for the last time. I wanted the show to go on and on, the robbing and shooting, the love scenes with Billie.

I always offered a short word of explanation before the finale. That night I made up something different. I stepped to the edge of the stage, requested quiet, and made a speech.

"You know what's going to happen to me, folks. You've

read about it in the headlines. It's the moral of our story. It's the message we're bringing you. You get it in church, you get it in your newspapers, and you're getting it here. Crime does not pay."

Their eyes were on me, the same ones that had watched Harry fall.

"Crime does not pay? What does pay? Does selling off your life by the tablespoon pay? Does spending all your time counting what you've got to lose pay? Does locking people in cages like animals pay?"

I was shouting. My voice filled the tent.

"I'm not John Dillinger! John Dillinger is dead! They killed him. They hunted him down like a dog and killed him.

"What happened? The Lady in Red, a cathouse madam they were trying to send back to Romania. He trusted her. She took the deal to the police in East Chicago. And they wanted to get him. Fair trial? Forget it. Give a man a chance? That's not how they work. Kill him like a dog? That's what they wanted. That was the deal.

"They took it to the cops in Chicago. Forty men had been tracking Johnnie for eight months. They wanted him bad, but say what you will about them they wouldn't agree to murder. We'll give any man a chance to turn himself in, they said. So the Indiana boys took the whore's deal to Hoover.

"And what did Hoover say? What did J. Edgar say? He said, of course. Sure. Set him up. Shoot him down. Don't give him a chance. He's a troublemaker. The people love him too much. They admire him too much. Let's show them. Show them crime does not pay. Let's kill him.

"So they set him up. And they were waiting outside that theater that hot night."

*   *   *

267

Anna Sage she called herself. She understood men, the way a mother does and the way a whore does.

"I'm going out for some beer," she told John and Polly when they emerged from the bedroom. "You'll like some cold Schlitz before we go. Did you decide yet?"

"What do you want to see, Polly?"

"That Gable picture."

"You think Gable's so good-looking, Anna?"

"Compared to you? Why—"

"Here's something for the beer."

She stopped at a drugstore on the way. The air inside the phone booth smelled of grease.

Everyone condemns betrayal, yet there's something sweet about it, something tragic. Judas, they say. But remember Judas repented what he did. He brought the pieces of silver back to the priests and threw them on the floor and went and hanged himself.

I've never damned Anna. It was the government men who now checked their ammunition. It was Hoover who waited on a telephone line in Washington. Waited to give the order.

Lincoln Avenue was crowded that night. The screams of hot children rang out from the alleys. Radio music seeped from the beer gardens. Old men sat on chairs in front of candy stores puffing cigar smoke into the stifling air. A Polish woman in a sheer slip leaned out a window on her elbows. A black man on his way to deliver two bottles of gin to a party on Belmont looked up at her as he mopped his forehead with his bare hand.

They descended the stairs from Anna's apartment. The Biograph was a short walk away. John went in his shirtsleeves. It was too hot for a coat. He wore glasses. He carried a .32 automatic in his pocket.

Under the yellow lights of the marquee Anna's bright mandarin-orange dress looked red. Her face showed no sign of what she might be thinking. Only once did her eyes dart up the avenue, searching.

Polly shined. The heat turned her into a furnace of high young beauty. Her white arms swung loosely from the fluttering silk of her short sleeves. As she waited for John to buy the tickets she lifted the hair from her neck and waved her hand lazily to stir the air on her nape.

I imagine John looking at her and thinking of all the wasted beauty in the world, of all the elegant, precious women working in Woolworth's or waiting tables.

Polly deserved to have her face projected on the silver screen, to have the world sit in darkness and watch her eyes and lips portrayed in dancing light.

I'd managed to get hold of a poster that advertised *Manhattan Melodrama,* the film they were showing at the Biograph that night. To play Anna Sage I used a girl named Wilma Cathcart. She was twenty-six, but she could pass for forty-five. She was a comely, shy girl who kept herself puffed up with fat.

She had a tough role. When she appeared for the final scene she drew hisses. She was the Lady in Red. They hated her.

I told her to play up the double cross. She would smile and soothe as I strolled toward my doom. Meanwhile she would turn to the audience with an oversized wink. Once somebody threw a tomato at her.

That last night Ivy held my arm more tightly than usual as we stood outside the imaginary movie theater. She was tired. She had just buried her husband. And no matter how much money he'd left her, she must have smelled the emptiness in her future.

Her small face, softened by grief, impossibly tender, looked up at me as I bent to give her the final kiss before we entered. We held our lips together for a long time. The lust was gone. It was replaced by a feeling that melts even deeper, the mutual melancholy of two people whose paths cross and who continue on. There were no hoots from the audience that night.

In the basement of the Biograph they had big chunks of ice. Fans would move air over it and blow it up through ducts. It took the edge off the heat. But it was a dank kind of cool, with some of the metallic flavor of a cold-storage locker.

Betty Boop vamped through the cartoon. The Movietone covered the bloody San Francisco longshoremen's strike, Nazi storm troopers, and Dizzy Dean's unbeaten streak that was to run seventeen games.

The sweet smell of popcorn suffused the theater, a kind of magic vapor that entranced the eager watchers, transported them to a black and white world where anything could happen.

Much was made in the papers later about the fact that John watched a gangster film that night. That he watched Gable rise to a pinnacle of crime, then suffer the righteous consequences of his sin and finally meet his end in the electric chair.

In fact, John hardly paid attention to the movie. To the average person a movie like that might have represented a stark reality. But to someone who knows, someone on the inside, it's only another cartoon, a distraction.

John sat in his aisle seat holding Polly's hand. He looked around occasionally at the light-washed faces. He glanced back at the entrance. He closed his eyes and remembered Polly's full curved body lying on the rippled sheets. He even dozed briefly, awoke with a start as the screen voices went suddenly very loud in his ears.

270

*   *   *

They didn't want to take the chance of touching off a bloodbath inside the dark theater. They would wait for him to come out.

Sam Cowley was in charge. A somber Mormon, he'd been sent to Chicago by Hoover with the express mission of getting Dillinger. He was a heavyset man who, when he looked at an attractive woman, made a funny twisting motion with his mouth and immediately looked away. The hunt became his obsession.

Melvin Purvis was another whom Dillinger's falling star would briefly illuminate. A Southern gentleman. Special agent in charge of the federal men in Chicago. A small man. Mild. A spiffy dresser. He'd taken to wearing a boater during the long hunt because Dillinger himself often sported such a hat. Later Hoover would force him out of the bureau for seeking personal publicity. He would become the Post Toasties G-man, with his own Crime Busters Club. He would shoot himself in 1960 with the gun he carried that night on Lincoln Avenue.

And a dozen others. In doorways. Lurking behind the theater. The Biograph manager had called the police because he thought hoodlums were preparing to rob the theater. Two Chicago detectives were questioning a group of federal men when Dillinger walked out.

Purvis was standing just past the theater entrance. When Dillinger passed him, he was to light his cigar. That would be the signal to close in.

Now, I understand that those men were scared. They were being paid to enforce the law, but they wanted to go home to their families at night. Just like you and me. They wanted to go home and read the paper and smoke a pipe and eat pot roast and tell their children fairy tales. They had not signed

271

on to play the life-and-death game. They were men with futures. Just like you and me.

They had had Dillinger in hand before. He had escaped. Men had died. So these men were scared.

But God damn it, nobody forced them to strap on guns. You have a job, you do it right. You don't appoint yourself executioner. You're a professional. You follow the rules. You give a man a chance. That's what I say.

"They shot him down like a dog," I shouted at the audience that last night. "The man wasn't robbing Sunday schools. He wasn't sticking up church picnics. He was walking into heavily guarded banks with iron vaults. He was facing armed men ready to shoot down anybody who tried to take those pieces of paper. Oh, those precious pieces of paper."

I mopped my forehead.

"Who are our heroes? Actors? Movie stars? Bankers? The bankers who stole people's farms and people's dreams and never once had the courage to face their victims, to come down out of their mansions and say, I robbed you with a fountain pen, what are you going to do about it? The speculators? The money changers? I'm no preacher, but I know Jesus spit on the money changers. He took a thief to heaven with him, but he turned his wrath on those parasites, those butter-and-egg men.

"Who are our heroes? People loved John Dillinger. They love him to this day. Because he dared. He dared to do something. He didn't lie down and take it. He didn't hang his head over hard times. He didn't bemoan his fate. He carried his courage into the world and he took what he wanted. And they shot him down."

This wasn't part of the act. Yet they sat there, silent, listening, wondering. I don't know if they understood what I was saying. I only half-understood it myself then.

"Ladies and gentlemen. Don't walk away tonight thinking, Crime does not pay. When you tell the story to your children, when you tell them, I saw the Man Who Looks Like Dillinger, tell them the truth. Tell them Dillinger was a man who loved. He was a man who had the nerve to do what thousands would have done, but were afraid to. Tell them he was a man with spunk when the world needed some spunk. Tell the truth."

The image of Clark Gable walked toward the electric chair. People began to come out of the theater. Each face briefly assumed a stunned look. Wrapped in fantasy inside the cool darkness, they'd forgotten the dirty, overheated reality that awaited them: the yellow light, the grinding engines of cars passing, the hard concrete in which little flecks of mica glistened.

The southern sky glowed, the lights of the Century of Progress illuminating the haze. Down there thousands danced to hot brass bands, or drank beer under strings of bulbs, or watched sweating women prance naked on spotlight stages.

And out in the vast sweltering lands beyond the city, men in blackface strummed banjoes in minstrel shows. Old men sat on porches smoking cherry tobacco. And young girls kissed their boys, hesitantly at first.

Anna had been worrying a hangnail all during the movie. She dug at it, tried to bite it, felt it bleed, sucked the blood, then compulsively started picking again.

She was worried about Polly. Seeing the younger woman emerge from the bedroom earlier, the way she glowed, that dream in her eyes, that special lilt in her voice when she spoke to him, the gestures and looks that she thought were secret, it made Anna realize how tender Polly was, how easily bruised.

Polly had been married. She wasn't above acting as evening escort to a hardware merchant up from Cairo. Accepting his generosity, offering her own. Yet she still thought that the right man, the right circumstances, and her life could crystallize. And it would happen. Sooner or later it would happen.

Now it had happened. This man they called Jimmy was the answer to her midnight prayers, even if not the answer she had anticipated.

And now, Anna thought, Polly was going to learn. It was a lesson that a girl had to learn: that there is no answer. That you'll always be weeping and asking at midnight. That the finer your dreams, the more easily they shatter.

One thing, Anna didn't want Polly to be hurt. There was no reason the girl should go to jail. She was smart enough, at least, to deny knowing who Jimmy really was. But Anna was worried. The cops told her just to walk away. But you couldn't always trust police.

She wished to God they'd picked him up before the three of them had entered the cinema. All through the movie she had felt a tickling pressure at the back of her neck. Every time someone walked down the aisle she had to fight not to turn her head around to look.

Now she was wondering if the whole thing wasn't a gag. They were playing with her. They were afraid to take him, or didn't want to take him. The fix was in. They would turn *her* over. His gang would strangle her. Asthmatic as a child, she had a special fear of being suffocated. That was it. A guy like Dillinger owned the police.

Anna's eyes flashed around Lincoln Avenue as they emerged into the humid air. There were too many people around. Her heels clicked, clicked as they turned to the left and began to walk slowly toward the corner. At an alley halfway down the block they could cut through to her apartment.

A man in a straw boater just past the theater glanced at them. He put a cigar to his lips. He opened a box of matches. Two of them fell. He broke a third trying to light it. Finally he struck a flame, sucked it to the end of the cigar three times, blew smoke.

Purvis stepped out onto the sidewalk behind the man and the two women. He drew his gun. Two other agents closed in beside him. Others were crossing the street. Several were stepping from doorways in front of the strolling trio.

Death wears many faces. It is a fearsome chasm. It is a majestic conclusion that ennobles a person's chaotic existence. We imagine all the events of our lives flashing, gathering in that instant. We anticipate a revelation of the meaning of all faded hopes, lost opportunities, empty dreams and unrequited loves.

During his life John heard a voice. It spoke to him as he whipped a baseball around the infield, as he gripped the bars of his prison cell, as he strolled the magic streets of Chicago. It spoke most loudly when he walked into a bank and took control with an attitude and a gun. He heard it at Crown Point. It spoke through Red Hamilton's lips as he lay wounded. It whispered every time he turned his eyes to a beautiful woman.

And all the time he struggled to know what the voice wanted. And finally he came to know that it wanted only one thing: It commanded him to act. To dare.

His nerves now sensed that the street was alive. The windows had eyes. The pavement prickled.

His mind automatically formed a plan. Where he would run. How he would reach his car. Where he would drive to. The route he would take. A plan.

275

He took another step. His brain interpreted the scrape of feet, the paths of several grim-faced men, Anna's sudden dropping back. He loosened Polly's hand from his arm.

His muscular legs propelled him toward the alley. Running. Reaching into his pants pocket. For the pistol.

Ducking.

A gunshot is a flat sound. Flat and loud and awful. An inhaled sound more than a blast. It doesn't ring out. It gasps.

The first bullet hit him in his left side. He stumbled forward. They shot him in the back. He fell to the pavement. They shot him again. Again. Again. One bullet came out through his right eye.

When they shot me in the show the choreography was more spectacular. I grimaced. I fired my own gun wildly. I spun in a slow pirouette. I slumped. I tried to rise. I stumbled a little farther. Finally, clutching my belly, I collapsed. All the time the swarm of thugs playing the G-men continued to bang at me. Ivy ran, knelt, clasped her hands over me, appealed to heaven.

I tried to imagine what the bullets felt like. Poisonous stings. Sudden stabs of heat.

The way the audience reacted to this scene was always confused. In some towns, maybe those where the Methodist and Presbyterian ministers had cowed their faithful into piety, nothing but applause followed. This was the right ending, the proper repayment for a life of crime. For crime, the townies knew, did not pay. Dillinger had sinned. He had coveted. Another man's money, another man's woman.

But in most places they hissed the G-men. Frontier independence, resentment of any type of authority, or natural orneriness—whatever the reason, folks had sympathy for the slain outlaw.

That last night—it had happened before—neither cheers nor jeers followed the fusillade. Instead, an uneasy silence settled as I lay crumpled on the stage. Ivy wept real tears. Some of the women in the stands joined her, sobbing quietly. The curtain was drawn. The show was over.

Then I had to get up. I always found it difficult. Every time, but especially that night, I felt the weight of my own life pressing me down. I felt, for a brief moment, the lush attraction of death.

No such burden weighed on John that hot July night in 1934. The wing tip toe of Purvis's shoe prodded him daintily. John's cheek lay pressed to the warm bricks that lined the alleyway. He died on the threshold of escape.

Anna, as soon as she saw him fall, began to run. She pulled Polly after her. They ran to the corner, past a woman who sat on the sidewalk grinning hysterically at her bullet-pierced leg. They rounded the corner, separated, continued to run. Polly, who knew so little, knew enough to run.

The agents, guns drawn, sweat stinging their eyes, gathered around the bleeding prize. They pushed back the curious. The dutiful Cowley went to call Hoover in Washington.

Like a crackling brushfire the word spread up and down the street. Dillinger! They got Dillinger! Dillinger's dead! It's Dillinger!

Hundreds ran to see. By the time they arrived the body was gone, taken in a van with five agents. The onlookers pointed to bullet holes, pointed to the blood.

One young woman, a steno girl in the accounts department of Marshall Field Company, pushed through the milling crowd. She had strawberry blond hair and was wearing a sleeveless navy-blue dress that looked almost black under the lights. She pulled her skirt above her knees and knelt on the bricks. She gathered the lace hem of her slip and touched it to the blackening blood. It made a stain.

Swatches of cloth soaked in Dillinger's blood would be hawked for years afterward. I sold them myself after the show. All phony.

But her gesture was genuine. Her grandchildren would find the slip in a steamer trunk after she died.

25

A PERSON'S LIFE is a show, a creation, not an endurance contest. You are what you do. History records not what you dreamed, but what you dared.

Dillinger was thirty-one years old when he died. Barely a year later, while I was still strutting for the crowds every night, pretending to be him, I passed that age myself. I became older than he'd ever been.

"Yer lucky," Ivy told me when I mentioned it to her.

Yet it was a strange, lonely sensation, something like the way I felt when, later, I passed the age at which my father had died.

And so I carried Dillinger's face into the uncharted future. On me it grew old. On me the hairline continued its retreat. The cheeks sagged. Women lost interest in the face. But that easy, crooked smile I shared with him, that arrogant, boyish smile, I kept that. I always kept that, until finally it etched my face with its wrinkles.

Many have asked since then, Why did they kill him in public? They knew he was in Anna's apartment, that the three of them would leave from there. Why not grab him as he emerged?

Or barricade him inside? Stake out the route to the theater? Why apprehend him on a busy street? Why wait until he was in the middle of a crowd of exiting moviegoers?

But it had to be because it was part of the show. The events demanded a public execution. The movie theater, the *Manhattan Melodrama*, the fusillade without warning—they were elements to complete the drama.

And the denouement. The news spread by word of mouth. In the heat, people hopped streetcars, or drove or walked or ran toward the Biograph. Everyone said to himself, This is real. This is happening in my lifetime. I want to touch it.

The federal men arranged with the Chicago Police to move the body to the morgue on the floor of a paddy wagon. The crowds rushed downtown.

The van backed down a ramp. The basement receiving room was crowded with policemen, reporters, and politicians. Formaldehyde and cigar smoke mixed in the hot air.

They removed John's white buck shoes. They removed his trousers. They unknotted his tie. They unbuttoned the shirt still damp with his sweat under the arms. They rolled the limp corpse from side to side as they undressed it.

More than two thousand citizens gathered outside. A teenage girl wearing white knee socks squatted at a barred basement window. Her straight hair draped behind her ears, she peered through glass grimed with coal dust.

"There he is!" she screamed. There was a rush. She was pushed roughly aside. A shade was drawn. The girl hopped on one foot, giggling. She'd seen him. Naked.

The next morning they put the body on display. Viewers, many of them women, waited in the pulsing heat for an hour, two hours, before they could shuffle past the lifeless body draped with a sheet. Some walked back and got on line again. What did they see? A short man with a dyed mustache and a bullet hole under his eye? The embodiment of some vision? Were the women looking at the flesh of a figure who'd inhabited their imagination on sleepless nights? Did the men contemplate how ordinary he was and think, Couldn't anybody have done what he did?

When they brought the news that night, his father was sleeping on the lawn because of the heat. He rode from Mooresville in a decrepit hearse. The elder Dillinger had last been in Chicago for the Columbian Exposition thirty years earlier.

"They shot him down in cold blood," he said. "That ain't fair."

That was all he said. He buried his son beside John's mother in an Indianapolis graveyard. The day of the funeral was a stormy one. Torrents of rain fell on the mourners. Lightning flashed.

In August three policemen trailed Homer Van Meter to a house in St. Paul where he'd been living for several weeks. Ordered to surrender, Van Meter pulled a pistol, fired and ran. The police chased him up the block and into an alleyway. As he turned to fire again one of the officers opened up with a machine gun. His body was riddled. He dropped down dead.

Like Dillinger, Homer had dyed his hair black. The tattoo of an anchor on his left arm, with the word HOPE in a scroll below it, had been obliterated with acid.

In September Pete Pierpont and Charles Makley tried to emulate Dillinger's escape from Crown Point. Both were locked on death row in a Columbus, Ohio, prison. They carved chunks of soap into guns. Makley fashioned an automatic, Pete a revolver. They blackened the realistic models with soot, used cigarette foil to add glints of metal.

As a guard was delivering his meal, Pierpont drew the fake gun and demanded the key to his cell. Unlocked, he freed Makley and the other eight men waiting to die. They used the guard as a shield and demanded that the watchman outside open the metal door that would free them from death row. Instead of opening the door, this man sounded an alarm.

The prisoners smashed apart a large table and used the pieces to try to batter their way out. A riot squad of eight guards with rifles formed in the corridor. At a signal, the steel door was flung open.

In a final game of pretend, Pete and Makley lifted their toy guns. The guards fired.

Makley died an hour later.

That same evening Pete was back in his cell. A bullet had torn his spine, paralyzing his right side below the waist. He wept. "I want to die," he said. "I want to die."

Three weeks later he traveled the same corridor that Clark Gable had in *Manhattan Melodrama*. But it was no movie. No one yelled, "Cut." They sat him down in the chair and electrocuted him.

An era ended. Another generation of men took up weapons during the following decade, but they fired their tommy guns on Corregidor and Omaha Beach.

As for myself, I saw where show business was heading. I took the little I'd saved from the Dillinger Alive show and traveled west. There were openings in Hollywood then—there still are—for guys like me. For anybody who knew how to turn a tip, pack the house, and separate the marks from their precious greenbacks. For anybody who knew how to put on a show.

You've probably seen some of my movies. Gangster stuff. Shoot-'em-ups. Cold-eyed men and tough-talking broads.

If Ivy had ever come to me looking to be a star I think I could have made her one. Her face had that dreamy quality the camera loves. At least, that's how I remembered it.

But she never called, I never sought her out.

By that fall of '34 only one was left. Hoover promoted Lester Gillis to the top of his public enemy list. Baby Face Nelson. Five foot five. Twenty-six years old. Mad dog.

At four o'clock on Tuesday afternoon, November 27, Lester was driving south from Wisconsin to a house he'd rented near Barrington, Illinois. He'd spent three days in Madison living in tourist cabins. He'd been scouting a bank that he planned to rob.

His blond wife Helen sat beside him in the stolen Ford V-8 sedan. She was watching the drab scenery, her pale face serene. She turned to him, raised her eyebrows. Without actually smiling, she ignited the dimples in her cheeks. He loved that look. It communicated a secret erotic message to him. He looked ahead at the road, then back to her. He pursed his lips slightly.

Behind them was Paul Chase. Chase was a thin young man. The two sides of his face didn't match up and he never seemed to look directly at you. He was a lieutenant in what would come to be known—Lester was sure of it—as the Baby Face Nelson Gang. Lester was getting used to that name, Baby Face. He liked reading it in headlines. The mockery in it had been replaced by a sinister tang.

He needed more recruits. Being targeted by the federals had its disadvantages. Many of his cohorts in the underworld felt that Lester was bound to explode. They had no desire to be in the killing zone when it happened.

In other words, they were yellow. That's how Lester saw it. They didn't understand. Lester knew how to work it.

283

"You run away, lie low, hide out, that's when they get you." He was explaining it to Chase as they drove. "That's how they got Dillinger."

"Because he hid out."

"Exactly. You don't hide, you attack. Stand there and let them have it. They'll always back off. They'll always back off because they figure they've got more to lose. You turn tail, that's when you're in trouble."

Chase agreed. He agreed with everything Lester said. A few more good boys like him, and Lester would have a gang that was invincible. They would sweep right across the country. St. Louis, Denver, Sacramento. Pretty soon nobody would remember Dillinger. Dillinger would be small potatoes. Everybody would be talking about Nelson. Nelson.

The day was mild for November. One of those empty, in-between days when fall is spent and winter hasn't yet gotten a grip. A very quiet day with a slate sky overhead.

"Les," Helen said. "They have a new Philco model out where they say you swear Little Jack Little is right in the room with you. I was thinking—"

"Wait a minute." Lester swiveled his head at a green Ford coupe going in the opposite direction. "What the hell are you looking at, you son of a bitch?"

The man stared at him as the cars passed each other.

Lester had spent his life looking up at people. He knew they often signaled to each other over the top of his head, the way adults do over the head of a child. Signaled secrets about him.

"And they have these walnut cabinets," Helen said. "Like a piece of fine furniture."

Or they stared at him. Tried to make him do things by looking at him. By looking through him. Sometimes on the street in Chicago he'd catch somebody in a third-story window. Staring. Watching him. Or in a tavern. Eyes focused across a room.

You couldn't let them get away with it. Not even from a passing car. You had to be on guard.

"He's turning," Chase said, watching out the back window.

"That son of a bitch is thinking. What are you thinking about, you son of a bitch?" Lester crunched the car onto the gravel beside the road and spun a quick U-turn.

The cars approached each other slowly for a second time. The green car's windscreen reflected the bright sky. Lester caught sight of the eyes of two men as the vehicles crossed paths.

"Oh, these jokers are really out to see the sights." He immediately whipped the steering wheel hard. The Ford's tires squealed. They fell in behind the other car now.

The landscape was a succession of second-growth woods and deserted farm fields overrun with weeds. Stands of naked ash and sumac alternated with stripped plots of corn. In one field a scarecrow lurched like an inebriated farmhand.

They came to a town. The few houses and stores were mute, the street deserted. They quickly passed back into the countryside.

"You ready?" Lester shouted.

"Whaddaya mean?" Chase said, his voice breaking.

"With the gun." Lester snapped his head around. Chase's mouth was open. He licked his lips.

"Okay," he said finally. They'd gotten hold of an army-issued Browning automatic rifle. Chase pulled off the piece of carpeting that covered it.

The roadway stretched dead straight in front of them. Lester was following four car lengths behind the coupe. He gave the Ford more gas. He told his wife to open her window. They pulled up close behind the other car. He swung into the left lane and drew even. He looked around Helen's blond head twice. She was staring forward, tense.

Lester yelled, "I want to talk to you! Pull over!" He motioned with his hand.

The coupe continued at a moderate speed. The two men inside looked at each other briefly.

Lester let off on the accelerator. He swung his vehicle back in behind the other car.

"Helen," he said. She had an idea what was coming. The bones of her face stood out in a white outline. "Duck down, lover."

She ducked.

"Okay." Lester wasn't yelling now. His words to Chase were almost gentle. "Give it to them."

Chase swung the heavy rifle barrel over the front seat. He sighted, fired through the windscreen.

The blasts shook the car. Helen put her hands to her ears and screamed.

The coupe surged ahead. Its own back window shattered as one of the men fired from inside with a pistol.

Lester pressed his accelerator pedal to the floor. Wind blasted the open windows and whistled through the jagged holes in their windscreen. The car shook with speed as they roared along the strip of concrete.

They came closer to the speeding coupe. Lester reached out the window with his left hand and fired four times with a revolver. Chase let loose another blast from the automatic rifle. The right panel of the windscreen blew to pieces. Helen huddled on the floor.

The hump of a small knoll lifted them all into the air and slammed them back down. The car tore forward, then bucked once. Lester swore.

Chase was trying to line up the car ahead in his vibrating

286

sights. They heard a crackling sound behind them. A blue Hudson was bearing down on them. A man was leaning out one window and pointing a rifle at them. A trap.

Their car bucked again, slowed for a second.

Lester yanked the steering wheel. One foot worked the brakes while the other held steady on the gas. The car went into a slow slide. It darted forward on a road that led into Barrington. The Hudson followed.

Chase now swung the rifle around to fire out the rear window. The big engine suddenly lost power. There was a sickening, weightless feeling. It caught again and lurched forward. But the Hudson was gaining.

They passed a Sinclair gas station. They were losing speed.

Without warning Lester turned onto a gravel road to the right. He stopped, one tire in a ditch. The car behind skidded. It came to rest a hundred feet away on the other side of the main road.

Chase flipped a machine gun and an extra canister of ammunition onto the front seat. Helen opened the door and ran. Across the dirt road she stumbled, fell onto her hands and knees in a clump of withered goldenrod. Weeds pricked her palms. She struggled to breathe.

Lester gripped the Thompson gun and climbed out the passenger door. He moved along the ticking, overheated hood of the Ford.

Silence settled on the scene. It was a silence that seemed to extend forever, as if everyone in Chicago, in Milwaukee and St. Paul, in the entire Middle West, had suddenly stopped what he was doing and stood listening.

The men in the first car were, as Lester had suspected, federal agents. So were the two men who now scrambled from the car opposite. One was Sam Cowley, the chubby Mormon who'd served as Hoover's contact at the Biograph. The other

287

was Herman Hollis, one of the men who had fired at Dillinger as he lay in the hot alleyway. Hollis had just celebrated seven years of marriage to his young wife.

Lester broke the silence. He leaned around the front of his disabled car and blasted a metallic scream from his machine gun.

Chase fired from the rear, letting his gun empty in a continuous roar.

Glass clinked in the federal car. Then a fast drumroll of shots flew back at them. And the round boom, boom of a shotgun. A deep thud sounded in the far door of their car. They could hear pellets scampering underneath between the tires.

Chase reached inside for more ammunition. He passed two more canisters forward to Lester. He ducked around to fire another volley at the agents. They answered with shots of their own, Cowley from a ditch, Hollis still firing from behind the car. Bullets slashed the air.

Chase looked over at Lester. Lester was blinking his eyes like a man just awakened from deep sleep.

"I'm gonna go down there and drill those bastards," he said.

He stood. Behind him, bare elm trees made elegant silhouettes against the sky.

The two men who now trained their weapons on Lester were doing their duty. They were moral men, men without imagination. They had been hired by the bankers and politicians, the speculators, the shopkeepers and the ordinary citizens, to hold back wildness, to rid the world of ogres. Now they faced an ogre.

In the show we never reenacted the scene that followed. It has been reenacted far better, from that day to this, by little boys with sticks and tin guns. For them, playing the G-men is fine. Playing Baby Face is fine. Playing cowboys is fine, playing Indians is fine. All that matters is the battle. All that matters is the shoot-'em-up.

Lester's walk that afternoon inspired a thousand thousand boys to face an opponent's guns head-on with eh-eh-eh! or pow-pow-pow! or rat-atat-tat!

Quick bursts, like gulps, blasted from Nelson's gun. He stood in the open, on the pavement of the main road. He walked toward the agents' car.

Chase fired. The government men fired. The combined sound was the earth ripping open.

Cowley took aim from the ditch. His gray suit was smeared with autumn mud. He aimed at Lester's belly. At an academy back east he'd been taught to aim for a man's belly.

Lester kept coming.

Hollis emptied both barrels of his shotgun at Lester's legs. The pellets tore away fragments of cloth and bloodied the fabric.

Lester kept coming.

Drawing his pistol, Hollis ran for a telephone pole behind him.

Not aiming, Lester held the machine gun at hip level and swept it back and forth, spewing fire and bullets.

Lying in the ditch, still shooting his own gun, Cowley felt a metal finger pierce his ribs. He felt hot liquid seep across his belly. He felt his leaden limbs press into the earth. His face pressed against the clay. A humming sound came from inside the clay. He tasted clay in his mouth. He heard more shots. They echoed from the top of the sky.

Lester always wore shoes with an extra half inch of heel. He inserted wedges inside them to boost him a fraction of an inch higher. As a result, he walked with a slight forward tilt. He walked like a man who is not connected to the earth.

289

He walked that way now. It was almost a mincing walk. He did not crouch. He did not run. He just kept walking forward, step by step.

How long does it take to walk across a road? Hollis hadn't yet reached the cover of the telephone pole. Lester's gun kicked, kicked. A bullet caught the agent in the back. Another slammed into his skull, shattering it.

Lester climbed into the agents' car. He started the engine. The November sky was darkening. He backed up to the cross-road, stopped beside his own car.

While Chase transferred their arsenal into the government car, Helen's blond head emerged from the weeds. A ringing silence stinking of hot metal hung in the air. She ran to her husband.

"You better drive," Lester told Chase. "I'm hit."

He'd been shot seventeen times.

The next day the police, tipped off by an anonymous phone call, found Lester's body in a Chicago suburb. It had been laid by the side of the road, stripped naked. Baby Face Nelson was dead.

The Wild West was over.

The curtain came down that November day on an outlaw era that had begun with Jesse and Frank James. New laws and two-way radios put an end to the kind of hit-and-run tactics that Dillinger had perfected. Our criminals became punks, bit players, grifters.

And yet today, on the firing range of the FBI academy at Quantico, Virginia, the recruits still look down their sights at paper targets printed with the image of John Dillinger.

*   *   *

The show's the thing. You get one chance to strut and fret before the curtain drops, the reel ends, the houselights rise. Your performance is all they judge you on.

You enter a bank. You face a cop with a gun. You walk a wire strung across your death. You shoot blanks pretending to be a famous criminal. It's all for the show.

Did you give your audience some laughs? Thrills? Tears? Hope?

Did you try, at least? Did you dare?

Of all the stories, the one I remember most vividly was one Sparky Masterson told me. He was managing his first circus not long after the World War. They were touring jerkwater. towns in the Ohio Valley.

The show featured an equestrian act. The star was a girl, Angela May Sommers. Just twenty-three, a fragile redhead, she was a natural bareback artist. Slim. Astonishingly limber. She just floated on the backs of those thundering grays.

Her people were circus people. She herself was shy.

"She would cover her mouth when she laughed," Sparky said. "Like a kid. And I've never seen a person blush so easy."

She had married a fellow in the show, a clown. He was devoted to her.

She tried stunts in her act that had not been seen before, flips and jumps people said were too dangerous. But she performed with utter confidence. The horses never frightened her.

One night she was approaching the climax of her act when one of the stallions misstepped. Just for a second. The horse didn't even go down. But he lurched enough to throw her. She landed in the sawdust. The fall broke her neck.

Her husband, in his clown suit, was the first to reach her. He knew right away she was gone.

He immediately turned to the crowd and twisted his features

into a sad-sack grimace. He scooped up the body, draped it over his shoulder, pranced across the ring.

Some kids giggled.

He stopped at the ramp. Turned. Spread a big smile across his face. Lifted her limp wrist. Waved a comical good-bye.

The audience, relieved, laughed and laughed.